Sister Girls 2

Also by
Angel M. Hunter

Sister Girls
Around the Way Girls
Faking It
Turned Out

Sister Girls 2

ANGEL M. HUNTER

www.urbanbooks.net

HUN

Urban Books
1199 Straight Path
West Babylon, NY 11704

ISBN-13: 978-1-60162-044-6
ISBN-10: 1-60162-044-6

First Printing March 2008
Printed in the United States of America

10 9 8 7 6 5 4 3 2 1

This is a work of fiction. Any references or similarities to actual events, real people, living, or dead, or to real locales are intended to give the novel a sense of reality. Any similarity in other names, characters, places, and incidents is entirely coincidental.

Submit Wholesale Orders to:
Kensington Publishing Corp.
C/O Penguin Group (USA) Inc.
Attention: Order Processing
405 Murray Hill Parkway
East Rutherford, NJ 07073-2316
Phone: 1-800-526-0275
Fax: 1-800-227-9604

Acknowledgments

I thank my husband, Tony Irby, for his support and his suggestions, for sitting up with me and helping me type when I couldn't press another key and for being the example of a "good man". God graced me with your presence and love. I appreciate you.

To my son, Anthony Shacquille Irby, you are growing into a kind, gentle, strong and handsome young man. I am proud of you and your talents.

TO MY READERS:

You are responsible for your life and how you use your power. We all have it. The power to succeed, fail or prosper. Many times we come across challenges, people, places and things that stop us in our footsteps that try to block us and hold us back and keep us from moving forward. Trust me, I speak from experience. Please know that this is Gods way of getting our attention and making us realize that we are strong and capable, that we can grow. You just have to believe it, the power of your thoughts, words and actions create your experiences. So don't focus your energy on what's outside, focus it on what's inside. Thank you for supporting me and "getting it".

Love, Peace and Joy, Angel M. Hunter-Irby
msangelhunter@aol.com

ACKNOWLEDGMENTS

To my mothers: Barbara Hunter, Norma Turner and my mother-in-law, Cora Lee Irby.

To my father, James Guy Turner Sr. and my father-in-law, John Irby.

To my brothers (all great men, contrary to popular belief there are still some in the world ladies) Antonio Pierre Hunter, Lushawno Duvall Butler, James Guy Turner Jr. and Russell Irby. Oh yeah, I can't forget my nephew Jason.

To my Sister Girls . . .

Lucretia Willis, Angel Elliot, DaNeen Wyche, NeeCee Dorsey, Paula Woodhouse, Quassmirah Baten, Stephanie Dawson, Tonya McGhee, Faye Wilson, Verna Lee, Tammy (my typist), Natalie, Ingrid, Jolyn, Amber Chaney, Trina Dorsey, Tonya Rice, Sonya, Yolanda, Kelly, Monica, Sabrina, Gail Robinson, Cassandra Giglio, Jasmine Giglio, Jonte Giglio, Camille Butler, Lekenta Robinson, Stephanie Johnson, Dominique, Melissa, Michelle, Tara, Sharon, Alicia, Tia, Melena, Monica, GeeGee, Jackie, Tia, Tracy, Kimesha Hunter, Thomasina Hunter, Tee Tee , Sherry, Tanya, June, Sonya, Vesa, Tracey, Samantha, Barbara, Sharon, Kiari, Tameko, Shannon, Pamela, Erica and. My sisters in spirt . . . Debbie Allen (who I wish one day to work with), Jada Pinkett Smith, Erykah Badu, Patti Labelle, Oprah Winfrey, Lena Horne, Dana (Latifah) Owens, Mary J. Blige, Diana Ross, Janet Jackson and Gladys Knight.

(If you feel I forgot you, I apologize; you are in my heart where it counts the most)

In memory of Phyllis Hyman, Dorothy Dandrige, Billie Holiday, Lisa "Left Eye" Lopez and Aaliyah.

SISTER GIRLS 2

THE OLD AND THE NEW

ESSENCE BESTSELLING AUTHOR
ANGEL M. HUNTER-IRBY
msangelhunter@aol.com
www.myspace.com/angelmhunter

Dear Readers:

all the negativity and negative influences from your life
ELIMINATE
show your enemy by succeeding
DEVASTATE
when making major decisions, don't be emotional
HESITATE
do this daily
EDUCATE
act as if until you
MAKE IT
don't show the struggle
FAKE IT
all the
CONFUSION
is just an
ILLUSION
you know who you are suppose to be
don't
HIDE
don't
COMPROMISE
be
WISE
don't be taken on a guilt trip
or made to feel as though you're
MORALLY CORRUPT
if it's meant to be it will
there is no such thing as
LUCK

be true to you
BELIEVE
put action behind your dreams
ACHIEVE
please
don't stay
LOCKED
in the soap
BOX
Keep your
HEAD UP and you HEART OPEN.

DEDICATED TO THE TWO LOVES OF MY LIFE

TONY B. IRBY and ANTHONY S. IRBY

And to my mothers:
Barbara Hunter Jones
Norma Turner
Cora Lee Irby

I'd also like to thank:
Carl Weber Arvita Glenn Roy Glenn

FEEL FREE TO E-MAIL ME
AT
MSANGELHUNTER@AOL.COM

A LETTER FROM ELSIE

Well, I'm back and it's been a minute, we have some catching up to do. I've made a lot of changes in my life and I'm thinking it's time to bring you up to speed.

There are also some new people you'll be meeting this time around and the story will focus on them.

I think it's time some new lessons are learned. Before you find out about these new people, we must play "catch-up."

Me? Well, I'm no longer working with Crystal, Susan and Jewell at the law firm. I decided to move on and do something different, something I feel will make more of a difference in the lives of people. I've started a nonprofit organization.

My love life? Well, I'm still gay. I'm also single. Summer and I, as some of you may recall, are no longer together and a year later, I still struggle with that decision.

Crystal? Well, she and Lange called it off. Most of you know that when they first started messing around, he was a married man. It's no secret that relationships that start off as affairs rarely work out.

Susan? She's still drug-free and loving Timothy every day. Her life has definitely changed for the better. You never know what hidden addictions people have. That's why you have to watch the ones you love closely. It was such a relief that things worked out for her because she was on a road of self-destruction. It goes to show that if you really want to change, you can.

And finally, Jewell, with her crazy ass? She has really grown up from the chewing gum, snapping her fingers and cursing-you-out female to a mature woman. When people grow, re-

spect follows. She and King worked things out and moved in together to raise Tyson. She's now a paralegal and couldn't be happier.

So that brings us to today and the new group of women you'll be meeting. Don't fret, my old friends are still around and you will be hearing from them. But this time, like I said earlier, we're going to focus on Bella, Faith and Harmony and of course me.

Who are these people and where did they come from? They all have something to do with the Essence of Self Center, my nonprofit.

Bella is a pastor whose past continues to haunt her.

Faith remains in an adulterous marriage because of guilt.

Harmony is a young mother with three kids who is struggling to keep her family together.

I hope the ladies' stories assist you on your journey of life and give you some insight into the everyday situations we all experience.

Keep Growing, Elsie

BELLA

Bella was lying in the bed with her eyes closed, naked. Her sexual urge had taken over once again and she couldn't stop it.

No, she didn't want to stop it.

She moved her fingers over her body, touching her breast, where she stayed for a brief moment, squeezing her nipples, making them as hard as possible. There was a time when men paid to do that, but now she did it to herself.

Her hands trailed down her stomach, stopping on her pussy. Did she really want to do this? Was it a sin? Even if it was she couldn't stop if she wanted to.

It was time to feed the beast.

HARMONY

Harmony watched as Shareef came towards her. His dick was hard as a rock, sticking straight out, as if it was saying "hello." She hoped he hadn't taken one of those stay-hard-all-night-long pills again. His ass always wanted a session and she just wanted maintenance.

She knew just how to get this over with. She'd turn over, stick her ass in the air and open wide. That way when he approached the bed, she would be ready and it would also let him know that this is the position we'll be doing tonight.

"Come hit this pussy," she'd told him.

Harmony knew the dirtier she talked the quicker he would come.

FAITH

Faith's pussy was exhausted and pulsating. In her fantasy with LL Cool J, he was *doing it and doing it and doing it well.*

She had taken in as much of him as she could. "Harder," she told him, "deeper." The deeper he thrust, the more aroused she became watching his Adonis-like body move inside her.

When she looked up at him, he licked those luscious lips of his and she knew it was about to be on.

It was a damn shame that it was just a fantasy and that she wasn't an around the way girl.

It was also a shame that the man she married was never around when she needed him. She knew it was time to put an end to her marriage. If only she had the courage.

CHAPTER ONE

BELLA

Dear Journal,

I really need to let go of the past, I can't continue to live nor dwell there.

I can't continue to feel the guilt and the shame of what's done and over with. Guilt will kill you and shame will hold you back. So why do I continue to do it? It's so easy to not let go, but why do what's easy.

I've never taken the easy way out before. Look at me, I've turned my life over to God because it's said he forgives all, I preach forgiveness; I preach letting go and moving forward.

Why can't I do it?

Peace and Blessings, Bella

Bella got into prostitution because she thought no one wanted her and that she wasn't anyone special. Sex made her feel extraordinary. She had something men would pay for and yes, she admitted sometimes—even women.

This is why she did not preach on such topics as homosex-

uality because she had been there and done that—it was her belief that what mattered most is what's in a person's heart. She just wished others believed this as well because the world would then be a much better place.

The word had also gotten around how liberal her church was. You can come dressed up. You can come dressed down. You can come looking any way you like as long as you did not come naked and that was enough to pack a full house every Sunday. She was proud of this. Her ability to keep up made her uncertain.

Bella questioned whether she deserved the life she was living; based on her past, she felt she did not. She knew God forgave all sins, and if you let her tell it, her sins were of a magnitude that required constant prayer even years later. It was a good thing God was her savior because she didn't think anyone else would know how to handle her.

Bella sat up in the bed. There was no way she was going back to sleep so she might as well do something productive, like clean the house before she went to the opening of the Essence of Self Center.

Insomnia is a bitch, Bella thought to herself, but not without adding, *Lord, forgive me.* Every now and then an occasional swear word came out, usually when she was alone. Once again, she asked for forgiveness. Sometimes Bella had to laugh to herself because it seemed like she was always asking for forgiveness. She wondered what her congregation would think of that.

Bella did the same thing in the same order every morning. She got on her knees and prayed for about thirty minutes, not that she timed her prayers. It just always worked out that way. It was like clockwork or maybe it was the inner workings of the Lord. Then she would pull out her Bible, read, take notes and work on her sermons.

Afterwards she would make herself a light breakfast and a cup of tea. She'd relax for a little while and then get up to do charity work or go on various appointments.

Bella couldn't believe this was her life. She couldn't believe that she wasn't running from anyone, that she wasn't hiding out, and that she wasn't selling her body. All those things were in her past.

A miracle, that's what she considered herself and her life.

Bella never had a childhood. If she did, she didn't remember it. She actually didn't remember anything prior to the third grade.

Where she lived, who she lived with, it was all a mystery to her. Who her parents were and what they looked like were also unknown.

Bella was all alone in the world. She never really had a place to call home. She'd never really had a family to call her own. She never had much of anything. She grew up feeling like it was her against the world. Now she felt like it was her and God trying to conquer the world.

What she did remember is going from home to home as a foster child, being either abused, mistreated or made to feel as though she were a maid.

One family she stayed with made it no secret that they were just in it for a check. They never took her anywhere, bought her the basics of the basics, the necessities and that was that. She yearned for love. She yearned for someone to tell her she was worthwhile and that she meant the world to them. This never happened. There were many nights when she lay in bed crying and wondering why she was even born.

When Bella turned fourteen, she decided enough was enough. She was fed up with being an afterthought. She decided to make a plan and run away. *I can take care of myself.*

Bella figured that what her foster parents did for her she could do for herself. She looked older than her age, so finding a job shouldn't be that difficult. She could go to school during the daytime and work at night.

All she had to do was come up with some money that would tie her over until she got settled. She needed money now, she needed money yesterday. Babysitting was one way. She couldn't really think of another, unless it involved stealing.

Bella thought about the girls she went to school with. The girls everyone wanted to be around, who always had on the fly gear. These girls boosted for a living. They would find out what people wanted from the mall, take orders, go steal it and charge them half of what they would normally pay. From what she heard in the hallways, they were making a large profit.

Bella wondered if that was something she could do and get away with. Would they say yes to her if she went up to them and asked if she could be down? Would they laugh or would they kick her ass?

She didn't know but she was willing to find out. Her life, her very existence depended on it.

Before approaching them and asking if she could be a part of their posse, Bella decided she would try her hand at stealing, to see if it was even something she could do on her own.

She chose a Saturday to attempt it. She was home alone the majority of the day, all she had to do was sneak out, catch the bus to the mall and proceed from there.

That whole week, she'd been collecting change from around the house and taking a dollar here, five dollars there out of her foster mom's purse and as luck would have it, one of the neighbors came by Friday in need of an emergency babysitter.

"Please, can I do it?" Bella begged. She was certain her fos-

ter parents would say no; after all, they didn't let her do much of anything.

To her surprise, they said yes. When she thought about it later, she shouldn't have been surprised, because she knew to them it meant more time for her to be out of their way.

That evening she watched the clock. Every time she looked up only fifteen minutes had passed. So to make the time go by quicker, Bella went to her room and tried to lay down for a nap.

As she was dozing off, her foster mom walked in her room. She never knocked; after all this was her house, she was fond of saying over and over.

"Aren't you supposed to be babysitting?"

Bella looked at the clock, it was time for her to leave.

As she walked to the neighbor's house, Bella tried to think of things she was going to do with their two kids, who were six and four. She hoped they knew how to entertain themselves.

When she arrived next door, Mr. Lee let her in. "Hi Bella, we're glad you could do this."

"I'm glad I could too," she told him. "I really need the money."

"You're saving up for something?" Mr. Lee asked.

Bella wanted to say, "Yeah, I'm saving up to move the fuck out," but being the respectful fourteen year old that she was trying to be, she just told him, "yes."

Mr. Lee followed Bella into the house.

Bella could practically feel him on the heels of her sandals, he was walking that close to her. If she stopped, he might have run into the back of her.

"So, how long has it been since you've been with the Reeds?"

"Almost two years."

"Are they are treating you good?"

"As well as can be expected." *Why was he asking her all these questions?*

By this time they were in the living room, Bella looked around. "Where's the kids?

"My wife is bathing them, we're leaving right afterwards."

"What time will you be back?" Bella found herself crossing her arms because if she wasn't mistaken, Mr. Lee was staring at her breast.

"Probably around midnight, you might want to see if you could spend the night."

On that note he walked off.

About ten to fifteen minutes later, Mr. Lee, his wife and the kids appeared.

"Here's the number you can reach us at in case of an emergency. Remember we'll be late returning, so see if you can stay over."

"I will, and don't worry, I'll take good care of your babies," Bella assured them.

When they walked out the door, Bella turned toward the kids. "So, what would y'all like to do first?"

As it turned out, it went smoother than Bella expected. All the kids really wanted to do was play games and watch television.

Around 10:30 PM, the Lees called and told her they'd be back around one in the morning, so she got permission to stay the night.

When the Lees returned home, the kids were in bed and Bella was asleep on the couch. Mrs. Lee covered her with a blanket and went into their bedroom, so Bella thought.

Sometime in the middle of night, Bella felt someone star-

ing at her. When she opened her eyes, she saw that it was Mr. Lee.

"Yes?" she asked in a low tone and feeling uncomfortable.

Mr. Lee whispered, "You're a beautiful girl, Bella, do you have a boyfriend?"

Bella sat up. She wondered why he was asking her this question in the middle of the night.

"Thank you and no." What else was there to say? She could tell he was up to something, but she felt paralyzed, as though she couldn't move.

Mr. Lee sat on the edge of the couch and touched her leg. "Do you want to make some extra money?"

Bella wasn't stupid, she knew what he was getting at, and she wondered what made him think he could ask her something like that?

"Why?" Even though she was only fourteen, Bella had a little experience not in traditional sex but in oral. One of the boys in school that she had a crush on asked her to suck his dick in the locker room and she did. She thought it would make him like her back, but it didn't. At first she was devastated but then she was thankful because it was short of a miracle that he didn't go around bragging.

"There's something I would like for you to do," Mr. Lee told her.

She really needed money so she could run away. Would whatever he asked of her be something he'd be willing to pay for?

Mr. Lee took her hand and placed it on his penis. He waited to see what she would do.

Bella looked towards the bedroom. "I'm not sleeping with you."

"I'm not asking you to, I just want you to touch me and show me your stuff."

Bella looked toward the bedroom again. She knew what "stuff" he was talking about.

"You don't have to worry about my wife. She's sound asleep," Mr. Lee assured her.

Bella knew this was wrong, she knew she should get up and leave but she also knew he would be willing to give her some money, he'd said so himself. So she reached over and squeezed his penis through his pajama pants.

"Let me see your pussy," he told her.

Bella closed her eyes, took her hand off his penis and pulled her dress up. She moved her panties to the side.

She didn't know how she was supposed to feel, a part of her wanted to cry but desperate times called for desperate measures.

That night, on top of her babysitting money, she received an extra fifty dollars, just for letting him masturbate while she rubbed on herself.

This soon became a routine of theirs. He often asked her to babysit or when his wife wasn't home he said he needed someone to watch the kids while he worked around the house.

Between Mr. Lee wanting to see her again and her making money off of stolen clothes, she figured she just might be able to move in two months' time, three at the most.

Bella knew she was wrong for what she was doing but all she was thinking about was survival, hers.

Stealing was easier than she thought, especially when the stores were busy. She discovered she didn't have to be down with anyone, she could do this on her own.

Over the next couple of weeks Bella wore her new clothes to school. When someone complimented her on her gear,

she let it slip what she was doing. She even cut her price under 50 percent to beat out the competition.

Bella tried to justify what she and Mr. Lee were doing by telling herself it wasn't that bad because she wasn't having sex with him, he just liked to see her naked and play with himself. If he tried to take it further, she was going to end it. Actually, it depended on how much he would offer her.

It didn't take long for her to find out. After a month of seeing him about twice a week, he finally asked for sex. Scared because she was still physically a virgin, she told him no but when he told her to name her price, she decided to reconsider.

This just might be it, this just might be my opportunity to leave.

"One thousand dollars," she told him while she thought there was absolutely no way he would agree to it.

To her surprise he did and they arranged for her to cut school so they would meet at a hotel.

This was not the way Bella thought she would lose her virginity but at least she was being paid for it.

She put it in her mind that she was going to have to lose it one day anyway and at least this way it was all under her control.

That day they met at the Holiday Inn, Bella was scared out of her mind. How bad was it going to hurt? How would it happen? She asked herself all these questions and more. Not that it mattered because her clothes were packed. After this was over, she would not be returning to the Reeds' home.

Before anything happened, she asked him for the money. He handed it over. He also pulled out a little yellow pill.

"What's that?" she asked.

"It's something to ease your nerves."

"I don't do drugs."

"It's not really a drug."

Bella gave him the *I'm not stupid look.*

He insisted that she take it. "It'll take the edge off," he told her. "You'll be more relaxed."

After taking the pill and having a couple of drinks, Bella lost her virginity, all for the sake of cash.

When they were done, Bella saw the blood on the sheets and told Mr. Lee that she was ready for him to leave, that she needed to be by herself.

Of course, he begged to see her again. She just looked at him. She knew she'd never be returning to this place or be in his presence anymore.

Bella didn't remember a thing about the sex and that was a good thing, but when she saw the blood on the sheets she cried, stood up, took the sheets off the bed and stuffed them in the garbage can. She then went into the bathroom to take a bath.

As she waited for the tub to fill with water, she thought to herself, *I have over three thousand dollars in cash and the ability to steal, what more could a girl ask for?*

That day was the beginning of a new life for Bella. It was the day she lost her virginity, the day she turned fifteen and the day she left the Reeds.

CHAPTER TWO

ELSIE

Dear Journal,

Today I am starting a new venture—not only am I starting a new venture, I'm ready to make some serious changes in my life. I'm ready to share my life with a child. How is this going to happen when I'm a gay woman? Well, it's happened for many other gay women. I just need to look into the options that are available and God willing, I'll be a mother.

Today I'm opening my nonprofit organization called the Essence of Self Center. I'm so thankful to be given this opportunity to assist in the growth of young women. We should be willing to give back because what goes around comes around and when you help others good things come your way. It's called karma.

This past year has been one of growth, setbacks, heartaches, heartbreaks and bullshit, but I've overcome and I'll continue to overcome.

So, journal, I start this morning off by thanking you for

being the one consistent thing in my life that I could turn to and talk to without judgments.

Everyone should be so lucky.

Your friend, Elsie

Elsie found herself thinking about babies constantly. She was ready to be a mother, a birth mother, not an adoptive mom, not a foster mom and not a godmother. She wanted her very own child and she wanted a baby to come out of her womb. The question remained, how it would get there, because she wasn't up to fucking a man, that wasn't going to happen.

Elsie was seriously considering getting a sperm donor. Once she got the Essence of Self Center up and running, she was going to start researching the process.

Every morning when she woke up, her mind was on motherhood. Perhaps it was because she often dreamed of her ex-girlfriend Summer and her daughter Winter. If she had not been such an asshole and they would have stayed together, they would be a family. She would be a mother by extension and then maybe, just maybe, she wouldn't be so pressed to have a child.

It was five in the morning when Elsie glanced at her clock. She hadn't even set her alarm; it was like her body knew she was on a mission that morning. Elsie stretched across the bed and let out a big yawn.

"God, I thank you for another day," Elsie said out loud just before she climbed out of the bed. She walked into her bathroom, flicked on the light, opened the doors to her shower and turned the water on. She had quite a morning planned and there was nothing like a cool shower to wake her body up.

She took off the only thing she wore to bed, her panties,

climbed in the shower, stood under the water and let the coolness hit her body.

She threw her head back, allowing the water to hit her face and run down to her throat, while she psyched herself up for the hour and a half that lay ahead. She was meeting with Angel, her personal trainer, at the park.

Elsie reached on top of the door for her rag, grabbed her peppermint body gel and wiped her body down while inhaling the scent, invigorating her mind.

Ten minutes later she dried off and threw on some deodorant, sweatpants, a sports bra and a T-shirt.

Why she let Angel talk her into doing a boot camp workout, was beyond her. She was comfortable sticking with the treadmill and free weights; too bad it wasn't enough. She wasn't seeing the changes in her body she wanted to see.

When she told Angel, "I work out almost five days a week. I've improved my eating habits but I'm not getting the results I want," Angel told her, "you should never get too comfortable with your workout because once you do your body gets comfortable, and that's when you'll stop seeing changes. What good is it to do all this work if your body stays the same?"

Elsie had to admit, Angel was on point with that one because whenever she looked in the mirror, she saw a lot of changes she wanted to make. Okay, maybe not a lot but a few like the age-old slimmer thighs, flatter belly and tighter ass, every female's wish list.

When Elsie pulled up to the park, she noticed that Angel was already there and had the audacity to be stretching out.

"What the hell?" Elise asked, as she approached her. "Did you sleep here?"

Angel laughed. "I figured I'd get here first and get a little

run in, plus when I show up before my clients, it looks good."

Elsie chose Angel as a trainer because at the gym, she always seemed personable with the people she was working with. They also seemed to be having a good time. If someone could make working out seem like fun, then that's who she wanted to train her.

"All right, are you ready to burn fat, build muscle and sweat for the next hour and fifteen minutes?" Angel asked, as she jumped up and down and warmed up her body.

"I'm always ready," Elsie lied.

"That's what I like to hear."

Elsie looked at Angel and just like she did at every session wished Angel was gay, but she learned a while ago that wasn't the case.

"I'm strictly, dickly," was Angel's response, when Elsie asked her if she'd ever been with a woman.

For the next hour and fifteen minutes, Elsie ran, jumped up steps, squatted, lunged and did so many push-ups that she had convinced herself she'd lost an inch from that workout alone.

After they walked around the track one final time for a cooldown, Angel hugged Elsie. "Congratulations, girl, today's your big day, you're getting ready to change lives with your organization."

Elsie liked the sound of that. "Yep, I am."

After they said their good-byes, Elsie went home to get started with the rest of her day. Exhausted and hungry from the workout, she threw some frozen fruit and protein powder in the blender and took another shower.

While in the shower, Elsie placed her hands on her stomach. She was doing all this work to have flat abs and a toned body just to lose the results by eventually having a baby.

What was the point, she wondered; it didn't make any sense, but then again it did, because when she finally got pregnant she wanted to be in the best shape possible.

After her breakup with Summer, Elsie didn't know what she was going to do relationship-wise. She knew she needed to take time for herself and that's what she did. She didn't date or have casual sex. She was never one to do that anyway. Being alone allowed her time to think about her life and the direction she was headed in. That's how the whole nonprofit organization idea came up.

That's not the only idea that came up. It was then she realized that she wasn't getting any younger. She also realized that marriage didn't look like it was going to be in the picture and because of these two issues, she was going to miss out on something wonderful and that's a child.

An hour later when Elsie arrived at the Center, she was the first one there as planned.

Crystal, Susan, Jewell, her pastor Bella, who was coming to bless the building, Faith, a counselor she hired with Susan's referral, a couple of reporters and a photographer were all coming a little later.

Elsie was proud of what she turned from a thought to reality. Every little detail was carefully thought out, especially the location of the center, which was in Asbury Park, New Jersey.

Asbury Park is a small suburban town that's two square miles. This small town has had its share of ups and downs. The Center was housed in a building that was a few blocks down from the beach, which was a shadow of the past. It used to be a tourist site but times had changed due to riots and other negative activities in the 1970s.

The reason Elsie chose Asbury Park for her location was because there had been some resurgence in the Asbury Park

real estate market and it was in the process of being redeveloped. She wanted to be a part of that redevelopment. She saw big things happening there. She knew it would be a struggle but she was here for the battle.

It bugged Elsie out how on one side of town, people were out and about shopping and strolling, stores were open and it looked like a little city. While on the other side of town, just two physical blocks over, it was the hood. There were run-down homes and people hanging on corners obviously selling drugs, because they knew no other way of life. A local store called Sheffields was the main hangout for teenagers.

Would that ever change? She didn't know, but she hoped. Elsie's goal was to bring the two sides together and to assist the women who were struggling to survive, maintain or just keep it together in the community.

She believed that when you change, educate and uplift one female, you were changing, educating and uplifting a generation.

Elsie paused at the door and ran her hand across the sign that read THE ESSENCE OF SELF CENTER. This was an important moment and she wanted to take it all in.

She pulled her key out of her bag and opened the door. She turned on the lights and glanced around. As the first one to enter the center she looked around the room to see what impression the others would receive when they arrived.

She wanted the reception area to be welcoming, more like a guest area as opposed to a waiting area. She chose warm, serene blues and comfortable furniture. She didn't purchase regular chairs, she chose two loungers and a chaise. You sank when you sat down in them. There was also a coffee table with magazines and uplifting books on display and two end tables. Up against the wall, she placed two bookshelves, with a variety of authors. The reception desk was facing the

door on a slant, she didn't want the receptionist to be up in people's faces the second they walked through the door. Elsie was pleased with her design.

So pleased that she wanted to cry tears of joy but she would save that moment for another time. She wanted to be clear-eyed when people arrived.

Elsie walked from room to room, office to office, thanking God for the space, for the chance, for allowing her to be in this position and for the opportunity.

She then sat in the guest area and meditated for fifteen minutes in the silence of the room, bringing positive and peaceful energy to the space. Afterward, she went into her office and sat behind her scroll-carved mahogany desk, the most expensive item in the center. It was an antique that still had its original knobs. She saw it on a recent trip to Los Angeles. She shipped it to herself as a gift. It was a celebration of a new beginning.

Elsie pulled the day's schedule out of her desk and went over it. She thought about what she would say to the press, how she would thank her supporters and the board members for assisting her. Anything else she had to say, she'd flow naturally. She didn't want to sound rehearsed in her responses.

As Elsie looked over her paperwork, she heard the front office door open and the sound of footsteps.

Elsie moved from behind her desk and went to see who it was when she heard, "Elsie!"

It was Crystal. Elsie met her in the small hallway.

"Hey girl," Crystal reached out for a hug.

"You're early," Elsie told her as she hugged her back.

Crystal glanced at her watch. "Only by thirty minutes. I thought I'd come see if you needed any help."

"Actually, I do. The caterers will be here soon, you can show them to the conference room and—"

Crystal cut her off. "Look at you, hiring caterers, having a press conference, I'm so proud of you."

Elsie waved the compliment off. "Girl, please, had you not helped me get it together and agreed to be the board president, I don't know what I would have done."

Crystal smiled and replied, "You would have done just what you're doing, your damn thing."

Elsie wasn't too sure about that; after her breakup with Summer, she surprised herself by going into a depression. If Crystal hadn't been there to talk her through it and had she not invited her to church, Elsie didn't know what the outcome would have been.

Elsie thought about the day she was in her office with the door locked. For weeks she had been feeling listless, she didn't feel like doing anything, much less coming to work representing people in the court of law. Law wasn't in her spirit; she was so ready to get out of that field of work. She questioned how she could continue being a lawyer, representing others when she was barely representing her true self.

Elsie was putting up a front on a daily basis. It was taking everything in her power to come into the office.

On top of being lonely, the one escape she thought she had, which was her work, was becoming a burden. At night her mind was always racing, thinking of what she could or should be doing with her life and on top of everything else, she wasn't sleeping well.

One day while sitting in her office with the door locked and her head down, there was a knock on her door.

"It's Crystal, let me in."

Not wanting to be rude, Elsie let her in.

Crystal knew that Elsie wasn't one to shut herself in, to not

give anyone access. Out of all the women in the office, Elsie was the one you could count on, the one that had your back, the peacemaker when someone started to get on your nerves. Crystal was concerned and wanted to know what the hell was going on.

"May I take a seat?" Crystal asked.

"Of course," Elsie told her.

Crystal sat in the love seat Elsie had in her office. Crystal and Susan thought Elsie had lost it when the love seat was delivered. They wondered why she was putting a love seat in her office and not a regular table, with four chairs for clients to sit at. When they asked her, Elsie told them she wanted her clients to feel comfortable. "As their attorney, they need to feel free and trust me, to be able to open up and by them being comfortable, it will allow them to do so."

"So, you want to be a psychological attorney?" Susan joked.

As it turned out, Elsie's idea was a great one and her clients referred others because they felt like not only did Elsie represent them, but that she genuinely cared.

Crystal and Susan followed her lead and made their offices more comfortable and welcoming.

"So," Crystal started as she relaxed into the comfort of the love seat, "what's going on with you?"

"What do you mean?"

"You seem detached, like you have a lot on your mind, like you're not at peace."

That was all it took for Elsie to break down. Prior to that moment, Elsie had not realized she'd been holding so much in.

Was that all it took, for someone to ask how she was doing for her to fall apart? Normally she was the caretaker, the one asking how the other was doing.

"Girl, I don't know what the hell is wrong with me. All I know is that I'm tired, that I am mentally drained and I feel like something is missing from my life."

"Well, you are single,.maybe you miss having a companion," Crystal suggested.

Elsie shook her head. "No it's not that, it's deeper than that. What I'm feeling is not about being relationship-free. I mean, yeah, I get lonely but I can find things to do to occupy my time and fill the space. It's more like an inner sadness. I feel like I'm searching for something and just don't know what it is and for some reason I can't figure it out."

Crystal could relate, she knew what Elsie was talking about because she'd been there herself and the thing that got her through or should she say the place, was church. The turning point for her was not religion but getting in touch with her spirituality.

"Remember when I came back from visiting Mom?" Crystal asked.

"How can I forget? You were an emotional wreck."

"Yeah girl, you don't know the half of it." Crystal had went to see her mother, something she hadn't done in quite some time only to find out that her mother had cancer, which thank God was now in remission. On top of that, her mother had married the stepfather of the boy that raped her when she was in high school. Do you want to talk about a shock to the system?

"Well, what got me through," Crystal went on to say, "was God."

The last thing Elsie was in the mood to hear about was religion. She did not feel like being preached to.

As though Crystal could read her mind, she told her, "Now don't think I'm going to sit here and preach to you, that's not who I am. That's not what this is about at all, but

what I am going to do is quote a Bible verse, 'If God is for us, who can be against us?' "

Elsie looked at her like *that's suppose to move me, that's suppose to make me feel better?*

"Why are you looking at me like that?" Crystal asked.

"Because you're really sitting here quoting scripture to me like I'm just suppose to get it." Elsie wasn't a religious person nor was she a spiritual person. She had to admit that she just kind of existed.

Church was never really an option for her, she wasn't raised in church and she didn't attend now. Occasionally, she would turn on the television and catch a sermon. Every now and then, she'd surprise herself by being moved by something that was said. Sometimes she even found herself sitting down on the edge of her bed and listening to the whole message.

"I'm not really into religion," Elsie told Crystal. "I hear too much about pastors messing around, having babies by members of their congregation, women hating on one another and talking about each other behind their backs. I'm sure you've heard the same stories. Haven't you?"

"I have," Crystal admitted, "but I don't go to church for the people, I go for the message."

Elsie didn't have a response for that.

"You do believe in God, don't you?" Crystal asked.

"Of course," Elsie responded. She didn't tell Crystal that there were times when she wondered about his existence. There was so much evil, destruction and craziness in the world, that she wondered how can someone that's suppose to be the supreme being, the embodiment of all great things, the one who represents love, exist at all.

Was she alone in wondering if God was a physical being, a spiritual being or was he just someone that was a figment of

someone's imagination, made up and passed along through word of mouth? Was the Bible fiction or did all that it say really exist? How many hands had it passed through, how many people had tampered with it?

Eventually, Elsie had to accept that she'd never have an answer to her questions. So, instead of doubting, she choose to accept and believe.

It was better to live on hope and faith, to live as if there was a heaven and hell, then not. The way Elsie figured it is, she knew the basic rule of the Bible, which she interpreted as "do unto others as you would have them do unto you" and Elsie prided herself on being kind and respectful to all.

"You don't go to church to pay attention to what's going on around you. You don't go to church for the people, you go for the word, you go to feel peace in your spirit, you go for yourself," Crystal told her. "I know that's why I go and it's helped me through some moments that I otherwise would not have been able to get through."

By the time Crystal left Elsie's office, Elsie had promised her she would go to church with her on family and friends day.

It seemed like that day came sooner rather than later. When it arrived, Elsie wanted to call Crystal and pull out. She wanted to renege on her acceptance of the invite but she didn't and today, she could honestly say she was glad she didn't, because it was the day her life changed. It was the day she received some clarity on the path she was supposed to be taking.

So, for Crystal to be sitting next to her on the day she was opening the center, telling Elsie how proud she was, didn't make any sense to Elsie. What made better sense was for Elsie to tell Crystal how much she appreciated her for being there when she needed her the most.

When she told Crystal this, Crystal waved her off. "Girl, that's what friends are for."

Crystal was right; that is what friends are for, to pull each other up and to listen without judgment.

It was at that moment the phone on Elsie's desk rang.

"The first ring of the day," she said as she picked up the phone. "The Essence of Self Center, how may I help you?"

Crystal stood up and mouthed, "I'm going to look around."

On the other end of the phone was Susan. "I'm parking my car and I'm on my way up."

"I'll be waiting." Elsie hung up the phone and walked out of her office to find Crystal showing the caterers the way to the conference room.

Elsie went to greet Susan, only to find the reporters and the photographer trailing behind her.

"I bring with me the press," Susan said by way of greeting.

After the reporters left and everyone ate, Elsie, Crystal, Susan, Jewell, Bella and Faith were in the conference room for the center's first official meeting.

"Have you found a receptionist yet?" Jewell asked Elsie.

"I called a temp agency and asked them to send me someone that can answer phones and do secretarial work until I have a chance to do interviews."

"Well, my cousin is going to call you about the position."

"Is she dependable?"

"Of course, she's family."

"Not that, that means much," Susan joked.

"Ha! Ha! Ha!" Jewell said. "I love you too."

"Well, tell her to come by here tomorrow and I'll interview her," Elsie offered.

"Thanks, I appreciate it."

What Jewell hoped was not only would her cousin Har-

Angel M. Hunter

mony get the job but maybe working here and being around positive people would assist her in her growth.

"You're welcome," Elsie responded.

She looked at all the women around the table and thanked them individually. Each of them bought something to the Center that she alone could not provide.

Faith would counsel.

Bella would uplift.

Crystal and Susan would be there for administrative support as board members.

Elsie felt good about her new family, her family in spirit.

24

CHAPTER THREE

HARMONY

Dear Journal,

I don't know what the hell I was thinking having all these damn kids, this shit is hard as hell, even with a man. If I had it to do all over again, I would have been on like three birth controls, the pill, condoms and the sponge. I know people say you shouldn't live with regrets, but I do. Am I wrong?

Am I the only one that gets tired of her kids? Am I the only one that wants to up and disappear? It's not that they're disruptive or disobedient. Because believe me, I know some people with some badass kids that need to be knocked upside the head.

It's just that motherhood is all-consuming. It's like your life is no longer your own, you have to be concerned with another person all day, every day and you no longer exist as an individual.

I know, I know, I made the decision to have my babies, but damn, can a sister get a break?

Your homegirl, Harmony

As usual, Harmony was running late but it was hard to be on time when you have three kids. Her boss never took that shit into consideration. The last time she came to work late, he called her into the office, slammed the door behind her and told her if she was late one more time, it was a wrap. He was going to fire her ass and she knew he meant it. Harmony couldn't think of anything to say to make him change his mind because in a way, she was hoping he did just that. She was tired of her job and tired of being under his perverted-ass supervision.

When she glanced at the clock, Harmony cringed; damn, she was already more than forty minutes late, by the time she walked through the door, she'd be more than an hour and a half late.

Shit, she didn't know why she was even going in. Maybe she should bite the bullet, accept the inevitable, call out and deal with being fired.

As she was thinking these thoughts, her phone rang. Shareef had taken the kids to school and she was home alone. Normally, when she was trying to get ready for work she'd let it ring, because she knew once she started talking, it was no telling how long before she hung up.

Harmony looked at the phone, should she answer it, risk having a conversation and risk losing her job?

Yes, she should because the truth was her mind was made up, that half-ass job could kiss her ass. Yes, she needed the money, but on the real, she was tired of putting up with her boss's bullshit and harassment.

She knew he wanted to sleep with her because of things he would say, sexual innuendos and whatnot. Just last week he tried to brush up against her. She'd already made up her mind if he did that shit one more time, either she was going to beat his ass or worse, let Shareef know and then he'd get the real beat down.

Harmony walked over to the caller ID and saw that it was her cousin Jewell.

She picked up the phone. "What's up, ho?"

Jewell laughed. "You're the ho. What are you doing at home anyway? Aren't you supposed to be at work?"

"If you know I'm suppose to be at work, why the hell are you calling me?"

"Because I know you and your late ass."

Harmony laughed. She couldn't respond because Jewell spoke only the truth. "So what's up?"

"I know you've been looking for a new job and I just might have an opportunity for you."

"For real?" Harmony felt the anticipation rising. She hoped Jewell wasn't playing her, but then again, her cousin would never do that.

"Yes, for real."

"You know I love you, right."

"Yeah, yeah. I just figured since you're ready to move on and up, whatever I can do to help, I will. We both know that working at a cabstand isn't going to get you anywhere near where you want to be."

Jewell was right, working at a cabstand just wasn't the move anymore. She needed to be an example for her kids and one of the ways of doing so would be to get a more professional job.

"So where is it?" Harmony wanted to know.

"Elsie is starting a—"

Harmony cut Jewell off. "Ain't that the gay chick you used to work for?"

"She's my friend."

"And?"

"You know what, never mind about the job, you're not ready yet, if you're going to have that attitude, maybe they're better off hiring someone else."

The last thing Harmony wanted Jewell to do was hang up. She needed this opportunity.

"I'm sorry, I'm sorry. That was ignorant. I didn't mean anything by it."

"Dang," Jewell joked. "I always have to bring a bitch up, don't I?"

Harmony knew Jewell was half-joking and half-serious with that comment. She was always helping her mature. Although Jewell was her older cousin, she acted more like a sister. She did a lot for her, when they were younger and as they got older. She was her best friend, her rock, her support and her kids' godmother.

Harmony used to feel like there was nothing she could do for Jewell to compensate for her love.

"I'm not there for you to get something in return, I'm there for you because we're family," Jewell would tell her.

Harmony still wanted to return the favors and when Jewell finally came to her a year ago for advice, she was more than happy to give it.

Even though it was relationship advice she was asking, something Harmony really wasn't qualified to give, she did it the best way she knew how, by being honest, raw and straight to the point.

Jewell was torn between two men: her baby's daddy and a white man, Evan, who treated her like a queen. After thinking about and talking about it constantly, Jewell ended up staying with King, her son's father, because to her, it was the right thing to do. Plus, she still loved him and for her son Tyson, keeping her family together was worth it.

"What's the job? Is it at the law firm?" Harmony hoped not, because she didn't feel ready for that, it was over her head.

"Would it matter if it was?" Jewell asked. She knew why

Harmony asked. "You never give yourself any credit. You're smart, Harmony, if you don't believe it, no one else will."

"No, it wouldn't matter," Harmony responded with hesitance in her voice.

"Good, I'm glad to hear that. But it's not, it's at the Essence of Self Center.

"What's that?"

"Elise started a nonprofit organization. She's going to be helping women and girls get ahead by offering workshops and having a place to meet."

"Shit, it sounds like the place I need to be. I'm past ready to better myself and stop depending on a man."

"Good for you, Harmony. But you know Shareef is a good man and you really shouldn't knock or belittle what he does."

"Oh, hell no! I'm not knocking it at all. I'm just ready to achieve something on my own, I'm ready to upgrade. I'm even thinking about going to back to school."

"For real?" Harmony could hear the approval in Jewell's voice.

"Yep," Harmony continued. "I think it's time for me to get my GED and maybe even register for college."

As Harmony said the words out loud, she found herself feeling both excited and anxious. To say the words out loud was one thing, to put action behind them was another, but she wasn't going to let fear stop her.

What if she failed the GED test? What if she found that she wasn't as smart as she thought she was? What if she turned out to be a dumb ass?

Harmony was fed up with being a statistic, with being just another black girl who had babies way too young by different men. She was tired of being a young black girl who didn't finish school and started fucking way too early. She didn't want to be another black girl that wasn't going anywhere in life.

"What's the position?"

"Administrative assistant."

"Does that mean I need to know how to type?"

"Do you?"

Harmony, embarrassed, answered honestly, "Not real fast, I have to look at the keys a lot."

"Well, here's what you do," Jewell advised. "Go to the library, get one of those learn-how-to-type programs—better yet, download one from the Internet and start practicing right now. You need to know how to type and not just for this job, but most jobs require that skill. You're also going to need it if you plan on going back to school."

Harmony knew her cousin was offering good advice and she was going to take it.

"So," Harmony asked, "should I call and set up an interview?"

"Yes, she's expecting you."

"Thank, cuz, this means a lot to me."

"Now, Harmony, this doesn't mean you got the job, it just means you got the shot at an interview."

"I understand."

"And dress professionally, be on time and don't speak that hood shit."

Another person would have been insulted but Jewell had traveled the road Harmony was taking now. Therefore, whatever Jewell told her to do or not to do, it was in her best interest to listen.

"I'll call this afternoon."

"Good."

Harmony felt a sense of relief, because maybe this was a sign that she was on her way to bigger and better things.

Changing the subject, Harmony asked Jewell about King. "How are things going between you two?"

SISTER GIRLS 2

"Girl," Jewell said, "things are what they are."

"What the hell does that mean?"

"It means we've fallen into a rut, the relationship rut."

Harmony knew just what she meant because she and Shareef were in that rut as well. For them it was the sexual rut. Hell, they were lucky if they made love once a week.

Harmony could tell that Shareef was getting pissed off about not having sex. What was she to do? She couldn't help it when her mind was preoccupied with other things like life, school, her kids and moving out the hood. When her mind raced this way the last thing on her mind was sex.

"I can't stop thinking about Evan," Jewell admitted, interrupting Harmony's thoughts.

"See, I knew that shit would happen especially after you ran into him those ~~few~~ times. Your ass better be careful, because like you told me, you have a good man."

"You ain't telling me anything I don't already know. But girl, that white boy knew he could eat some pussy."

Harmony laughed. "Are you saying King can't?"

"I'm not saying that at all, but with Evan, it was different, he devoured my shit."

"Good pussy eating does not make a good man, look at Ny'em. He tore my shit up when he did it and he ended up being an asshole. You and I both know you made the right decision by staying with King. If I had it to do it again, I would have chosen to have my kids by a man as good as King."

"You have a man as good as King right now and he acts likes a father to all those knuckleheads," Jewell reminded her.

"That I do and that he does."

Shortly after they hung up, Harmony thought about the job Jewell was trying to hook her up with. She was definitely

31

going to call. If she got the job, maybe she could get some sort of counseling while she was there. She needed someone to help her figure out her life.

Jewell didn't call her job, she knew her ass was fired, so she figured *why bother, it was time to move on anyway.*

CHAPTER FOUR

FAITH

Dear Journal,

How do I go on pretending? Why should I go on pretending? I'm tired of people looking at me thinking I've got it together, I don't have shit together.

My marriage is practically nonexistent. Raheem and I are basically roommates. Yes, he pays the majority of the bills, yes, I've been a kept woman for the past twelve years and yes, he was there when I needed him most and for this I'm grateful.

But now I want something more in a marriage, I want time and I want monogamy. I'm getting neither and it's no secret. He continues to hurt me and he doesn't even acknowledge it. I don't know how much longer I can take this.

I know I can't continue to do this shit! I can't continue living this way. I feel as though I'm compromising my dignity. This man doesn't even love me anymore. Why does he even want me here? For appearance sake? Definitely not for the sex because it's been a long time since that has happened. I need to get up the courage to leave his ass, but then what would I do?

Am I really ready to start over?
I'm stuck between a rock and a hard place and I'm determined to get out of it.

Forever yours, Faith

Faith sat on her patio, threw on her Gerald Levert CD, laid back on the lounger, closed her eyes and listened to it from beginning to end.

What a waste, she thought. *All that talent, all that fineness, gone.*

She let the music take her away, away to a place other than where she was and away to another reality. Faith felt like a fake and a phony. Here she was counseling, mentoring and guiding people's lives, when hers was a complete mess.

She'd been married for years. She and Raheem had been through it, in it, under it and around it. Her advice to people getting married was to think it through. Ask yourself, do you want another job, because that's what marriage is: work, overtime, extra hours and then some. If anyone says differently or feels differently, she wanted to know their secret.

Faith met her husband, Raheem, when she was deep into her addiction. She was actually high the day they met.

She remembered it, like it was yesterday. It was late at night and Faith was high as hell. It just happened to be the night she was contemplating ending her life. Faith had gone out and purchased a gram of cocaine, sniffed it up in under two hours then went and purchased another gram.

She was all alone getting high and pissed off at herself, because even though she wanted to stop snorting, it was out of her control. She didn't know why she continued to get high. It's not like she enjoyed the high anymore. She would just become more depressed but even depression didn't stop

her. Faith had started to wonder if she was an addict. If she was, she wasn't ready to admit it.

All she knew was earlier her man, John, broke up with her. He was the one that got her hooked and here she was all alone. She'd lost her job with the hospital as a counselor because she was late and absent more than she should have been.

It had gotten so out of hand that earlier that day her boss pulled her to the side and told her she best not return to work until she got her shit together. She told her that she needed to discontinue whatever she was doing and whomever she was doing it with because it was ruining her life and her career.

Faith tried to pretend like she didn't know what her boss was talking about, but she knew. She also suspected that her boss knew she was getting high and this suspicion was confirmed when she pulled open her drawer and pulled out a pamphlet.

"Here, I think you should take this."

Faith glanced at it and noticed the words *Narcotics Anonymous*.

"I don't need that," Faith told her, looking indignant.

Her boss looked at her and placed it on the desk. She stood up and said, "I'm going to leave it here in case you change your mind."

As she started to walk toward the door, she told Faith, "Don't come in tomorrow, I think you need to take a leave of absence."

"A leave of absence? For how long?"

"Indefinitely."

So there she was without a job. When she left the hospital that day all she could think about doing was getting home, calling John and asking him to come over to keep her com-

pany. Maybe they would even take a hit of cocaine together. Now mind you, she wasn't an addict but a hit would help her think clearer and decide what her next step would be, so she believed.

When Faith arrived home, she picked up the phone and dialed his number, only to find that it was disconnected.

"What the hell?" Faith then tried his cell number.

"Speak." John was always blunt.

"What's up with your phone being disconnected?"

"Obviously I didn't pay the bill."

"Must you be so nasty?" Faith asked. This was definitely not the mood she wanted him to be in when she called. All she wanted was his company and to have a good time in his presence.

"Why don't you come over tonight? I'd like to see you."

There was no response.

"John, didn't you hear me?"

He cleared his throat and told her, "Listen, I don't think this is working out."

Faith moved the phone from her ear, looked at the phone and put it back. "Excuse me?" She knew she must have misheard him.

"I don't want to see you anymore."

"What do you mean, you don't want to see me anymore? What did I do wrong? I don't understand. How are you going to spring this on me with no warning or anything?" Faith felt like she was begging and she didn't like the sound of it. "You know what?" she told him. "Let's have this conversation tomorrow."

"Won't be any need to. I won't be seeing you tomorrow."

"Huh?" Faith just knew that he was tripping.

"I'm ready to move on."

As much as she wanted to black out, scream and yell, she didn't. "It's just that easy for you, huh?"

"I don't think of it as being easy, I think of it as being what's best."

Unable to stop herself, Faith asked, "Please just tell me why."

"I've found someone else."

Faith wasn't stupid. What he meant was, that he found another bitch that would carry his ass. When she really thought about it and when she got honest with herself, it was the same thing in every relationship. She just couldn't seem to get it right. She was always choosing the same sorry-ass man in different skin. It was like they were drawn to her, and she was reeling them in, men who wanted to be carried, men who wanted their woman to foot the bill, men who were just plain ol' sorry. What the hell was wrong with her? Maybe it was the counselor in her. That was the only excuse she could come up with. She refused to believe she was like some of the patients she saw that felt unworthy.

The next time she met a man, Faith decided, she'd look him in the face and ask, "Are you him with a bigger penis? Are you him with a bald head? Are you him with an agenda?"

At some point, she knew she was going to have to step back and take a look at her choices. It's just that she'd always been a caretaker. She'd always been there for the underdog.

Maybe that's what made her fall apart and turn to drugs, being there for everyone and having no one to really be there for her. She tried to please everyone. Yep, that's what she was, a people pleaser.

The day John broke up with her, Faith decided enough was enough; she was tired of feeling used, of allowing her emotions and her neediness to get the best of her.

So off she went to get a fat-ass package of cocaine. She didn't want to feel anything; the only thing in her mind was being numb.

She picked up her package and pulled up alongside the

beachfront. This was her sacred place, her place to think, her place to unwind, her place where if she chose to end her life, this is where it would happen.

Faith sat in her car, stared at the ocean, ran through her list of men and saw how alike they all really were. It wasn't a short list either, it was a fucked-up list. Had she ever chosen a good man, a man that would take care of her, support her and not dog her out? It appeared not. Now what kind of shit was that? *Damn,* the realization hit her, *I do think I'm not worthy, that shit must have come from my father.*

"You're never going to amount to shit," he would tell her over and over.

"You're going to be just like your mother, worthless."

"When the hell are you going to grow up and move out?"

"Your mother should have taken you with her."

On and on he would go, tearing her apart with his words, breaking her down, belittling her and acting as if it was her fault her mother left.

She wanted to yell back at him, *Mommy left because of your sorry ass!*

It wasn't a big deal to see her mother get smacked in the face for something real simple like a spot on the dishes. He wouldn't let her mother have any friends or company. One time, when she was on the phone speaking to the one friend she did have, he hid in the attic listening and just as the conversation started getting good, just when her mother was laughing, he came out of the attic, took the phone from her and threw it across the room.

He kept her mother cooped up in the house. Simply put, she was his slave.

"A woman's place is in the house. A woman's place is in the kitchen. A woman's place is beneath her man," he would rant and rave.

Faith grew up hearing about a woman's place so much, she started to wonder, where the hell was *her* place. The older she got the more afraid she became of her father. He started to look at her in a way that made her uncomfortable and he'd taken to drinking more than usual. He'd come home from work drunk and talking a lot of shit.

"Look at you, growing titties and shit, you think you're a woman? Is that what you think?"

"I know you're sleeping around," he'd tell her. "Well, ain't no daughter of mine going to be sleeping around with these little knuckleheads."

One night when she was in the bed asleep, she woke up feeling as though someone was watching her. She turned over to see him standing at her bedroom door.

Oh, hell no, this cannot be happening. Faith had just turned sixteen. She'd had enough. She was not going to sit around this house another minute and wait for him to molest her. That shit happened to other people, not her. Faith was tired of being treated like a second-class citizen.

My father is wrong about me, and I'm going to prove it.

Faith ran away. She ran away to find her mother. She recalled hearing her mom talk about a sister that lived in New Jersey.

Faith stole the two thousand dollars her father thought he had hidden in his room and caught a bus to New Jersey. It was then that she found the town called Asbury Park.

Faith wasn't a dumb girl, she was more intelligent than most girls her age. She knew how to get around on her own. She knew enough to stay at one of those pay-by-the-week motels and most importantly, after taking a cab through the town and seeing how small it was, she figured everyone had to know one another, which meant someone had to know her mother.

All she had to do was go around and ask if anyone knew

Norma Stallworth. Surely, someone would. She tried not to think too hard about this chance she was taking, a sixteen-year-old, living in a motel, going around asking if anyone knew her mother was not the safe thing to do.

What would happen if she came up on the wrong person? What would happen if someone purposely lied to her and tried to get her alone and harm her in some way?

What would happen if someone actually said yes, they knew her mother and took her to where her mother was? What would happen if her mother told her she didn't want her around?

Wasn't it obvious that she didn't, after all, she just left her with her father, knowing the type of man he was. There was never a phone call and never a letter. She just straight abandoned her. Her mother left without a look back.

The more she asked herself these *what-would-happen* and *what-if* questions, the more she doubted herself and her abilities to see it through.

Maybe she was a jackass, maybe she wasn't going to be shit like her father said. Maybe the best thing would be to realize that she'd made a big-ass mistake coming to this town.

Even as she thought these things, she knew there was no turning back. She was in this town to find her mother and she would. She was just going to have to deal with whatever the consequences were going to be.

On the beach Faith sat, after losing her job and her man, reminiscing about the past. She finished sniffing her coke as she thought about the day she'd finally met someone that knew her mother.

It had been four weeks of fear, of doubt and of asking herself, would there really be a happy ending. Faith had gotten a job at Fayva, a shoe store in Seaview Square Mall.

Every now and then someone would come into the store

and she'd strike up a conversation. This one time, Faith noticed a woman that kept staring at her.

"Do I know you from somewhere?" Faith asked her.

"You look like a younger version of someone I know," she responded.

Not one to throw words to the wind and because she was in Asbury Park on a mission, Faith said, "Well, my mother is from this area."

"Who's your mother, dear?" the woman asked with an intense look on her face.

"Norma Stallworth," Faith told her.

The lady brought her hand up to her chest and if Faith wasn't mistaken, the lady's eyes watered up.

"Are you okay?" Faith asked her.

"Faith? Is your name Faith?"

Faith's heart started to race a mile a minute. She knew something major was about to happen, that whatever this woman was about to say would change her life forever.

"Yes, I'm Faith."

Before you knew it, the lady came around the counter and drew Faith into her arms.

Faith pulled away from the lady. "Who are you?"

"I'm your aunt."

By now, people in the store were looking, whispering and wondering what the hell was going on.

"My aunt?" Faith repeated.

"Yes, I'm your Aunt Gail."

Faith tried to remember if her mother had said that her sister's name was Gail. She couldn't. "You're my mother's sister?"

"Yes, sweetie, yes."

"How do I know if what you say is true?" Faith didn't really doubt her because what reason would this woman have to lie to her?

The woman took her purse off her shoulder, laid it down on the counter, opened it and pulled out a small photo album. "Take a look."

Faith took the photo album and started to look through it. What she saw overwhelmed her. There were a couple of pictures inside of her mother when she was younger, pictures that Faith had seen in her own household. There was also a picture of Faith and her mother sitting in a rocking chair when Faith was a toddler.

Faith looked up and stared at her newfound aunt and she could actually see the resemblance. After getting over the initial shock of this news, Faith asked about her mother. "Where is she? Where's my mother? She left us, she abandoned me, did she come here?"

Taking another hit of her coke, Faith thought about the emptiness she felt when her aunt told her that her mother had passed.

Her aunt reached out and took Faith's hand. "I'm sorry to tell you this, dear, but your mother died last year. She had diabetes and high blood pressure, sweetie. She went to be with the Lord."

Faith just stood there and looked at her aunt, trying to will her to take back what she just said. But from the look on her aunt's face, Faith knew it was true. Faith felt numb. She felt like all the air had left her body. There was no way this could be true, there was no way she could have gotten this close to finding her mother only to find out that she was dead.

The emptiness she felt that day was something she carried with her into adulthood. She was now an orphan. She felt as if she had no one.

Faith was hurt because she would not get the chance to ask her mother why she never came back and rescued her.

She'd never get the chance to ask her why didn't she take her when she left. She knew she left her in hell.

"Who are you here with? Is your father here? Where are you staying?" Her aunt fired off these questions quicker than she could respond.

Still in shock, Faith took down her aunt's number and address. She told her, "I'll call you or come by sometime this week."

As Faith said these words, she didn't know how true they were. Hell, she didn't know if she was going to be able to make it through the rest of the workday.

Somehow she did and when she got back to her motel room, she sat on the edge of the bed, looked at the phone and went back and forth in her head. "Should I call her or should I just let it go?" She really didn't want to let it go, but she didn't want to be hurt either.

There were so many questions going through Faith's mind. Would her aunt invite her into her life? Would she ask her to come and live with her? Did her mother tell her how abusive her father was? What could she tell her about her mother? Was she happy? Was she content?

Thinking back to that day, Faith had to be honest with herself and say it was the one time she had made the right decision.

She called her aunt, went to see her and ended up living with her. Her aunt never called her father and for the first time ever, Faith felt like she belonged somewhere, like she was wanted, like someone loved her.

There was one rule her aunt insisted upon, and that rule was college and in order to go to college, you had to finish high school, which Faith didn't have a problem with. She wanted to go back to school. She did and she excelled. She graduated at the top of her class.

But being book smart, having street wisdom and man/ relationship sense were three different things and just because you excelled in one, it definitely didn't mean you would excel in the other.

Faith's first real relationship was mentally abusive and the cycle continued. No, it may not have been physical abuse but verbal, financial and mental abuse was just as destructive.

Faith knew that she was repeating the same cycle over and over but for some reason she couldn't stop herself. It's like she was pressing the repeat button. Even as she sat on the beachfront getting high, Faith analyzed herself.

Her diagnosis was her father was to blame. It was because of him she felt like she didn't deserve happiness.

Faith wanted to stop trying to prove that she was worthy. She was tired of buying men, of overdoing everything to be with them. She was tired of letting men walk over her.

These thoughts and numerous others ran through her head when she noticed she was out of cocaine.

Faith looked out toward the ocean and contemplated walking into it. She wanted to let herself be taken away. Better yet, maybe she'd take her car and drive off the bridge.

Right when she was thinking these thoughts, there was a knock on her car window. Faith looked up and noticed a man bent over and peering in the window with a frown on his face.

She wanted to ignore him but knew that wouldn't do any good because he didn't look like someone that could easily be ignored.

Faith rolled down her window. "Yes?"

"Are you okay?" he asked.

The next thing Faith felt were the tears, which were running down her cheeks. She must have cried buckets of water. She was damn near wailing and she knew these crazy emotions were coming from her high.

"Open the door," the man insisted.

Faith looked at him and wiped her face. Just because she was high, it didn't mean she was crazy.

Faith turned the key in her ignition, pulled off and left the man standing there. The man was Raheem.

A week later, she returned to the beach.

This time she was sober as she sat on a bench and stared out at the ocean as she tried to figure out what she was going to do with her life.

"So," Faith heard a man's voice say, as he sat beside her. "No tears today?"

Faith looked up and thought to herself, *why is this man acting like he knows me, I don't know him.*

"Do I know you?" she asked, poised to leave the bench.

"Last week, here at the beach, you were in your car crying. When I asked how you were doing, you drove off."

Talk about embarrassed, if she could crawl under the bench she would have. Faith recalled being high as hell that night. When she made it home safely, she cleaned the house top to bottom as she tried to get the suicidal thoughts out of her head.

"Oh, yeah, I remember."

"So, are we feeling better?"

Better? At that point, Faith didn't know when or if she would ever feel better. What she did know was that she was willing and ready to take the necessary steps to making it happen.

In her hand Faith held the Narcotics Anonymous pamphlet her boss gave her. She didn't even recall sticking it in her purse, but she must have, because earlier that week when she was cleaning it out the pamphlet stared up at her, the pamphlet and a cut-up straw, which is what she used to do her lines of cocaine with.

As she stood looking from the pamphlet to the straw she

knew it was time to make a choice. She threw the straw away and stuck the pamphlet back inside her purse. With that action, her decision was made, now all she had to do was get up the nerves and actually go through with it.

When Faith looked up at this stranger talking to her, she noticed he was looking at the pamphlet in her hand.

Embarrassed, she covered it up.

"I—I have to go," Faith stuttered.

"Well, can I at least know your name?" he asked.

Faith saw no harm. "Faith."

"Well, I hope to see you again, Faith." He took a business card out of his pocket and handed it to her. "I'm Raheem, call me if you need a friend."

When Faith left the beach that night, she attended her first Narcotics Anonymous meeting. She also met Susan, someone who would become a lifelong friend.

CHAPTER FIVE

The week the Essence of Self Center opened exceeded Elsie's dreams. She was concerned that it would take a while for the word to spread that there was a location for young women to come and talk things out, to get advice, hang out, read, do homework or whatever would keep them out of trouble and out of the streets.

To her surprise, by day three they had received a number of phone calls and a few drop-bys. She still hadn't hired anyone yet and was hoping that Jewell's cousin would be the person. The day they were initially supposed to meet was postponed because one of Harmony's kids was sick. So they ended up rescheduling.

Tonight, Susan was having a little get-together at her house. When Elsie pulled into the driveway, she saw Crystal's car, Jewell's car and a few cars she didn't recognize. She was looking forward to this little get-together because recently Elsie felt like she had shut herself out from everyone and she thought it would be nice to actually be around some people.

Elsie parked about three houses down the street. By the time she reached Susan's house, Susan was standing at the door waiting on her. "I saw you when you drove by. Come on in," Susan greeted.

Elsie could see that the get-together was in full swing. There appeared to be a houseful of people.

"What did you do, invite everyone you know?" Elsie joked.

"Girl, these are Timothy's people. Had I known he was going to go out like this, I would have been better prepared. I thought we were having a small dinner party."

Elsie followed Susan into the living room and looked around. "Where is Timothy?"

"He had to run out and get more food."

"Elsie!" Crystal approached them. "It's about time you got here." Crystal started pulling Elsie into the "conversation room" where people were gathered and seemed to be deep into a heated conversation.

Elsie turned to Crystal. "What did I step into?"

"A battlefield, girl."

Elsie felt someone tap her on the shoulder. She turned around and was surprised to see Bella standing there. "I didn't know pastors went to parties," she joked.

"I just thought it was a dinner party. I didn't realize it was going to be so testosterone driven," Bella offered in way of explanation.

Even if she had known, the truth was Bella probably still would have showed up. She didn't feel like being alone tonight. Yes, she could go visit the unhealthy and those in need of prayer but for once, she felt like being around people that didn't want her to heal them or expect much from her. She just felt like some good company.

"Just because you're a pastor, it doesn't mean you can't enjoy an outing as much as the next person."

"You are right about that," Susan chimed in as she walked up behind them.

Elsie was about to step out the room and go into the kitchen to get something to eat when she heard a man's voice say, "Heck, you might as well call me a lesbian, I love women too."

On that note, Elsie, Bella, Crystal and Susan moved closer to the conversation.

"I know that's right," Timothy's friend Malik remarked. "You just don't know what you're getting into nowadays as far as relationships are concerned, everyone appears to bisexual, men and women."

Bella looked at Susan. "I think that may be my cue to leave."

"You don't have to leave, it's only a conversation."

Malik went on to say, "I think it's a damn shame, it's like being gay is okay. All this openness and acceptance is crazy. Every time I turn on the television, there's a gay character prancing around, whether it's a talk show, a television show or a reality show. What kind of shit is that? What kind of example are we setting for our kids?"

Elsie did not want to get involved in this conversation but she couldn't hold back. "You sound like you're homophobic. Do you have something against gay people?"

Susan looked at Elsie as if to say, *why did you even go there, why are you egging this asshole on.*

Malik told her, "I have nothing against anyone, I'm concerned for the next generation, that's all I'm saying."

Bella knew that Elsie was one of the gay members of her congregation. They'd talked about her sexual preference in private and they were developing a friendship outside of the church. "What do you mean, you're concerned for the next generation? Do you think that not accepting people for who they are is setting a good example?" Elsie asked.

"What I'm talking about," Malik tried to point out, "is the world is crazy enough without mixing up our babies. If we allow same-sex relationships, how do men learn how to be men and who teaches a woman how to be a lady and stay in her place?"

This touched a nerve in Faith. "What the hell do you mean, stay in her place?" Faith heard that shit growing up, she didn't want to hear it at a place where she was supposed to be having a good time.

Bella also put her two cents in. "Yeah, what do you mean by 'her place'?"

None of the other men in the room were saying a word, they were letting Malik stick his foot in his mouth.

"In my experience as a pastor, having counseled same-sex couples, I've come to see and understand that in their relationships their roles are clearly defined," Bella told him.

"Not to mention last I checked," Faith added, "many of you so-called men are not doing such a great job anyway."

Malik ignored that remark and looked at Bella. "So you don't think homosexuals are hell-bound?"

"I think anyone, regardless of their sexuality, could be hell-bound, as you say, if they are not doing the right thing. I don't believe you can go to hell based on who you love."

"What I don't understand," one of the other male guest decided to contribute, "is why when a woman wants to be with a woman, they end up with a woman that acts and looks like a man."

"Yeah," Malik said, "That shit just don't make sense to me."

Everyone looked at one another. It seemed no one had an answer, not even Elsie, who preferred feminine women.

"You know what," Susan said, "I think part of the problem between male and female relationships is sometimes you

men get so caught up in being the alpha male that you forget that women are your partners and not your property or servants."

Timothy looked at Susan, surprised that she would say such a thing. "Is that what you think I think?"

Susan smiled to reassure him. "Sweetie, you are one of the exceptions to the rule."

"But must you blame the man for the failure of today's relationships?" Timothy asked. "I'm a good man, who's to say that most men are not."

Malik didn't give Susan a chance to answer. "I don't think it has anything to do with the man at all. I think the problem started when someone thought of that equal-opportunity shit."

Crystal finally cut in. "What the hell are you talking about now?" She looked around at all the women and asked, "Why are we even entertaining this person?"

Malik went on. "The problem started once you women started working and earning a paycheck. When this happened, you started to believe we were equals." He looked at Bella. "On this, the pastor would even have to agree. It says it in the Bible, the man is the head of the household."

When these words come out of Malik's mouth, comments were heard all over the room.

"He done lost all his mind."

"Being head of the household is something you have to earn."

"We had to start working out of necessity, because of the sorry-ass men out there."

On and on the comments went, until Faith threw up her hands and said, "I'm a counselor and just the other day one of my clients came into the office in tears, distraught. She went on to tell me her man constantly cheats on her, he does

drugs, he's not attentive to her needs, a terrible lover, and most of all not bringing home enough money to take care of his family."

"Well, if it's that bad, why don't she leave!" someone yelled out.

"Because she believes she owes him for all the good he's done in the past. When they first got together, when she was down and out and he stood by her."

"That sounds like my sister!" someone called out. Everyone laughed, easing the tension.

Faith waited to see if anyone had anything else to say. She was hoping to get some insight to her situation, but it went unrecognized.

Bella looked at Malik and said, "Before I leave, I want to say this to you. You are correct in stating that the Bible suggests that the man should be the head of the household. However, he cannot be the head of the household if he is an incompetent, inept and unqualified leader."

"I know that's right, you tell him, sister," someone yelled from across the room.

Malik stood up and realized that he was losing the argument, and announced, "I have to piss, y'all can continue this conversation without me."

Once he had left the room, Timothy tried to redirect the energy and asked if anyone wanted to play spades. A few people said yes.

In the meantime, Bella tapped Elsie on the shoulder and signaled her to come into the kitchen. Faith followed

"Can you believe that character?" Faith asked them.

"At this point in life," Elsie answered, "I don't put anything past anyone. The world is messed up and people are screwed up in the mind, look at the news and read the paper. Shit, if he wants to know why women are turning gay

in record numbers he should look in the mirror, that's his answer right there."

A couple of hours passed by before Susan grew tired and ready to end the night. She motioned for Timothy to come into the kitchen.

"What's up?"

She looked at her watch. "How much longer?"

"Another hour or so."

Susan rubbed her neck and told him, "Let's make it thirty minutes."

"We can do that," Timothy agreed.

Susan leaned into Timothy and whispered, "You need to get someone to take your boy Malik home, he's had more than his share of drinks."

Timothy informed her that she wasn't telling him anything he didn't already know and that he had it all under control.

As people were leaving, Elsie asked Susan, "Do you want me to help you start cleaning up?"

"Yeah, girl, maybe people will get the hint and hurry it along."

A short while later, the house was empty and Elsie was helping Susan wash the last few dishes. "Thanks, girl, I appreciate it."

"You'd do the same for me," Elsie responded.

"And more," Susan told her.

Later that night, while Elsie lay in bed, she thought about what Malik said, about the examples that were being set for kids regarding sexuality.

Maybe that should be a discussion amongst the teenagers in the program, she thought, but she knew she would first have to get permission from the parents.

After listening in on the kids' conversations, she discovered that alot of the kids who were in middle school and high school were confused about their sexuality, that they didn't know the difference between experimentation and making a choice.

CHAPTER SIX

ELSIE

That following day after the party, Elsie decided it was time to admit the inevitable. It was time for Elsie to do what she'd been putting off doing for quite some time and that is to make a decision about the baby she so desperately wanted to have.

She knew she couldn't do it on her own, that she was going to need a man's seed. The question that remained to be seen was how was that going to happen? She couldn't remember the last time she had a dick up in her.

She could always adopt a baby, but that was a process that Elsie wasn't sure she wanted to go through. She also wasn't sure how she would feel about raising another person's child. What if she fell in love with the child and when they got older they wanted to find their birth parents, how would she feel about that? What if the child grew up full of resentment because she wasn't the kid's real mother? How wrong would it be not to want that information exposed?

Plus, Elsie wanted a child that resembled her. Would she be able to find one? What were the odds of that happening?

Could she and would she be willing to adopt a kid of a different race? How open was she to that?

What about a sperm donor? Would she really be able to step through the doors of a sperm bank, look through some strange man's file and say, he's the one, that's the man I want to have a baby by? Who's to say when the man was filling out his papers that he wasn't lying, building himself up to be the man he wanted to be and not the asshole he was.

What a person puts down on paper and who they are in the actual flesh can be two totally different things. What if the sperm was contaminated? What kind of tests did they run? Was she really willing to take that chance? There were a thousand and one questions Elsie needed answers to before she could make the proper decision.

Elsie knew she was panicking, she was almost certain that the men were checked out thoroughly before being allowed to donate sperm.

One of the things that bothered her about doing it that way, is that it was so damn impersonal. Maybe that would be best, that way the child would belong to her and only her, she wouldn't have to worry about child support and other things women worry about when having a baby by a man they know.

She was more than willing to raise a child all by herself. She was willing to be a single mom. Elsie knew she was capable.

Later in the week she would look into the whole sperm-donor situation a little more. It wouldn't hurt, even if she decided not to do it, at least she'd have the information.

Elsie was driving to For the Soul, a bookstore that had just opened at the mall.

Her mind was so preoccupied with these thoughts, that she was startled when she heard a horn blowing behind her.

Elsie looked in her rearview mirror and the woman behind motioned to the lights. Elsie looked at the light and said, "Oh shit." It had turned green without her even realizing it.

Elsie looked back in the rearview mirror. She could see that the woman was getting impatient because she was all frowned up, so Elsie pulled off. A short while later Elsie noticed that the car that was behind her at the light seemed to be following her.

"What the hell?' Elsie said out loud while thinking, *there was no way in the world this woman was following her to curse her out.* Shit wasn't that serious and if it was, Elsie would handle it.

When Elsie pulled into the parking lot of the mall, she turned off her engine and looked around to see if the car was anywhere in sight. She spotted the lady parking a few spots down from her.

Okay, maybe she wasn't following me. It is likely she was coming to the mall just like I was.

Elsie leaned over, grabbed her purse off the floor in the back and noticed that on the backseat of the car, the magazine she'd been meaning to read was opened to a page that advertised for foster care. Was it a sign? She wondered. Elsie sat back up, pulled out her lip gloss and put some on, while thinking, *is God trying to tell me something?* She placed the lip gloss back in her purse and got out the car.

Shopping was something Elsie hadn't done in quite some time. She had more than enough clothes from her days of modeling but that was some time and a few pounds ago. She needed to update her wardrobe, but today wasn't the day for that. She came to the mall with two stops in mind: the bookstore and Victoria's Secret.

When Elsie walked through the entrance to Macy's, she was in her own world. She didn't look behind her to see if

anyone was entering after her, she just let the door go and as it was closing, someone grabbed it.

Elsie turned around to apologize and saw the woman that was behind her at the light. "Bet you thought I was following you."

As Elsie let her pass, she told her, "Well, it did seem mighty suspicious. I thought maybe you were pissed and wanted me to know it."

The woman laughed. "I wasn't pissed. Believe me, I've been preoccupied with other things when driving as well. You just need to be careful with your thoughts when driving because the next thing you know, you'll be going somewhere you didn't mean to."

Elsie looked at her and wondered, *what the hell is she talking about?*

"I mean, life is hard as it is and sometimes the only time we get alone is in the car."

Elsie thought it was best to stop this lady right now because it was a conversation she was not trying to have, plus she didn't know this woman and she seemed like she was on a roll with whatever the hell she was talking about. Elsie just wanted to go to her two stores, get what she wanted and get the hell out. To have a conversation with a complete stranger was not on her to-do list.

Just when Elsie was about to dismiss her, the woman said, "Oh, I'm sorry, I don't mean to go on and on, you don't even know me."

Elsie lied and told her it was okay.

"No, it's not," the lady said. "I must seem like some psycho bitch."

Together they laughed. "Well," Elsie was honest with her, "it was a little awkward."

The woman turned and faced Elsie. "I'm Savannah."

"I'm Elsie."

After they shook hands, Savannah took a step back and looked at Elsie. "You look familiar."

"Well, they say we all have a twin," Elsie told her.

"No, that's not it." Savannah shook her head. "I've seen you somewhere . . . oh, I know, you're the young woman that just opened the center downtown, the essence-is-something-or-another."

Elsie nodded and said, "the Essence of Self Center."

"That's a great thing you're doing. I'm a gynecologist, if there's anything I can do for you, let me know."

That was an offer Elsie was not going to turn down. To have a doctor on her board of directors would be an excellent addition.

Savannah handed Elsie her card.

"I'll call you," Elsie told her.

Once out the store, they went their separate ways and Elsie couldn't help but think *that woman is crazy but fine.* She wondered if this Savannah woman was gay. Would luck be on her side? She doubted it very seriously. Luck was never on her side when it came to relationships.

For the past couple of weeks, she had dreams about her ex-girlfriend Summer. She didn't know if the dreams were because she was thinking of her in her subconscious or if it was because she was horny. Whatever the reason, she wanted so bad to call her and catch up, to see how she and her daughter were doing.

As Elsie recalled, what she and Summer had was special and they promised one another that they would remain friends even though they were no longer together. Instead they drifted apart.

Maybe it was because they both figured, *what's the point.* Now when Elsie thought about it, she saw what the point

was. When you love someone, you don't just let them go. Yes, she was the one who broke it off. She was also the one that caused the pain and now she regretted it.

She regretted telling Summer that she should focus on her relationship with her daughter, who had just moved in with her, and that she needed space. It was all a lie.

What was really going on was Elsie was starting to panic, she was going into the "am I really capable of a healthy relationship, can I make her happy, how long is this really going to last" mode. Instead of talking about it, Elsie decided to run away from it, to get out of the relationship.

Elsie looked at her watch. She had just under two hours to get to the office. She was meeting Jewell's cousin, Harmony, at 12:30 PM. She already knew she was going to hire her. She was trusting Jewell's judgment. She just wanted to speak with her and find out what kind of person she was and why she wanted the job. But most important, she wanted to feel her vibe, see if she was the type of person she wanted to be around every day.

Elsie was standing in line at Victoria's Secret about to pay for some undergarments when she felt someone place their hand on her waist.

She turned around with the quickness ready to knock someone out, but was surprised to see Trey, an old high school crush, standing behind her with a big-ass smile on his face.

"Oh my God, Trey?"

Laughing, he removed his hand. "The one and only."

Elsie wrapped her arms around him. "You still look the same, plus twenty something years."

Trey looked her up and down. "As do you, but just ten plus years."

They stood and looked at one another for a couple of seconds and sized each other up.

"I was walking by and glanced in," Trey told her. "I saw your profile and was like, oh shit, she looks like Elsie from high school. I wasn't too sure if it was you so I decided to take a chance and see. I'm glad I did."

"I'm glad you did too," Elsie said. "But what if it wasn't me?"

"Two things would have happened. I would have been embarrassed or I would have gotten a phone number."

"Well, you almost got your head knocked off, grabbing me around my waist like that," Elsie joked.

"Still the same feisty Elsie, huh?"

Elsie smiled. "Some things never change."

"Um, excuse me," the lady in line behind Elsie interrupted, "the line is moving."

Elsie looked in front of her and saw a huge space. She stepped to the side and let the other customers go in front of her.

"What are you doing here in Jersey? I thought you had moved to Los Angeles and was producing movies."

"Wow, you've been keeping up with me?"

"No, I read the tabloids," Elsie teased.

"Well, you heard correctly. Actually, I just bought a house in Asbury Park."

"Really?" Elsie knew that most of the homes in Asbury Park now sold for over three hundred thousand. There were some that were going for close to a million.

"Yes, really; after all, Asbury Park is on the rise, why not invest?"

"I hear that." Elsie looked at Trey again, this time taking in his tailored clothing and expensive shoes and jewelry. She couldn't believe that he was standing in front of her. What a

coincidence and coincidences were something she didn't believe in.

"Excuse me," the cashier said as she looked at Trey the whole time, "May I help you? Elsie put her things on the counter and pulled out her credit card.

"Are you free right now, maybe we can grab a cup of coffee or brunch and catch up on one another?" Trey asked.

"I'm really not. I was running into For the Soul and then I have to get to my office."

"Well, let me take your number and maybe we can get together this evening. I'd love to catch up."

Elsie looked at Trey and realized that she would love to catch up as well. After all, he was her first male crush. A crush that didn't go far because shortly afterwards she realized she was attracted to women.

"Here," Elsie pulled a card out of her purse, "call me and I'll let you know when I'm free."

The cashier gave Elsie back her card, the receipt and handed her the bag. Elsie looked at receipt, stuck it in her bag and started walking out the store with Trey behind her.

"A nonprofit, huh?" Trey was reading Elsie's business card.

"Yes."

"That's decent," he told her. "I'm going to call you."

"I'd like that," Elsie responded. She could feel him watching her as she walked away and knew that she was going to have to break it to him that she was gay. It amused Elsie when men tried to press up on her. She wasn't one to play the "lead him on game," she wanted men to know from the gate that she was interested in women only.

Of course, she would get the *you don't know what you're missing* or *maybe I can change your mind* line. What was it with some men, thinking dick was the answer?

* * *

When Elsie arrived at the office, a young lady was standing by the door.

"Harmony?" Elsie asked.

"Yes."

"Come on up." Elsie opened the door and led the way upstairs to the office. "Make yourself comfortable and I'll be right with you."

"Okay," Harmony replied as she sat down in the guest area. She glanced around and liked what she saw. *I could really see myself working here.*

Elsie went into her office and pulled the résumé Harmony faxed over out of her desk and skimmed through it. It didn't show any administrative experience but that was okay as long as she knew how to type. Elsie noticed that the light on the phone, which indicated there were messages, was blinking. *I'll check that later.*

She walked back into the guest area where Harmony sat patiently with a nervous look on her face. "You can relax, everything is going to be fine, come on, follow me."

Harmony stood up and Elsie took in her black pants suit. *At least she knows how to dress for an interview.*

Harmony followed behind Elsie and tried to think of something intelligent and witty to say. Nothing came to mind, so she figured it was best to keep her mouth shut and speak when spoken to.

Elsie took a seat behind her desk and Harmony sat across from her. "So," Elsie started and asked the dreaded question, "tell me about yourself."

What should I say, should I say I'm a single mom, or should I talk about what I want to accomplish? Freak it, I'm just going to wing it. "Well, what is it you would like to know?" Harmony asked.

"Whatever you want to tell me."

"Well, I'm a mother of three."

"Three?" Elsie was surprised to hear this, for some reason she thought Harmony was a mother of one. "That must be a challenge?"

Harmony sat up straighter and said, "Sometimes it is, but they're my babies and I'm up for the challenge."

Elsie nodded. "Do you have a significant other?" Elsie knew these were not the type of questions you asked someone when you were interviewing them but then again, she felt that it was okay because she wanted her office to be like a family. She needed to know as much as possible about the people she was going to be surrounding herself with.

"May I ask you what that has to do with the job?"

Elsie didn't respond immediately.

Scared that she messed up her chances, Harmony said, "Listen, I don't mean to be smart or anything, it's just that I really want this job and I hope that my having three kids won't jeopardize you considering me. I'm responsible, dependable and my children have never interfered with any job I've ever had."

Damn, this girl reminded Elsie of Jewell and her approach when she was first interviewed at the law firm. "That's not why I was asking. It's just that sometimes you may have to work in the evenings and when we have fund-raisers I'll need your assistance. Of course, that'll be later down the road but you should know this in advance. I don't want it to interfere with your family life."

"It won't interfere," Harmony let her know. "I have a great support system. I'll be available whenever you need me, if I'm your choice."

"Why this job, why should I hire you?"

"I know what the agency stands for and I would like to be a part of it. I'm trying to change my life and better myself and the way I figure it is by my being in the type of environ-

ment that promotes growth, it will make it that much easier for me to do." Inside Harmony was smiling her ass off. She impressed herself with that answer.

Elsie leaned back in her chair and Harmony could tell she had her attention.

"Can I keep it real with you?" Harmony asked.

"Yes, of course."

"I've been through a lot and for a long time I blamed other people. Nothing was ever my fault, my getting pregnant or my dropping out of school and now I realize that I have choices, that my past is just that, my past. It's time to leave it behind and move on. My future is up to me and I really hope you consider me for this position. I want to surround myself with positive women and according to Jewell, you are just that."

"Are you in school now?" Elsie asked.

"I'm studying for my GED and once I pass it, I'll be registering for college."

Elsie really wanted to hire someone with at least a high school education, but she was taken by Harmony and she felt like she could help her.

"Good for you," Elsie said. "Can you type?"

"Yes."

"How fast?"

"Over fifty words a minute and I'm getting faster every day. I've been practicing." Harmony had taken Jewell's advice and downloaded the typing program from the Internet.

"When would you be able to start?"

"As soon as possible."

"How about Tuesday morning at 10:00 A.M.?"

Harmony wanted to jump up and throw her arms around Elsie, but she remained calm. "I'll be here."

"Good. Faith, our therapist, will be here as well. You'll come in, I'll show you what I would like for you to do, we'll

go over the employee manual and then there will be a meeting with the board members. You'll get a chance to meet them all. How does that sound?"

Harmony felt tears welling up in her eyes. She was finally being given a chance. *Don't cry, do not cry.* "That sounds good."

Elsie stood up and held out her hand. "Welcome to the Essence of Self Center."

Harmony stood up and instead of shaking Elsie's hand, Harmony hugged her. She looked Elsie in her eyes and said, "Thank you. Thank you for giving me this chance."

Elsie felt good about her decision in hiring Harmony. She could tell that Harmony was sincere in wanting to change her life and if she could assist her in that process, she would. After all, that's why she started the agency.

The rest of the day went by without event. Elsie put together a marketing plan for the agency. She wanted to get the word out to schools, shelters and other centers about their services and she made a list of agencies she could collaborate with. A couple of people called and asked questions about their services. Two people left messages about needing therapy and wanting to know if their counseling fees were based on a sliding scale. That was something she and Faith were going to have to sit down and discuss.

By the time 5:00 PM rolled around, Elsie was hungry and in need of coffee. She decided to close the office and pick up something to eat on her way home. She had made up her mind to call Summer, now she just had to get up the nerve. As she was walking towards the door, she heard the office phone ring. *I'll let the service pick it up and check the message from the car.*

In the car, before pulling off, she checked the message and was pleased with what she heard.

"This is Trey, calling for Elsie, just wanted to say, it was a pleasure seeing you today and if you get this message before the night is over, please feel free to contact me."

Elsie had to listen to the message twice to write down the contact information he'd left. She called him back and agreed to meet him for dinner. What the hell, she didn't have anything else to do.

CHAPTER SEVEN

BELLA

Dear Journal,

Last night, I've found my thoughts slipping, turning and tossing, going in a direction they have no business going in. God, I ask for your forgiveness.

I ask that you be with me when I have lustful thoughts. I think I've become consumed with sex. I think about it often and want it even more. I'm human and I have needs. Thankfully, I can control those needs.

Living by fleshly desires is a thing of my past, something I've left alone and behind.

But I have to be honest, God, or keep it real, as the young folks say. I miss sex, I miss companionship and I miss having a body laying next to mine. It seems as thought my libido is working overtime.

Right now, my hormones are out of whack and the only thing I can do about it, the only thing I can do to stop the urge is masturbate.

Why?
Because prayer alone simply ain't working.

Love and Peace, Bella

Bella finished writing in her journal, the one she carried with her when she needed to vent. She put it in her purse, placed it in her desk and locked it.

Bella wasn't paranoid nor was she a fool. She kept her desk locked at all times, not only because her journal was in it, but the sermons that she was working on and notes on the members of her congregation that came to her for counseling were kept in there as well.

She did this because prior to someone coming to their counseling session, she liked to review her notes that had important details on them. Things her congregation would only tell her. It still surprised Bella some of things people would confess or reveal to her. It was almost like they were asking for her forgiveness.

She could understand it, though, because when you tell someone your dirt, when you have a secret to reveal or when you've been keeping something inside that has you so ashamed, you always feel better once you get it out in the open, even if in the open is to another person. She wasn't just talking about telling God in prayer, either.

Of course, that's the first person she would tell someone who was sitting in front of her to do, *tell it to God and he'll help you work it out.* It's just that she understood the wanting to talk to a physical person, someone in the flesh, a therapist or something.

But people didn't want to go to a therapist, they instead wanted to come to her, and being a minister, she didn't turn them away. Instead she listened, prayed and never judged.

It didn't take long for the word to get out that Pastor Bella accepted all, that she made herself available to the commonest of man. It also helped that the location of her church was perfect. When she first started looking for a location, she was growing frustrated because no place spoke to her soul or her pocket.

Bella wasn't assigned to a church like most ministers were, she was starting her church from scratch and would be renting the space in which to house it.

Her initial plan was reach out to the homeless, the addicts and the prostitutes. She wanted them to know there was a way out of their current situation.

One morning she was taking a walk along the beach, when she saw a storefront and an older couple that was putting up a going out of business sign. Not able to believe her luck and hoping that God was on her side, she walked across the street to inquire.

They allowed her to look around inside and she saw potential. She saw what she could build through God's eyes. She would definitely need him to make it work. There was also land in the back where she could add onto the building if she so chose.

God was by her side, because initially, the owners of the space were going to put the building up for sale, but after speaking with them and telling them her plan, they decided to rent the space to her for an unbelievably low amount. They also agreed to allow her to rent with an option to buy.

Bella had money saved up and was expecting grant money to come in for her start-up. How she was going to get a congregation remained to be seen, but she believed if she could change her life completely, then she could do anything.

She used grant money she received and hired contractors to come in, knock down walls, and put up a podium, among other things. Her church was starting to take form.

She opened in the summer and because out of towners frequented the beach, they would stop in to hear a sermon. Locals being curious would stop in as well. It wasn't long before the church ended up taking a life of its own.

Bella couldn't believe what was happening to her, she never thought that life could be this good. She never thought that she would be the one making a difference. When she thought about her past life and present life, all Bella could do was be thankful, grateful and full of appreciation. Yet and still she wasn't content, when she should have been ecstatic.

Bella was living a second life, she was being given a second chance. Hooker to heaven, working the streets to working the pulpit wasn't anything but a miracle.

God saved her and she chose to spread the word about him because if he could save her and pull her out of the depths of an everyday hell, he could do it for anyone.

Bella knew that most people, at least once in their life, have had an all-time low, a rock-bottom moment, a moment when they had to make a decision that could move their life forward, keep it stuck or knock it down a notch. Hers came later than she would have liked, but she was thankful when it did and thankful that it came at all, because had it not, she would not be alive.

Bella sold her body in order to survive as a teenager. She didn't stand on the corners but the man she thought was her boyfriend later became her pimp. It was an age-old story.

Leon, at one time was her knight in shining armor or so she thought, but he quickly went from being her light to her darkness. He was nothing but evil.

Bella recalled one night when she was exhausted and just did not have the energy to meet with a "client."

Bella told Leon she wasn't feeling well.

"Well or not, you're fucking going out to make my money."

It seemed like the words *my money* echoed over and over in her ears because that's just what she was doing: making "his money;" money that went into his pocket.

He did buy her clothes, shoes, jewelry, and food but she sometimes had to beg for those things. She rarely had money of her own to carry around, yet Leon's pocket was always full, always fat.

She was growing tired of the whole thing. She was tired of depending on him. She was tired of fucking for him and she was tired of taking orders from him.

"I'm not going," she told him, unsure of how he would react but willing to take whatever he was going to give out.

Leon looked at her like she'd lost her mind. "Excuse me, what the fuck did you say?"

"I said, I'm not going." The fear of these words was reflected on her face and in her tone, but she was not going to back down.

Bella expected for them to argue back and forth. She didn't expect for him to haul off and hit her. He punched her over and over with his fist.

Just when Bella thought he was done he took off his belt and beat her some more, like she was a child. The whole time he was beating her, he was careful not to touch her face.

When he finally grew tired of the physical beat down, Leon stood over Bella, who was balled up on the floor in tears.

"Now go get your ass in the tub, soak for a little while, put on something sexy and go do what I said. This is a new client, a high roller. He's got a lot of fucking money. Treat him right and fuck him in the dark so he won't see your bruises. I'm running out, I'll be back in an hour, you should be dressed by then," and he walked out the door.

Bella stayed on the floor for about ten minutes after Leon left, trying to get herself together. Leon told her that this new client had a ton of money and knowing him, that meant he was probably charging this new client a few hundred bucks for the night.

Bella put it in her mind that she was going to take the money and run. As a matter of fact, she was going to take all Leon's money and run. She knew where he kept his stash. He didn't know she knew, but she did.

How was she going to do it without getting caught and without getting her ass kicked or killed, she didn't know, but she would figure it out.

Bella half-walked and half-limped to the bathroom to run herself a quick bath.

How dare that motherfucker beat me like I'm a child, she thought to herself as she started to cry again.

Bella took some Epsom salt and lavender oil from beneath the sink and poured it in the tub. She hoped that it would relax her and soothe the bruises.

Bella stepped out of her clothes but not before going into the kitchen and pulling out a bottle of wine.

Once in the tub, she lay back, closed her eyes and let the lavender and Epsom salt take over. Every now and then she would open her eyes and take a swig from the wine bottle.

When the water started turning cold, Bella climbed out the tub and rubbed her body down with some baby oil.

While in the tub, she developed a plan to get Leon's money and get him fucked up. This would be done without her being killed.

All she had to get was in touch with Rock and Ramsey, two thugs she purchased ecstasy and cocaine from and make a deal.

They were straight hustlers. If something financial was in

it for them they were bound to help out. After all, Ramsey and Rock loved the dollar more than the average man and she would be willing to split it three ways with them.

By the time Bella finished dressing, Leon had returned. "God, you look good," he had the audacity to tell her.

Bella ignored him.

"So you're ignoring me now?" He walked in front of her so that they were facing one another.

Bella refused to look at him. Instead she looked down at the floor. She saw his hands reaching into his pocket.

Bella followed his hands as she thought to herself, *this is the bullshit he always does, makes me feel like shit and then goes out to buy me something like that is going to make it all better.*

Sometimes it did, but this time she wouldn't allow it because she was more than physically hurt.

Yet, when he handed her the box, she found herself taking it and promising herself that after this, she would never take another thing from Leon, and by *never* she meant physically, mentally and verbally.

"Mr. Black is going to send a car for you in a half an hour, do whatever he tells you to do and I'll see you tomorrow."

"I take it you've already gotten paid," Bella remarked.

Leon didn't feel the need to respond, which Bella took as a yes.

"I'm going to run downstairs and get me a snack," Bella told him.

Leon waved her away. "Go ahead and make it snappy."

Bella couldn't get out the condo fast enough. She wasn't going for a snack. She was really going downstairs to look for Rock and Ramsey. She hoped they were in the neighborhood.

It's as if all the planets were in alignment because she didn't have to look too hard. When she entered the convenience store, there Ramsey stood, looking like the fine thug he was.

Bella and Ramsey had a brief affair a short while back. Truth be told, they almost fell in love with one another. No one knew about it, it was their secret. Eventually, they ended it because they both knew it wasn't going anywhere. The line of work she was in and the line of work he was in wouldn't allow it.

Bella walked up to him and asked in a whisper, "You got a minute?"

Ramsey whispered back, "Why are you whispering?"

Nervous, Bella looked around and told him, "I need to speak with you about something, something important."

"What's up," Ramsey asked. "You need a package on credit or something, because you know I don't do that credit shit for anyone."

"Nah, I've got a proposition for you and Rock, a proposition that will make you a large sum of money."

Ramsey raised his eyebrows. "Let's take it outside."

"I can't right now, but tomorrow, come up to the condo around midnight. I promise you, it'll be worth it."

She had his curiosity. "How worth it?"

"There's over ten thousand dollars in it for you."

When he heard that, Ramsey said, "let's talk about it right now, then."

"I can't, Leon is upstairs waiting for me and I have a date."

"I will be there at midnight, tomorrow."

"Good." Bella turned to leave but Ramsey grabbed her arm.

"Yes?" she asked as she looked him in the eye.

"Don't be playing me."

Bella knew that Ramsey didn't take kindly to being played, so she reassured him and placed one of her hands on top of his. "I'm not."

He let her go and she went back upstairs.

When Bella walked through the door, Leon looked at her

hands, which didn't have a thing in them. "Where's your snack?"

"I changed my mind," Bella told him and went into her room, where she closed the door behind her.

She sat on the edge of the bed and thought about her plan. Once completed, she was out of here and she was not going to look back. Bella looked around the room, stood up walked over to the closet, and looked at her wardrobe. There were only a few items she wanted to take with her, most of what she possessed, she felt, was paid for with her blood. *He can give this shit to another one of his hoes.*

Bella wasn't stupid, she knew he had another place of residence and that he had other women working for him. It was because of these reasons, she knew she would be home alone tomorrow at midnight. His routine never changed. When he came and went stayed the same, it was like clockwork.

The condo they were now in was his primary location, where he stayed the most, where he kept his most prized possessions.

So why didn't she just take the money while he was gone? Because he kept a lock on the safe, which was bolted down and he was the only person who knew the combination.

"Your ride is downstairs!" Leon called out.

Bella took one quick look in the mirror. Thank God he didn't hit her in face. She didn't know how she would be able to cover that up. Bella walked right by Leon without saying a word.

When she stepped outside she was surprised to see a Mercedes limo parked in front. There was no way this could be her ride. Leon simply didn't know this caliber of a person. So she looked down the street while wondering where her ride was.

"Bella?" the man from the car called out.

Oh shit, this must be my ride. Bella looked around to see if anyone was watching. They were. It seemed like the whole neighborhood was watching and wondering what the hell was this whore doing getting in that car. When did she become high-class?

When Bella stepped into the car, she didn't know it would be the last time she saw Leon.

"Welcome, I'm Black," the man that sat in the back introduced himself.

"I'm Bella," she told him as she took him in with her eyes.

As it turned out, Black wasn't like any other customer she'd been with. He was older, distinguished and his whole vibe was one of sophistication.

She thought they were going straight to a hotel but instead Black took her to see her first play. Bella felt like she was in a fairy tale and afterwards they went out to dinner. Black was a gentleman the whole time they were together. Bella wondered why the hell he had to pay for pussy.

Later when she asked him, he told her, "Because there is no work involved. I can leave town and do what I want with no ties and no commitment. Plus, I'm not a young man."

Bella was surprised to learn that he was in his fifties. There was something about Black that made her feel comfortable, like she could relax and didn't have to put on a show. She actually found herself laughing a time or two, something she never did when she was with a john. When he asked her about her past, she told him about her being a foster child and running away. That was something she never told anyone, especially a john.

That night as Bella was getting undressed she tried to hide the bruises Leon inflicted upon her but Black saw them and asked, "What happened?"

Bella was straight up and told him the truth.

"You're not going back there," he informed her.

Bella started laughing.

"What's so funny?" he asked.

Bella sat on the bed next to him and said, "This ain't some *Pretty Woman,* come-and-save-the-damsel-in-distress shit. You and I both know the circumstances in which we met, we both know I'm a whore and that I sell my body for money." She waited on him to say something back but he just sat there with a smirk on his face.

Bella stood up to leave. "What? You want to be my pimp now. Is that it?"

Black blocked her path. "You need to calm down and let me speak. Yes, I know the circumstances in which we met, but Bella, there's something about you, I don't know what it is, but you're special."

Bella rolled her eyes. She'd heard this shit from Leon when they first met.

Black smirked. "I see you rolling your eyes and that's okay, but I mean every word I'm saying. I'm not a pimp nor do I want to be one. I'm in town twice a month on business for three or four days at a time and I'd like company. I'd like to not have to go around looking for someone, I'd like to have someone waiting on me. Maybe you could be the one."

Bella sat on the bed and searched his face, she wanted him to be on the up-and-up, to not be pulling her leg. Could this be it? Could this be just what she needed to get out from under Leon, a sugar daddy?

Bella stayed the night and the next morning she told Black that she would like to be the one that waits for him when he returns. "But you need to understand that Leon isn't going to just let me go like that. It's not going to be that easy."

"Who said you had to go back there? You don't have to, I'll handle Leon." Black walked over to a suitcase that was in the corner and pulled out a set of keys. "I have an apartment

I rarely use." He threw the keys at her. "Here, take them, my driver will take you there when you're ready to go."

This shit doesn't just happen. Bella was in shock. She looked at Black and held back her tears. *Please let this be real, please let this be real.*

Bella took him up on his offer, but not after telling him that in the next day or two there were a few things she needed to wrap up.

Belle spent the majority of the day with Black, who took her shopping. Later when he had to go take care of some business, he told his driver to take her wherever she wanted to go.

That night around 11:30, Bella caught a taxi to the condo. Bella let herself in the apartment and was grabbing items such as her undergarments and jewelry.

At twelve on the dot, Bella heard a knock on the door. She knew without asking that it was Ramsey and Rock. She opened the door to let them in.

"So, you've moved up in the world, huh?" Ramey asked when he walked in.

"What are you talking about?"

"The vehicle that picked you up."

"All right, so tell us about this money," Rock interrupted.

Bella looked at Ramsey; she didn't really care for Rock. It was common knowledge he would do anything for money and dog anyone out to get it.

When she and Ramsey were seeing one another, she asked him why were they boys. "He's evil," she told him.

"He may be evil to some people, but we've grown up together, we've always had one another's back, he would never stab mine and I would never stab his."

Bella didn't say a word because she didn't put anything past anyone.

"Listen," Bella told Ramsey, "I'm leaving this area and this lifestyle alone."

"That what you called us up here to tell us?" Rock asked. He turned to walk out the door. "Come on, man, let's go, I don't have time for this bullshit."

Ramsey grabbed his arm to stop him. "Hold up, man, she's not done yet." Ramsey looked at Bella. "Are you?"

Bella walked over to the sofa and sat down. "No, I'm not." Bella took a deep breath and looked from one to the other. "I have a proposition but it must never leave this room, never and that's whether you agree to do it or not."

"Well, what the fuck is it?" Rock wanted to know, he was in a hurry. There was money to be made and he felt like time was passing him by fucking around with Bella.

"Promise me, give me your bonded word it won't leave this room."

"My word is my bond," Ramsey said.

Rock just stood there until Ramsey shot him a look.

"Damn, man, my word is bond as well."

"All right then, Leon keeps a safe here and I want you two to rob it, we'll split the profit three ways."

"How much are we talking about?" Rock wanted to know.

"We're talking over ten thousand dollars."

"Man, please," Rock waved her away. "That's only three apiece, it ain't worth it."

"She's talking about ten thousand apiece," Ramsey told him without taking his eyes of Bella. "That is what you're saying, right?"

"Yes it is," she told him.

"The safe here now?" Ramsey wanted to know.

"Yes, in the back room." She knew what was coming next.

"Well, why don't we just go get it right now?" Rock wanted to know.

"If it was that easy, do you think I'd be asking you two to help me? It's bolted to the floor and Leon has the one and only key to the lock, he carries it around with him and of course, only he knows the combination."

Ramsey and Rock took this in.

"All right, so what's the plan?" Rock wanted to know.

Bella went on to explain how she wanted them to give Leon a beat down, get the information they needed to open the safe and that they would meet up afterwards.

That was her biggest fear, them meeting up afterward. What if they decided to betray her and keep the money to themselves? That could happen, she wasn't trying to convince herself otherwise. All she could do was trust the situation and hope for the best.

She wanted to believe that Ramsey would do the right thing because of their past.

They made a plan to do it within the next day or two. Bella told Ramsey Leon's schedule. She also gave him the number to her beeper, the one Black gave her.

"Here's where you can reach me when it's done."

Ramsey and Rock said their good-byes but once Rock was out the door, Bella called Ramsey back.

"I really need this money, Ramsey, please don't disappoint me."

Ramsey knew that Bella was really asking him not to steal from her. "I've got your back."

Three days went by and Bella still hadn't heard a word from either of them. She was starting to suspect Ramsey of lying to her. She didn't want to go back to the neighborhood because she knew by now that Leon was looking for her.

After six days, she couldn't take it anymore, Bella had to

know what the hell was going on. She put on a sweat suit with a hoodie, called a cab and tried to go into the neighborhood incognito.

She had the taxi driver ride her around until she saw someone she recognized. "Pull over, pull over."

It was Willow, a young girl that ran errands for the neighborhood drug dealers.

With the hood on her head, Bella approached her. "Willow?"

When Willow saw who it was she said, "Oh my God, girl, where the hell have you been, everyone's been looking for you."

"Who is everyone?"

"The neighborhood, the police."

"The police?" Bella went into panic mode. *Please don't tell me Ramsey and Rock got caught and turned my name in.*

"Girl, don't you know Leon was killed?"

"Killed?" This is not what Bella wanted. "Killed?" "Killed?" Bella couldn't stop repeating herself. She was afraid to ask but she had to know. "Does anyone know who did it?"

Willow shook her head, "Nah, but—"

Bella didn't give her a chance to finish her sentence. "I've got to go."

"Wait!" Willow called out as Bella sprinted to the taxi.

"Please just take me back where you picked me up," she told the driver while in tears.

"What's wrong sister, is everything all right?"

"Does everything look all right?" she snapped.

"Damn, I was just being concerned."

Bella apologized. How could she tell this complete stranger that she may have had another man killed?

Maybe that explained why she hadn't heard from Ramsey and Rock, their asses were probably hiding out.

"Fuck! Fuck! Fuck!" Bella said under her breath. When she arrived at the apartment Black had her staying in she paid the driver, went inside and broke down.

She shed tears of frustration, anger, disappointment and yes, even sadness.

Although Leon mistreated her more than half the time, he took care of her the other half and if she was honest with herself, a part of her loved him.

She wished she could turn that part of her off but it wasn't that simple.

"What the hell did y'all do? What went wrong?" Bella yelled at the walls.

Just when Bella was feeling an anxiety attack coming on her pager went off. She took it off her hip and looked at the number.

The only people that had the number were Black and Ramsey. The number that showed up on the beeper did not look familiar, it could be either of them. In her panicked state, Bella thought to herself, "It could even be the police."

She did not want to call the number back. What if it was the police?

Bella started pacing back and forth when her pager went off again, this time with 911 at the end of the number.

Shit! Shit! Shit! What was she going to do?

"Fuck it!" Bella screamed and picked up the phone. She dialed the number and it was answered on the first ring.

"Bella?"

It was Ramsey.

"What happened? Leon's dead! Where's the—?"

Ramsey cut her off. "Where can we meet?"

Bella didn't answer. *What if he was setting her up?*

"Bella, where can we meet?"

"Tell me this, Ramsey, did you do it?"

Bella could hear Ramsey take a deep breath. "Would you believe me if I told you no?"

"Yes," Bella lied, "I would."

She could hear Ramsey breathe a sigh of relief.

"I have your portion of the money, let's meet."

Bella wanted so bad to believe him, she had to believe him. She told him where to meet her.

When Bella thought back to that day, she still wondered if Ramsey was honest with her or not. He told her that they whipped Leon's ass, they got him to tell them the combination and when they left him he was still alive. Ramsey swore to her neither he nor Rock killed Leon but it was no secret Rock was a killer.

Ruthless was his middle name. He gave Bella her share of the money, telling her, "I'll see you when I see you."

Bella continued to let Black take care of her and during that time, she saved just about every penny he gave her. She went back to school and got her high school diploma and then onto college. Black supported her every choice.

It was in college when she developed an interest in philosophy and religion, it was also what sent her on a quest for God.

Bella started attending various churches and Bible studies.

Black noticed the changes in her. He also knew it was time to let her go and grow. Plus, he found another woman, one that wasn't motivated to change.

To this day, Bella still thought about Black and how if he had not come into her life when he did, her life just might have been over. She was thankful for him and for a while they kept in touch. Black was more than a john to Bella, he was her guardian angel.

CHAPTER EIGHT

FAITH

Dear Journal,

Enough is enough, when he comes home I'm going tell him that I'm ready for a divorce. I just hope I can say it with conviction. How he's going to react? I have no idea but however he does, I'm just going to have to deal with it.

I'm tired of being a doormat, I'm tired of having sex with someone just because they think it's my duty. It's not even like it's that pleasurable and even though it's far and few in between, I no longer want to.

I'm in my thirties for goodness sake, and you'd think that with all I've been through, I would know better.

I do know better, it's just been hard to do better.

Your friend in need, Faith

Another hang up. Faith was tired of this shit. It'd been going on for so long now, too damn long and she was getting tired of the games, of pretending like things were

okay between them, tired of accepting the fact that he had mistresses.

She was his wife, damn it! It was either time to work it out or move on. Who was she kidding? There would be no moving on. The truth about their situation was there was nothing left to work on. The, I love you so much, I don't know what I'd do without you, feeling was gone. The "I can't live without you" had turned into "I'm grateful to you, love." That is not the type of love that kept a marriage together.

Faith refused to let Raheem walk all over her anymore. She refused to let him think he could see other women and that it was okay.

It amazed her the way some men seriously thought they could do whatever they wanted to and however they want to as long as they were paying the bills.

The night of Susan's party, listening to Timothy's friend Malik, showed Faith that this crazy way of thinking didn't only pertain to her household, that it was going on in a number of homes as well. Homes where the wives were treated as doormats, homes where they dealt with it because the men were financially well-off. Homes where outward appearances represented something different than what was actually going on, homes where the money was plentiful but the love was not.

The funny thing was when she'd counseled women that were in abusive relationships, women stayed in spite of what they were going through. She would try to convince them otherwise, she would try to talk them into leaving. "You don't have to live like that!" she'd tell them, but she was living the same way but under different circumstances.

Faith believed that she was getting too old for games, she wanted to be loved and cherished, not treated like a piece of property. She didn't want to feel like she was owned or like

she owed anyone. She didn't want to feel like she had to love someone because they helped her survive.

Faith finally beat her addiction and it had been years since she'd used. Put those years clean with years of use and you'd get a woman that still had inner struggles and inner demons. She wanted to rid herself of her personal demons; she needed to in order to continue helping others rid themselves of theirs.

On and off of cocaine for months at a time, a year off here and a year off there and a few binges in between had taken its toll on her physically, spiritually and mentally. Each time she returned to her habit, it had gotten worse. She attended meetings on and off, following a step here and a step there but never ready to surrender.

It was that *surrender* word Faith couldn't get past. Surrender to Faith meant giving her life up for someone else to run. She wasn't ready to do that.

What changed is when after a three-day binge, Faith got into a car accident and almost totaled the car. She didn't remember anything about the accident and that scared the shit out of her.

Faith decided to start attending meetings again and this time she was going to listen and learn instead of just sitting there and doubting. This time she was going to take part and tell her story instead of getting engrossed in others. This time she was going to get up the nerves and ask for a sponsor. That sponsor ended up being Susan and with Susan's support, her sobriety became a reality.

It was Susan that kept it gully and asked her how the hell she could be telling others what to do with their lives when hers was fucked-up. It was Susan that told her she was a fraud. Susan even advised her to take a step back from counseling and counsel her damn self.

It took a while for those words to soak in. But when they did, Faith went looking for an African American therapist, someone like herself, someone she felt would be able to better relate to her. It turned out the person's race didn't matter. She ended up using a black and a white therapist. They both offered something different.

It wasn't only therapy that helped her heal and become clean but it was also the prescription of antidepressants.

When they were first prescribed to her, Faith was like, there's no way she was going to take one drug to replace another. Hell, she wasn't so crazy that she needed a pill, she just needed time to get it together mentally, and she could figure it out on her own.

"Have you been able to figure it out yet?" Susan would ask her.

Just when she thought it was figured out, Faith would relapse. After going back and forth with sobriety and Susan finally saying she couldn't continue to be her sponsor if she didn't pull it together, Faith decided to give the antidepressants a try and this time to stick with it.

Maybe what she had was a chemical imbalance and if these little "helpers" did just that—helped her—then it would all work out for the best.

It did. The pills helped to balance her emotions and once that happened, she had clarity and once she had clarity she was able to make better choices and better decisions.

The funny thing about this was, when Raheem saw that she was doing better, that she was becoming stronger, he grew suspicious. He started going through her things and when he came across the antidepressants, he asked her, "What the hell do you need antidepressants for? You've got me to help you."

His reaction reminded Faith of something she'd heard in the NA room: very often people wanted a person to stay

where they were in life, even if it was stagnant, especially when they felt they had one up on you. Change made a lot of people feel uncomfortable, especially loved ones and when they saw that change for better was happening they often tried to jeopardize it in some way.

Faith was afraid that this is what would happen, therefore she tried to keep the fact that she was taking the pills a secret. She was also afraid she would be seen as being even weaker than she already was.

Faith was thankful for her "happy pill." She even noticed the difference in her behaviors. She wondered if it meant she really was emotionally unstable? How much longer could she have operated that way? How much longer before she was sent over the edge?

With Faith's newfound sense of self, she was ready to sit Raheem down and tell him what she'd finally realized and accepted herself, that she wanted a divorce.

There was some guilt with this decision because Raheem was an above-average provider. He did give her the option of working full- or part-time or not working at all, which is what happened when his kids from a previous marriage were living with them. She stayed home and took care of them. Now mind you, initially she was not feeling mothering someone else's children and she let Raheem know this.

"But that's what a good wife is supposed to do," Raheem told her. "I've taken good care of you, I've supported you and I've been there for you. I'm asking that you do this for me."

So she did.

When she left him, Faith knew that the financial security he provided her with, the lifestyle she'd grown accustomed to, would be a challenge giving up.

She had a top-of-the-line Mercedes, she lived in a house that realistically was too big for the both of them and he gave

her spending money every week, even with her earning her own money. She knew she should have stopped that a long time ago, but she loved having the extra money. Her situation was a fantasy to other women, what more could she possibly want? She had access to all the material things any woman would desire.

Faith realized this situation was about more than material things and status, it was about her dignity. It was about him respecting her as a person and not as property. It was about love, genuine love, real love, a love that surpasses all understanding, as the Bible put it. It was about the love she simply wasn't getting enough of.

In a way, Faith believed Raheem loved her but it was the love of a caretaker, not the love of husband and wife, not "till death do us apart" love.

Even with his other women, Faith allowed him to get up inside her. They made love once every couple of weeks, like it was a duty. She was a paid whore, at least that's how she was starting to feel. There'd been so many other women that she stopped caring. Faith started to accept Raheem for what he was. A provider only and in exchange for this provision she gave him the pussy.

Faith discovered his infidelities by the numerous hang ups on the phone, numbers he left lying around and whispered conversations she'd catch him having. She'd also had him followed on more than one occasion only to confirm what she already knew. Even with that evidence she wasn't ready to leave.

But for some reason, this morning was different. When the phone rang and she answered it, the silence on the other end didn't affect her the way it used to, it didn't upset her as much. Faith just moved the phone from her ear, looked at it, shook her head and just hung up. She was done. She was get-

ting too old to play these games. It was time for a confronta-
tion.

Faith looked at the time on the oven and saw that it was
nearing 6:00 PM. Raheem told her was coming home after
work. Whenever he made it a point to tell her this, she knew
what he was really saying is that he expected a home-cooked
meal on the table.

Well, too fucking bad, he could tell the bitch that hung up
on her to cook his dinner and Faith meant that from the bot-
tom of her heart. She would no longer hop, jump and skip
when he told her to. It just wasn't happening.

Faith was well aware that there would be a price to pay and
in her mind she was willing to pay it.

"A half an hour," Faith said out loud, counting down the
minutes before he arrived.

Faith thought back to the night they met on the beach
and he saw her NA pamphlet. Raheem was kind enough not
to judge or question her. What he did instead was ask her if
she wanted him to go with her. Faith surprised herself by say-
ing yes and together they found an open meeting that al-
lowed outsiders to attend.

All Faith did that first night was cry while Raheem held
her hand. After the meeting she went home with him and
she never left. Now in her thirties, Faith realized that she'd
never really been alone and on her own except for the time
she ran away.

After she moved out from her aunt, she went from man to
man, not allowing herself to get to know who she was as a
person.

Could she make it on her own? Would she fall apart?
Would she relapse or would she be the strong woman she
tried to counsel other women to be? Faith sat on the couch
and was dozing off when she felt someone touch her shoul-

ders. She opened her eyes to find Raheem standing over her asking, "Where's my dinner?"

Faith didn't answer him immediately. She was trying to get up the nerve to say to what she wanted to say.

He looked towards the kitchen. "I asked you a question."

Faith looked up at him and said, "Well, let me ask you a question. What bitch are you seeing now?"

Not one to deny or even try to play it off he said, "Listen, I don't have time for this shit. I had a long day at work. I'm here and hungry."

"Answer my question, Raheem." Faith was not going to let it go that easy. "How come every time I turn around, some skank is calling my house, breathing or hanging up in my ear?"

Raheem started walking towards the kitchen. "I'll fix myself a sandwich."

Not willing to back down, Faith stepped in front of him. "Who is she?"

Raheem fixed his gaze on Faith. "I don't know what you're talking about. Ain't nobody calling this house. You're always starting this shit, every few months, Faith, and it's starting to wear on me. I'm getting tired of it. It has to end, or else."

In the past when he would say something like that, it scared the hell out of her. She had a fear of being by herself and having to take of herself, but this time, she placed her hands on her hips and asked, "Or else what? Or else you're going to leave me?"

When he didn't answer her, Faith went on, "I'm getting tired of your empty threats. Say what you want to say, out with it."

Raheem told Faith to step out of his way.

"Or what, you're going to hit me like you used to?" This time she wouldn't allow it, she would fight him if necessary.

"What the hell has gotten into you? You're losing it,

Faith." Raheem frowned. "Are you getting high again? Is that it? Are you coming down from a high and that's what's got you acting all bold and shit."

She should have known he would throw that up in her face. "No, I'm not high, I'm not high at all, all I am is ready for a divorce." She waited on a reaction and there was none. So she repeated it: "I want a divorce."

Raheem sighed and moved past her. He walked into the kitchen with her following him. "Did you just say you want a divorce?"

"Yes." Faith was not backing down. "Look at us, Raheem; I mean, really take a look, are we happy together? Are we really happy? Or are we just passing each other by, pretending to be in a marriage? We're not a couple, we're living separate lives."

"That's never been a problem before." Raheem opened the pantry and pulled out some rolls.

"It's always been a problem, I've just never acknowledged it before."

He placed the bread on the island in center of the floor and told her, "I'm not going to give you a divorce, Faith; you might as well get that out of your head."

"Why not? You don't love me, you have other relationships, your kids are all grown, and why keep pretending?"

Faith sat down at the kitchen table and looked up at Raheem with tears in her eyes. "I can't do this anymore, I don't want to be in a loveless marriage. I don't want to be in an 'on paper only' marriage. I want more. I deserve more." Faith looked in Raheem's eyes, hoping to connect, hoping that he understood, hoping that he would be willing to let her go.

"You have other women, for goodness sake, you've had them almost our whole marriage. Why do you even want me here? I can move out and you can do you. You can be the bachelor you want to be."

Raheem left the rolls on the counter and walked over to Faith. He stood over top of her and what she saw on his face scared her. Before she could make a move or a sound, his hands were around her throat. He pulled her up to him and said under his breath, "I'm not going anywhere and neither are you." He removed his hands and told her, "Get a jacket, we're going out to eat," then he walked away.

Faith followed him while massaging her neck. It'd been a while since he'd put his hand on her. She knew why she allowed it the first few times. It was because of her self-esteem. Why she allowed it now when she knew better and wanted better was beyond her. As much as she told herself that if he put his hands on her ever again, she would fight back and call the police, she found herself doing neither.

Everything in Faith knew she should leave, just walk out, walk away but she couldn't make herself just do it.

The first time Raheem put his hands on her was when she confronted him about the "other woman." That was over ten years ago. He walked in the house full of life and shit, acting like he'd had the best fucking day in the world. Faith had been home crying her eyes out because once again someone called her, taunting her about the fact she was fucking her man and that he was going to leave the marriage, on and on it went until Faith had enough sense to hang up the telephone. She sat around all day and wondered why she continued to torture herself. That day she also purchased a gram of cocaine from her dealer on standby and got high.

So by the time Raheem arrived home, she was feeling like she could take on the world. Faith was ready to tear into his ass, she was not going to back down.

The second he walked in the door smiling like it was New Year's Eve and he'd just celebrated, Faith went and stood in

his face and said, "So you real happy you got your dick sucked today, huh?"

Taken aback, he asked her, "What the hell are you talking about?"

Faith did not back down. "One of your hoes called me and told me all about you and her sex life, about how good you be fucking her. Well, you know what, go and fuck her, go and fuck the shit out of her. As a matter of fact, bring her here and fuck her, I'll get out of your way." Faith brushed past him and went into the bedroom with him following close behind her.

She went over to the closet and started throwing clothes on the bed, she also pulled clothes out her drawers and threw them on the bed as well. The whole time she was talking shit, out loud and under her breath. She brushed past Raheem, who stood by the door and watched her every move with a smirk on his face. Faith came back into the room with a suitcase. She started shoving the items that were on the bed into the suitcase.

Finally done, she tried to push past Raheem but he pushed her back hard, so hard she stumbled. He grabbed her by the arm and pulled her up close to him; their noses were almost touching. Faith dropped her suitcase.

"Hand it over," Raheem demanded.

"Hand what over?" Faith asked while trying to escape his grip.

"Your package."

"My suitcase?" Faith wasn't stupid, she knew what he meant when he said "her package."

The next thing she knew, his hand hit her face so hard that she realized the saying, "I saw stars" was real. He smacked her again. "Give me the drugs and unpack your shit."

Faith tried denying that she had drugs and each time she

denied it, he would smack her. She just stood there and took it, too numb too react, while wondering how the hell he knew she had a package. She didn't care if he did know, she wasn't going to give it to him.

He grabbed her shoulders and spoke in a low tone, almost a whisper, telling her that she was leaving that house over his dead body.

In her mind Faith said, "If that's what it takes." Of course, they were just thoughts.

As Faith stood in front of him and told him she wanted a divorce, she wondered if she was going to have to kill him to get out.

"Get dressed, we're going out to eat. We can talk about us over dinner," he demanded.

What would he do if she said no? Did she really want to find out? Not tonight, she didn't.

So out to dinner she went against her will. It wouldn't be the first time but it damn sure would be the last.

"I'm getting out of this marriage come hell or high water," Faith said under her breath.

An hour later Faith and Raheem were sitting across from one another at a restaurant downtown, not saying a word.

Faith was sipping on champagne, looking across the room, when she saw Elsie walk in. She was alone.

Perfect, this would give her a reason to get up to leave his presence.

"So are you ready to talk?" Raheem asked her. She had been giving him the silent treatment since they left the house.

Faith ignored him and took another sip of her champagne.

"I asked you a question, are you ready to talk? You had a lot to say at the house, now you're all quiet and shit. What's up?"

Faith put down her glass and leaned over the table so he could hear every word she was going to say. "I'm thinking about the divorce I asked you for earlier. I'm wondering why you're trying to fight it. I'm thinking about you putting your hands on me and me calling the cops. You don't love me, Raheem. I can't help but wonder if you ever really did or did you just want to possess me?"

Raheem sat back and crossed his arms. "Do you really want to go there?" He looked around the restaurant. "You want to go there right here, out in the public?"

"Yes, I do, because if I try to 'go there' while we're here out in the public as you so eloquently put it, maybe you won't choke me up or smack me around like you did at the house."

Raheem shook his head and said, "You know what? I apologize for that but who was it that took care of you when you were too high to take care of yourself?" he asked.

Faith didn't say a word.

"I asked you a question. You're the one who wanted to go there, so tell me who took care of you when you were a drug addict."

"You did," Faith admitted with reluctance.

"Who took you in when you had nowhere to go? Who drove you to NA meetings and to your therapist?" He waited for an answer.

"You." Faith knew that he was running a guilt trip on her.

"Who helped pay your way through school?" He threw up his arms, exasperated. "Shit, who made you the person you are today?"

That comment pissed Faith off. "So what? I owe you my life? Is that what you think, is that what you want from me, my life? Yes, master, I owe you. Yes, master, you saved me from the depths of hell." Faith could hear her voice rising and scanned the room to see if anyone was looking at them.

The couple next to them averted their eyes. Faith continued. "Is that why you don't want to let me go, because you feel like I owe you, because you're keeping tabs, keeping count, adding up your points?"

Raheem started to say something but changed his mind.

"Go ahead, say it. What is it you want to say?"

"I'm not giving you a divorce. So you need to just let it go."

"I'm going to the ladies' room."

"When you get back, we're ordering."

Faith didn't plan on coming back, she was going to leave his ass sitting there and catch a taxi home.

If it meant him raising his voice, she'd deal with it, if it meant him raising his fist, she would not. This time he was going to have a fight on his hands and this time she meant it.

She was not a child and was tired of feeling like she was and now that she knew Raheem felt like she owed him. That just bothered her to the core of her being.

Wasn't that what marriage was about? Being there for one another, being supportive. She didn't ask him to carry her, he did it because he chose to, out of love, out of the kindness of his heart and she appreciated it, she still did, but it didn't mean that she had to repay him by staying with him and being unhappy.

When his kids lived with them, she took care of them as though they were her own, she never once complained after she accepted that this is how it was going to be. She never once asked when would their mother be returning, she loved them because they were a part of him.

She never threw that shit up in his face and here he threw up in hers all he did when she was struggling through her addiction.

"That's fucked up," Faith said out loud.

"What's fucked-up?" Elsie asked when she walked through the bathroom door. "I saw you leave your table, you looked upset, so I followed you in. Is everything okay? Is that your husband?"

"Yeah, we were just having a disagreement."

"Is there anything I can do?"

Faith almost told her she could take her home but decided not to involve her. "No, that's okay. I'm leaving his ass here."

Stunned, Elsie asked, "You're leaving your husband in the restaurant?"

Faith touched Elsie's hand. "Listen, I have to go, I'll see you tomorrow at the office."

Elsie watched with concern as Faith left the bathroom. *Damn, wouldn't that be something if the person I hired to help others needed help herself.*

But then again, Elsie thought, *no one had the perfect life, there was always something going on with someone.* Elsie went to the bathroom, washed her hands and walked out.

As Elsie walked to her seat, she looked over at Faith's table and saw her husband talking to the waitress. She looked around the restaurant and saw that Faith was nowhere to be seen.

Oh shit, she really left, Elsie thought.

Faith was already in a cab on her way home. She had to admit she was a little nervous about Raheem's reaction when he realized that she left him sitting there like a fool.

Good, maybe it was time for him to feel like a fool, she'd been one for long enough. As a matter of fact, maybe it was time for her to get out and do her thing, go out with other men. Maybe she should let him see how if felt. That is, if he didn't kill her first.

CHAPTER NINE

HARMONY

Dear Journal,

Sometimes Shareef's very presence gets on my last nerve. How can that be that when I love him so much? Is it possible to love someone all the time and not like them some of the time? I believe so. Is it possible to love someone and just want them to leave you alone? I believe so. Is it possible to want to walk out, walk away and take a break without saying a word? I believe so.

I also believe that people in relationships need time apart from one another, a time-out, but shit, even if I take a break or decided to just bounce, what point would it prove and could I really just leave my kids like that?

Sometimes I understand why women up and disappear, not that I would do it, but I understand it. I get tired of being all things to everyone and nothing to myself.

I want to be better, I want to do better, I will not let poverty or the hood dictate who I'm going to be or what I'm going to do with my life. I won't let it happen. So if sometimes I'm selfish

it's because I'm busy planning my future and the future of my children.

Peace, Harmony

Harmony could feel Shareef inching closer and closer. She tried tightening up her body as a way of letting him know she wasn't in the mood. He really shouldn't be surprised because lately, she was rarely in the mood. Her mind was way too preoccupied with all the things she wanted to accomplish in the next year. Sex was the furthest thing from her mind.

Of course, he did not take the hint because the next thing she knew he was rubbing on her shoulders, moving his hands to her back and down to her ass. She knew it wouldn't be much longer before he started rubbing on her nipples, like that was supposed to excite her.

Many moons ago it might have excited her. That is, before breast-feeding three kids and almost losing a nipple to one of them trying to bite the damn thing off. Now, it just irritated the hell out of her, sometimes.

Harmony covered his hand with hers.

"Can I get some?" Shareef asked.

Harmony turned over and looked at him.

Shareef could read the rejection all over her face. He sat up and threw his legs off the side of the bed as though he were going to get up. Instead, he turned to face her. "I'm getting tired of taking care of myself, you really need to know that shit."

Harmony knew he was saying that he was tired of beating his dick, but shit, sometimes you have to do and what you have to do and if that included masturbating, so be it.

Other women would think she was crazy for feeling that

way because they thought if a man felt he had too mastur-
bate to often, it would lead to infidelity.

Heck, Harmony masturbated and she didn't think of cheat-
ing so why would Shareef? Harmony saw nothing wrong with
pulling out her bullet and taking care of herself. At least she
knew her orgasm was guaranteed in five minutes, sometimes
less. It was her treat to herself when she knew she wasn't going
to have any alone time and wanted a quick release.

In the past, after discussing this issue with many of her
male friends, Harmony came to the conclusion that men
tend to believe that once they were in a relationship with a
female, the woman's pussy became theirs. They believed that
they had ownership over it and that just because they, as the
male, were in the mood for sex, then the woman is suppose
to be also, like the pussy works on demand.

Harmony felt it was her duty to inform them that their be-
lief system was not happening, nor was it true, nor would it
ever be. One too many times Harmony had sex when she
didn't feel like it, when she really wasn't in the mood. She
did it thinking this what you do for the man you love. Well,
that thought process wasn't happening anymore. At least,
she didn't think it was going to happen again.

But lying in the bed looking over at Shareef, she realized
that what one says and what one does are two different
things.

Lying beside her was a good man. She knew it and he
knew it. Hell, she had to start watching the few friends she
had because they knew it too. Eventually, she was left with no
friends because it became too much seeing them up in his
face and she could really see herself hurting someone over
them wanting what she had.

Shareef did everything in his power to make sure Har-
mony and the kids were comfortable and not in need for

much. Until he started a business with King, he'd work two, three jobs at a time, overtime if he had to, in order to provide. He took care of all the kids, treated them equally and even put up with Harmony's moodiness.

Now don't get it twisted, although he was a good man, he wasn't perfect. He still had his idiosyncrasies. Sometimes, not often, but once in a blue moon, he would speak to her as though she was a child and not a grown-ass woman and that irritated the hell out of her. But she dealt with it because she knew it was rare for a man to take care of another man's child like they were his own without any complaints.

On second thought, Harmony decided she might as well give him some, so she moved from beneath the blankets and pulled him towards her.

"What are you doing?" he asked.

"I can't change my mind?"

Shareef pushed her away gently, "Just like that, you go from cold to hot?"

"What? A sister can't change her mind?" Harmony leaned forward to kiss Shareef on the lips but he pulled back.

"What? You don't want to kiss me now?" Harmony asked, confused.

Shareef patted the spot next to him and Harmony sat up. "What?" she asked. "What's the problem?"

"Harmony, you can't do that."

"Do what?"

"Be on and off, think it's okay to say no one second then the next be like, come on. Do you really think I'm just supposed to be okay with that, because I'm not. I'm tired of trying to figure out when I'm going to get some ass. I'm tired of being afraid to ask for some pussy because you might give me the 'here we go' look. I think it's fucked-up that the only time we have sex is when you want to, when it's conducive to

your schedule." He waited on Harmony's response, but she didn't know what to say. "Something has to change, and fast," Shareef told her.

Damn, Harmony thought to herself. *Shit was serious.* Shareef wasn't one to speak emotionally, he never really let things bother him, his mode of operation was it is what it is.

Shareef took her hand and asked, "What's going on with you, Harmony? Better yet, what's going on with us?"

"What are you talking about?" Harmony did not feel like having a deep, let's-analyze-our-relationship kind of conversation, especially this morning when she had school to be concerned with. "Do we have to do this right now?"

Harmony could tell her asking that question pissed Shareef off. He stood up, shook his head and said, "So not only do we have sex on your schedule but we have important conversations on it as well. Fuck this shit." He started walking towards the bathroom.

"Shareef, that's not what I meant. It's just that I'm taking the practice test today for my GED and I'm on edge."

"Whatever," was Shareef's response, he wasn't trying to hear that. He walked into the bathroom and slammed the door behind him.

Harmony knew she had messed up. Shareef was not one to go around slamming doors, the only time he did anything remotely close to that was when he was trying to control his anger.

She knew the right thing would be to go into the bathroom, apologize, and start the morning over by giving him some head, but there was no time for that. She still had to get the kids together and get on with her own day.

She looked towards the closed door and tried to mentally draw Shareef out, so she could at least apologize, but it didn't work and she was too stubborn to make the first move.

I'll make it better this evening. I'll cook something I know he likes

and then I'll seduce his ass. He'll be okay afterwards. Harmony wouldn't allow herself to think otherwise because the truth is as much shit that she talked to her girlfriends about being able to do this thing called life on her own and about not needing a man, she knew it was lie.

She needed a man. She needed Shareef. He was everything her other kids' fathers were not. For one, he wasn't a dirty old man and two, he'd never been to jail.

Four years ago, Harmony and Shareef met at Jewell's house. Shareef and King were boys, they had a past together. It was Jewell's idea for them to meet.

Jewell and King were having a dinner party. There were about ten people in attendance. All the men were in the living room and the women were in the kitchen when Harmony arrived.

The first person Harmony noticed when she walked in the door was Shareef's fine ass. There really would not have been any need for an introduction because she was determined to introduce herself. That is, if the other women at the house stopped hounding him.

Jewell, who was peeping it all and didn't want him to end up talking to any of the other women, finally decided to put a stop to it and grabbed her cousin by the arm.

"I've got someone I want you to meet."

Harmony saw where they were headed and noticed that Shareef was in the middle of a conversation with a female friend of Jewell's. "I don't want to step on anybody's toes," Harmony told Jewell while following her and not meaning a word she said.

Jewell pretended like she didn't hear her. Two seconds later they were standing in front of Shareef.

"Shareef, I want you to meet my cousin, Harmony. Harmony, this Shareef."

The girl he was talking to looked at Jewell with a "that's messed up" look.

Jewell looked back at Harmony, took her hand and said, "I have someone else I want you to meet."

A second later Harmony and Shareef were standing there looking at one another, sizing each other up. It was making Harmony a little uncomfortable. She wondered if she looked as good to him as he did to her. "So tell me, how you know King?"

"We go way back, as matter of fact, we grew up together."

"Well, how come I haven't seen you around?" She definitely would have remembered seeing him.

Shareef was well over six feet tall, built like a basketball player and had the complexion of smooth chocolate. She wanted to eat his ass up.

"I just moved back into the area."

Not one to bite her tongue, Harmony asked him was that code for "I just got out of jail."

Shareef laughed. "If I told you yes, would you walk away?"

Of course she said no.

"Good," he told her, "although that's not the case."

"Well, where are you moving back from?" Harmony wanted to know everything about this man she could possibly know because she was going to make him hers. There was something about his spirit, something about the way he looked right into her eyes when they were talking that held her attention. It was like he wanted her to believe every word he said, like he was trying to hypnotize her and it was working.

"I moved down south, needed a change of pace and scenery. I was doing things here I shouldn't have been doing and was ready to change my life."

Harmony loved the fact that he was being up front with her, pulling no punches. Hell, she decided to do the same.

"I have two kids by two different men," she blurted out and waited to see his reaction. She waited to see if he would walk away. To her delight, he didn't.

He just said, "Okay, and?"

Harmony wondered why his response was so nonchalant. Was it because he had children too? she asked him.

"Nope, no kids."

For a second there Harmony didn't believe him because there was no way a woman would let a man this fine get away from her. She knew plenty of girls who had trapped their men by becoming pregnant.

"Well, that's a surprise," Harmony told him.

"Why is it a surprise?" he wanted to know. "Every black man does not have babies all over the place."

She wished she could agree but every male she knew over the age of twenty had at least one child. She hoped he wasn't just telling her what he thought she wanted to hear. It would not have mattered if he did have kids anyway. She was feeling him.

That night Harmony and Shareef never left one another's side. Jewell and King were peeping the situation and felt real proud of themselves because they knew Shareef would be good for Harmony.

Harmony got pregnant in year one of their relationship. The thing of it was Harmony wasn't trying to get pregnant either; the last thing she wanted was a baby. They weren't using condoms but she was on the pill. Just her luck, it didn't take.

Harmony could recall being scared to death to break the news to Shareef. She wasn't sure how he would react, if he'd think she tried to trap him or if he'd take her word for it that she was just as surprised.

Not having the nerves to tell him, Harmony took a preg-

nancy test at home and left it in the bathroom. She put it near the garbage can so it would look like she was trying to throw it away and missed the can. She knew Shareef would spot it.

Later that morning, she was in the kitchen fixing the kids some breakfast when Shareef approached her from behind.

"Harmony!" There was a tone is his voice that caused her to jump.

"Yes?" Harmony turned to face him, She looked down at her chest because she was certain her heart was coming through it.

"Is there something you need to tell me?"

Of course, she knew what he was talking about but all that came out of her mouth was "huh?"

"I said, is there something you need to tell me?"

"Um." Harmony was tongue-tied. She did not want to lose this man. He has treated her better that anyone she'd been with and he was good to her kids. She did not want this pregnancy to run him away and she had already made up her mind to have an abortion if he asked her to.

"When were you going to tell me you're pregnant?"

Harmony looked him in the eyes. "I was afraid to."

"Why would you be afraid to tell me something like that?"

All Harmony could do was shrug her shoulders.

"Pregnancy is not something you can keep a secret. You do know that, don't you?"

She finally looked up at him. "Yes."

Shareef pulled Harmony into his arms and asked her, "So when do I move in so we can officially start our family?"

All Harmony could do was cry, she wasn't sure how to feel, especially when Shareef wanted her to have the baby when she wasn't even sure she wanted to have it herself. But have it she did and when she looked back and thought about the

abortion she was considering having, she knew she had made the right decision.

After Harmony got the kids together, she went into garage, where Shareef had made himself an office space. He was putting together some paperwork and Harmony asked him, "Can you put that to the side for a minute? I have something I want to say."

"What is it, Harmony? I'm busy right now." He looked at his watch. "I thought you had to leave the house so quick."

Harmony saw that he was going to hold on to his grudge. That was okay, because she was still going to say what she felt like saying. "I'm about to leave now, I just wanted to apologize again for this morning and I wanted to assure you I will be more conscious of taking care of your physical needs." She waited on him to say something. When she realized he wasn't, she walked towards the door, looked back and said, "You have a nice day too."

The second Shareef heard the door closed, he went into the house to call his boy King. He needed someone to talk to before he did something he knew he would regret.

He knew King would give him words of wisdom and understand because just last week, when King and Jewell was having it out, King needed someone to speak to and as usual he picked up the phone to call Shareef.

As Shareef was dialing King's number, the doorbell rang and Shareef remembered that they had an appointment with a client that morning.

Shareef opened the door with his face all frowned up.

Of course, King noticed. "Damn, man, what's got you looking all tight and shit."

"It's Harmony, man, she's been acting all tight with the pussy and shit, keeping it hostage."

King followed Shareef into the office as he continued his rant. "I don't ask for much from her, as a matter of fact, she requires more of me that I do of her and I'm tired of her ass always talking about she's tired or got too much on her mind to take care of my needs."

"Damn, you're real pissed behind this, huh?"

"Yeah, it's driving me crazy. What if I was like all them other motherfuckers and went out and found some other chick to handle my business with. Now that would be fucked-up."

Shareef sat down and started to put his papers in his briefcase. King sat down across from him.

"Is that what you're thinking about doing, something you'll regret?"

Shareef stood up and looked at King with all seriousness. "I don't know if I'll actually regret it."

King knew what Shareef was getting at. "Man, sit your ass down, we need to talk this out."

Shareef shoved the last of the papers in his briefcase and sat in the chair across from King. "What?"

"Are you thinking about cheating?"

When Shareef didn't answer him, King knew he had his answer. "You know you're bugging, right? That shit ain't even you."

"How do you know what's me? Maybe I've changed."

"You know just like I know, you're a one-woman man. Your ass is too old, just like my ass is too old to be out here trying to play the field. What? You think you can go from, Hi, I'm Shareef that loves my wife to playa, playa at the drop of a dime?"

Shareef puffed up and said, "Yeah, actually I do. I get hit on every day."

King laughed.

Irritated, Shareef wanted to know what the hell was so funny.

"It's just that Jewell and I have went through this too. I felt like because I took care of things at home and was a good father, I should be able to get the pussy whenever I wanted it. It just doesn't work that way."

"Why not?" Shareef knew he was being an ass.

"Are you giving her anything to be excited about? Are you doing anything to turn her on or are you thinking because you're you that should be enough."

Shareef didn't respond.

"Brother, do you even bother to put on any smell good? When was the last time you called her just to tell her you miss her? When was the last time you two went on a date? When was the last time you two did something without the kids? Not only that, but what you need to think about is all the diseases and shit that's out there and how those women who won't think twice about trapping a man."

Shareef just sat there and looked stunned that King was dropping it so hard on him.

King continued, "Now don't think I'm placing all the blame on you, but before you complain you need to check yourself first. Women are very complicated. We all know that, but you've got to remember that women have an abundance of hormones and they change daily, their needs and their wants."

Shareef was silenced by all that King was saying.

"Look, man, I know your lady, I hear the conversations she and Jewell have about you. That girl loves your dirty, stinky-ass drawers. She worships the ground you walk on."

This was one of the reasons Shareef knew he could talk to King because the boy was deep, he knew his shit. "I love you, man," Shareef told him. "You always set my ass straight."

"Yeah, and you always do the same for me. We pull each other up when necessary."

"Yeah, and when I really think about it, I don't want to make the same mistake many men have made before me by messing up a good thing. Just because Harmony ain't feeling sexual right now, it doesn't mean I have to be an asshole either."

King playfully punched Shareef in the arm. "See, that's what I'm talking about. Call her up, take her to dinner tonight."

"You and Jewell are going to watch the kids?"

"Man, please, you better get a babysitter."

Together they laughed.

"See man, you ain't right," Shareef told him.

CHAPTER TEN

BELLA

Bella was preaching up a storm in the pulpit. Once again she was on the topic of forgiveness. She knew her congregation probably wondered why she preached so often on this topic, was it her favorite or what?

She wondered how they would feel if they knew it was because she needed to forgive herself for the lustful thoughts she was consumed with.

Sometimes when she looked out into the congregation, she just knew some of the people were wondering how the hell she of all people became a minister. She knew she wasn't the average-looking preacher, which to her was someone male, older, overweight and stuffy.

Bella was just the opposite, female, young, in shape and attractive. Maybe that was the appeal of her church, many people could relate to her because of her appearance. She looked like she could be their sister, aunt, girlfriend or cousin.

She knew she was known as the hip preacher, the one in the area that teens and young adults could relate to. She'd

been stopped plenty of times in the supermarket, mall or when she went on walks by people, who said just as much.

"I hear your church is where it's happening, I hear that a lot of young adults go to your church, I'm going to bring my son or daughter." A couple of ministers had even asked her what was her secret. Bella didn't mind catering to the young. However and whoever God wanted her to serve, she would.

As Bella wrapped up the sermon, she glanced through the congregation to acknowledge some of the familiar faces and guests. It was when her gaze hit the back of the church that Bella stopped mid-sentence. *No, it couldn't be.*

Bella noticed a couple of members turning to see what or who had captured her attention, so she quickly got herself back together, rushing through the rest of the service, and through prayer. She tried to slow down but she couldn't stop herself. She was relieved when only one person stood in front of the pulpit.

Focus, Bella, focus, she repeated to herself as she prayed for them. It took everything in her power not to allow her eyes to roam to the back of the church and see if he was still sitting there.

There was no way this could be happening. How did he find me? Oh God, please help me get through this meet and greet, so I can run to my office.

Bella was going into panic mode. She could not believe that her past was sitting in the pews. She'd recognize that face anywhere, even after all these years. Was it coincidence? She didn't think so, coincidences were something that she just did not believe in. It couldn't be God's doing, he wouldn't play this kind of trick on her. He just wouldn't. If it wasn't a coincidence and it wasn't God, then what in the world was Ramsey doing here?

Okay, don't panic, there's really no need to, he knows your history, you know his. People change, as do circumstances. It's been over fifteen years.

If only she could get herself to believe those words, especially right now. The line of people that wanted to speak with her was moving along. *Don't let these people have a lot to say.* Eventually Ramsey stood and got in line as well. He was looking at her the whole time, whenever he'd catch her eye, he'd smile.

What could he be smiling about? Does he think I'm glad to see him? Bella tried to avert her eyes but found that it was a challenge to do so. After every couple of people, she'd look up at him.

"Pastor Bella, if you have a moment I'd like to speak with you privately," the next person in line requested. It was Brother James.

This was perfect, she'd have just a moment or two to speak with Ramsey. She'd find out what he wanted and why he was at her church and then she'd politely inform him that one of the brothers of the church wanted to speak with her.

Before she knew it Ramsey was standing in front of her. "Wow, isn't this a surprise?" He greeted with his arms outstretched, expecting a hug.

Bella wanted so bad to push past him but with some of the members still around, Bella gave him a church hug, the real quick, pat-on-the-back kind and asked, "What are you doing here?" There was no need to beat around the bush, after all he knew her way back when.

"Is that any way to greet an old friend?"

"You're right. It's not. It just seems odd that after all these years we run into one another again."

Ramsey looked around the church. "Who would have thought you'd be preaching?"

"Well, you know what the Bible says, 'With God all things are possible.' "

Ramsey stepped closer to Bella, so close that a few people took notice. "You still look good, Bella."

Bella took a step back. "Ramsey, you need to tell me why you're here so I can get on with my day."

"Why do I have to be here for anything? Why couldn't I just happen to be in the area? I had no idea I was stepping into your church."

Bella didn't believe a word he was saying, but she decided to let it go. "Well, it was nice seeing you." She turned to walk away but Ramsey grabbed her arm.

"I'd like to see you again. Maybe catch up on one another."

Brother James, who was nearby watching the interaction, sensed that something was up and came over towards them. He looked straight at Bella and asked, "Is there a problem, Pastor?"

Bella shook her head. "No, Brother James, this here is an old friend of mine."

Brother James looked at Ramsey and they acknowledged one another with a head nod. Brother James then looked at Ramsey's hand, which was still holding onto Bella's arm.

Ramsey noticed the protectiveness of the look, not wanting to cause a scene and whip this man's ass in the Lord's house, released her arm.

"I'm not here to start trouble, Bella."

Brother James looked from one to another and wondered what the hell was going on.

"I really was in the area, passing through and heard about this church. I was just as shocked to see you on the pulpit as you were to see me."

Before Ramsey could say anything more, Bella told him, "I can talk with you tomorrow, here at the church, 1:00 P.M. How's that?"

Brother James had not moved from his spot.

"I'll take what I can get." Ramsey looked at Brother James, smirked and left the church.

Bella watched him walk out and noticed that the few women who were left in the church were watching him as well. She could understand why. Even she had to admit, he had not lost his swagger, he was still handsome, just a few years older. He definitely did not look like the drug dealer she knew many years ago.

"Do you mind my asking you what that was all about?" Brother James asked.

"Huh?"

"Your visitor, I sensed something there, something that had you on edge."

Bella touched his shoulder and told him, "Don't worry about me, everything is fine. He's someone I knew way back when."

"You do know I'm here in whatever capacity you need me in," he told her, while touching the hand that was on his shoulder.

Bella knew he was saying more that she wanted him to by letting her know, he was there for her. She chose not to respond and removed her hand. "Let me see everyone out and we can meet in my office."

About fifteen minutes later, he followed her into the office. "Have a seat," Bella told him as she went and turned on the coffeepot that was in the corner on a table.

Brother James sat down on the sofa that was against the wall and followed her every move with his eyes.

Bella poured herself a cup of coffee. "Would you like a cup?" she offered.

"No, what I would like is your undivided attention," he told her.

117

Sensing that he was about to confess something of a serious nature, Bella sat next to him on the sofa, but was careful to put some distance between them. "What's going on? What's bothering you?"

"I'd like to take you out."

Bella almost choked on her coffee. "Huh?"

"I'd like to take you out."

"Take me out where?" There was no way he was asking her for a date. Would he really be bold enough to do such a thing? Is this what he meant when he said he was available to her in any capacity?

"On a date, movies, dinner, whatever you'd like to do, I'd be willing to do, where you'd like to go, I'd be willing to go."

Bella was actually at a lost for words, she looked everywhere but at him.

"I know this is awkward for you," he continued, "but I've been holding my feelings for you in for quite some time. You're a very attractive woman, Bella."

When he said her first name without her pastoral title, she knew he was dead serious.

"We're both single and although I attend your church, I don't see what the harm would be in us dating."

Of course he didn't see what the harm would be, he was a man, it wouldn't be his reputation on the line. Bella finally found her voice. "I don't think us dating is a good idea."

"Why not?"

"I'm your pastor."

"And?"

"And it would be unethical."

"Would it? Think about it, how many ministers marry women from their churches, think about how often we hear of pastors playing the field."

She knew he was right, but he didn't know her past and if

he did, would he still be interested? Bella raised her eyebrow. "So are you saying I should marry you or that we should just play the field?"

"I'm not saying either."

"And just because others feel comfortable doing that, it doesn't mean I would."

Brother James stood up. "I'm not asking you for an answer right now. I don't want to put any pressure on you." He walked around the couch until he was standing behind her, and leaned over and whispered into her ear, "Just think about it. I've seen you looking at me and the way I interpreted that look was one of curiosity and maybe wanting to get to know me better. I hope I'm not wrong."

He was right, she had been watching him on what she thought was the down low. It obviously wasn't that low because he caught her. No use denying it, instead, she told him, "I'll do that, I'll think about it."

Brother James smiled and told her, "That's all I'm asking."

When he left the room, Bella dropped to her knees and prayed for strength. She knew that the devil was at work and trying to destroy her. He knew she was lonely and in need of companionship, he knew her body was in need of some loving. He knew that she was feeling weak and that he was trying to come on in and take her out.

Bella knew she needed to put her armor on and take heed to her message about spiritual warfare, because the war was on and she was losing the battle.

But even with knowing this, she wanted to tell Brother James, *Yes. Yes, I'll go out with you.*

After all, a date didn't mean they were going to sleep together. Bella tried convincing herself that a friendly dinner and possibly a movie wouldn't hurt a soul. It would only mean what she wanted it to mean.

Would it really? If that was the case, why was she thinking

ahead, wondering what would happen if someone in the congregation saw them? If she said yes, would they and should they keep their date a secret? If they chose to keep it a secret and it was something they couldn't do out in the open, she knew it was wrong.

Bella needed someone to talk this out with, someone that would not judge her. She knew she had the Lord and that he should be enough. But what she wanted was a real live person, what she wanted was a friend. Even in her hooker days, she didn't have many.

Right now, her journal was her best friend, she could write whatever she wanted to, her needs, wants, desires and fantasies. At least she had that release, but it wasn't enough. It was getting tiresome and boring. She needed feedback. Maybe it was time for her to take the first step and befriend someone. The question is, who would it be? The only people she really knew were members of her congregation and the group of women that were associated with the Essence of Self Center.

When she thought about it, there was someone that seemed real cool, that didn't treat her like she was God's answer and that someone was Crystal. Yes, she and Elsie had a friendship but there was something about Crystal that stood out. Bella felt like they had some kind kindred spirit. *I'll call her and see if she would like to have lunch or something this week.* Thinking about lunch reminded Bella of her unwanted and unexpected visitor, Ramsey. Whatever it was he wanted, she was sure to find out tomorrow.

Over the next three hours, Bella sat if her office, read the Bible and prepared her teachings for Wednesday evening. By the time she left, the only thing on her mind was food. Food and Ramsey.

Dear Journal,

All I want is for people to realize that being a minister does not make you immune to human error, that it does not make you any less lonely, any less in need of companionship, both mentally and physically. Sometimes I wonder if I made the right decision in becoming a pastor, if this was really my calling or if I went this way because of guilt.

I know it's time to come out of my shell, I know that members of my congregation shouldn't be the only people I'm in contact with.

I'm tired of hiding, I'm tired of not having anyone to turn to. I know part of it is my fault and that it stems from not wanting anyone to know my past history.

In a way I want to change that. Maybe I should give my story to the church and let them know that I'm nowhere near perfect, that I lived a life of sin prior to living for the Lord.

I know I've talked about some things like my drug use. But confessing that I sold my body, now that's on a whole other level, I'm not too sure if my congregation would be able to handle that.

Heck, I'm not sure if I could handle telling them.

Faithfully yours, Bella

CHAPTER ELEVEN

HARMONY

"Damn, what am I going to wear." Harmony was throwing her clothes out of her closet. Everything she had didn't seem work appropriate. She never realized how most of what she wore were tight jeans, tight shirts, short shorts and short shirts. She was disgusted with herself.

Today was the first time Harmony had taken a step back and evaluated her wardrobe. What she saw was a hoochie and if she saw it that way, Harmony could just imagine what others saw.

Yes, every now and then Shareef would ask her to put something else on, especially when they were going out with the kids. She never argued or questioned why because it wasn't that big a deal. But now when she gave it some thought she wondered if it was his subtle way of letting her know she dressed like a video ho.

Harmony picked up the phone to call Jewell. Maybe she had enough time to run over there and grab a suit. They were about the same size.

"Hello?" Jewell's son, Tyson answered.

"Tyson, it's Harmony, is your mom there?"

"No, but my dad is."

That wasn't who she wanted to speak to, but she'd take what she could get.

"Dad! The phone!" Harmony heard Tyson yell before she could get another word in.

"Hello?" It was King.

"King, I know Jewell isn't home but I really need something of hers to wear to work, I start a new job today and I want to look professional." Harmony figured if she got it out fast enough, King wouldn't tell her what she knew he was going to say and that's "You know how Jewell is with her clothes, I just can't let you come over here and go through her stuff."

"So, you're finally tired of wearing that tight-ass shit you be wearing, huh?"

Harmony sucked her teeth. "I did not call your house to be insulted. I called to ask for my cousin's help."

"Well, she's not here, call her on her cell and have her okay it."

Harmony glanced at the clock, she had under forty-five minutes to get to work. "Never mind, King, I'll make do."

Harmony hung up before he could respond and at the same time Shareef walked in the room carrying a Macy's bag.

"Aren't you going to be late? You don't look anywhere near ready."

Harmonys eyes welled up. "I don't have anything to wear."

"Wear something in your closet," he told her, as he held onto the bag.

"I can't, I want to make a good impression."

"Are you saying nothing you own will make a good impression?"

"That's exactly what I'm saying."

Shareef opened the bag and pulled out a simple cream-colored dress. "Well, will this do?"

Harmony looked up and saw what he was holding. "Where did you get that from?"

"Me." Jewell walked in the room with a shoe box.

Harmony started crying for real. She ran up to Jewell and gave her a tight hug.

"Damn," Shareef said. "Can I get one of those? I gave her the money to get it."

Harmony hugged him too. "I love you both," she said. "I just called your house," Harmony told Jewell.

"I know, King just called me on my cell phone. He said you hung up on him."

"Because I was mad and he called me a hoochie."

Harmony noticed that Shareef frowned. The last thing she wanted was trouble between boys. "Well, not really a hoochie. But he did get smart with me."

"That's because he knew I was on my way here." Jewell looked at Shareef. "You can leave the room now, we got twenty minutes to get her ready."

Shareef put the bag on the floor. "Well, excuse the hell out of me," he joked but left as requested.

When he was gone, Harmony looked at Jewell and told her, "You're my best friend, you know that. I appreciate you so much."

Jewell told her, "Girl, don't go get all mushy all on me."

"But I'm grateful for you, Jewell, you got me this job and—"

Jewell stopped her mid-sentence. "No, I got you the interview, you got yourself the job. Now get dressed so you can be there on time."

Harmony did just that and in record time.

* * *

When Harmony arrived downtown, she was surprised to see cars parked everywhere. She drove around the block a couple of times until she remembered that the building they were in had their own parking lot.

"It must be my nerves," Harmony said out loud.

She located a parking spot, turned off the engine, looked in the mirror, fixed her hair and reaffirmed out loud that she was going to do the best job she could do. *Elsie will not regret hiring me. This is a chance for a new beginning.*

After she made sure she looked good and felt confident, Harmony opened the door and stepped out of her old life and into her new.

"Are you ready for your first day?" Elsie asked Harmony when she walked into her office.

"As ready as I'll ever be."

"Good, I like hearing that. You'll be sitting in the front, answering the phones, meeting and greeting. We have a group of teenagers coming in today to hear about the programs we have to offer. They're from a group home and—" Elsie stopped herself, she looked at Harmony and said, "You know what, go ahead and make yourself comfortable at your desk. I'll come out in about ten minutes and let you know what has to be done."

Harmony thanked her, because she felt overwhelmed. She did need a moment to get it together.

Elsie sat down behind her desk and told Harmony as she was walking out, "Just to let you know, I'll be keeping my door shut. Just because it's closed, it doesn't mean you can't come in."

"Thanks," Harmony replied and went to her desk.

Harmony sat down in her seat and spun around in the chair. *My own desk and my own computer.* She felt so proud. *I'm going to have to put a picture of my babies on my desk.*

Harmony opened every drawer and noticed everything she needed was in them, pens, pencils,tape, stapler, scissors, and everything else she could have thought of. Harmony turned her computer on, her screen saver was a basic blue. She was definitely going to change that. *I'll put a picture of kids on my screen-saver.*

Harmony soaked in her environment for a few more minutes and looked towards Elsie's door. She was ready to get her day started.

Harmony was walking towards Elsie's office when the phone rang. Harmony picked it up and said, "Essence of Self Center, how may I help you?"

"Oh, I'm sorry, I must have the wrong number." The person on the other end hung up.

Elsie came out of her office. "Who was that?"

"Wrong number," Harmony told her and sat down. "Now, what were you telling me?"

"Well, we have a group of young girls coming in around 11:00 A.M. Place them in the conference room. Faith will also be here to facilitate. Other than answering the phones, I'm working on a grant I'm going to give you to type up and we'll take some time today so I can show you how to research grants."

"Just let me know when you're ready," Harmony told her.

Elsie walked around Harmony's desk and pulled open a couple of the drawers. "I tried to provide you with everything I thought you may need. Let me know if I missed anything. In your top drawer is a job description, read it carefully, so we won't have any misunderstandings about what I expect from you."

Harmony was listening carefully. She did not want to mess this up.

"Oh, and another thing, feel free to read or study at your desk. I don't want you to think you have to be doing some-

thing every second of the day. We won't always be busy and I might not always have something for you to do, just don't try to take advantage of these privileges," Elsie told her, as she moved from behind her desk. "Also know that I won't tolerate going on obscene Web sites. We are on a server."

"Oh, never that," Harmony told her.

"I also want you to read over the packet about the agency that's in your drawer. That way you'll be able to answer any questions anyone may ask."

"Will do."

"Okay, do you have any questions?"

Harmony couldn't think of any, all of her questions, which were about pay and health benefits, were answered during the interview. Harmony couldn't believe she was actually going to have health benefits. "Not that I can think of."

"Okay fine, I'm in my office, if you need me let me know."

At exactly 11:00 Harmony heard a ruckus in the hallway. She was halfway out of her seat when a group of girls came walking through the door.

"Oh hell no," one of them said. "You can't let him get away with that shit."

Harmony noticed that these girls looked young as hell and they were talking mad nonsense.

"How about not using that language in here," a young woman said, coming in behind the group.

Harmony did a quick head count, there were eleven girls. They were looking at Harmony like they could care less about her.

The woman stepped forward. "Hi, I'm Kretia, we're here for a meeting."

"Okay, let me show you to the conference room." Harmony came from behind the desk. "Follow me."

They did and loudly.

"Y'all really need to calm down, that's why we're here, so you can learn to be ladies," Kretia told them.

"Shit, I'm already a lady," one of the girls said as she smacked her gum as loud as possible.

Harmony heard, "I know that's right. Me too," and other statements coming from the girls.

Harmony had to laugh to herself because she remembered those days, when she swore she was grown and that she had all the answers to all the problems of the world. There was nothing anyone could tell her. Come to find out, she was wrong, because had she listened to an adult, she may not have become a teen mom. Harmony looked at the girls, and wondered how many of them were already mothers.

She let them in the room and told them, "Someone will be with you shortly."

Of course no one responded.

Harmony knocked on Elsie's door.

"Come in!"

She stepped in. "The girls are here."

"I heard them come in." Elsie glanced at her watch. "I wonder where Faith is. Look in your Rolodex and call her up, see if she's on her way."

"Okay."

When Harmony got back to her desk, a woman she hoped was Faith walked in.

She was out of breath and looked rushed. "Are they here yet?"

Harmony raised her eyebrows. "You're Faith?"

"The one and only."

"They are definitely here."

Speaking in a low tone, Faith asked, "Are they off the hook?"

Harmony looked towards the room and nodded. "You will definitely have your hands full."

"Thanks for the warning." Faith headed towards the conference room, did a quick U-turn and went to let Elsie know she was in the building.

Over the next hour plus, Harmony heard laughter, cursing and finally total silence. She wanted so bad to get up and see what was taking place with Faith and the girls. She knew there were some things she could teach them about life and wondered if maybe down the line Elsie would allow her to.

It wasn't until 12:30 PM when Elsie finally came out of her office. "What time are you taking lunch?"

Harmony felt her stomach growl. "Now?"

"That's fine."

"How much time do I have?" Harmony didn't want to be gone too long.

"Forty-five minutes."

Harmony was out the door and on her cell phone in five minutes flat.

"How's your first day at work?" Shareef asked the second he answered the phone.

"It's fine. Today's one of my short days." The arrangement Harmony made with Elsie upon being hired was flexible hours. Some days she came in early like today and left at 3:00 and other days she came in at 12:00 PM or 1:00 PM and stayed until the afternoon programs were over with and that was between 6:00 PM and 7:00 PM. This didn't pose a problem because Shareef had his own business and he was able to pick up the kids from school or their babysitter would come and watch them until someone arrived.

"What have you been doing all day?"

"Answering the phone, reading up on the company, secretarial stuff."

"Oh."

Neither of them really had much to say so Harmony cut it short. "I was just checking in."

"All right, I'll see you this afternoon, love you."

"Love you too."

"Harmony!"

He caught her just as she was about to hang up. "Yes?"

"Let's go out to dinner tonight, just you and I."

She liked that idea. "I'll call the babysitter."

"No, let me," Shareef offered. "After all, dinner is my idea."

When Harmony returned from lunch, Faith and Elsie were sitting in the front and the group of girls were gone.

"Teenage girls are a trip," Faith was saying.

"You don't have to tell me that," Elsie said, as she laughed. "I could hear them all the way in my office, with the door closed."

Unsure if she should take part in the conversation or not, Harmony decided to chance it and asked, "How did it go?"

Faith laughed. "It went. You know these teenagers today, they think they're grown as hell. They have so much to learn."

"That much was obvious," Harmony replied. "But with some guidance who's to say what could happen. They might do a complete turnaround and become more than they think they could ever be."

"That's why we have Faith," Elsie said. She liked what Harmony said and was pleased that Harmony "got it." "Did you have a good lunch?" Elsie asked.

"Yes, thanks for asking."

"I put some things on your desk I need typed," Elsie told her. "Faith and I will be in my office."

Harmony looked over at her desk and saw a small pile. "Okay."

"If you need me, just buzz me on the intercom."

"I'll do that."

When they stepped into Elsie's office, Faith collapsed on Elsie's couch and said, "I'm exhausted, those girls wore my ass out. I just hope I'm the right person to guide them."

"Why wouldn't you be?" Elsie asked.

Faith caught the message she was sending out and tried to play it off. "I'm sure I'm the right person, I just hope they connect with me, that's all."

Elsie didn't believe her. She could sense something was going on. She didn't know how deep she wanted to get with Faith, after all she only knew her through Susan and she wasn't sure if she wanted to mix business with personal issues, especially when Faith was going to be the counselor of the center. She didn't want anything clouding her judgment and making her question if she made the right decision in her hiring her.

After all, the counselor should be the one that had it altogether. That way of thinking was a load of crap and Elsie knew it. She knew it didn't matter what it looked like from the outside or what kind of profession you were in, it did not make your life problem-free.

When she thought about it that way, Elsie concluded that women needed to be there for one another and she would mix personal with business, she would show support for whatever Faith might be going through. She knew she was struggling with something. That much was obvious when she left her husband in the restaurant.

Before Elsie could ask what that was about, Faith said, "Okay, let's go over the plan for the girls."

Elsie was a bit relieved that they didn't have to go into the "what's going on with you "talk" because as much as she wanted to show sister-support, Elsie had her own shit to worry about.

CHAPTER TWELVE

FAITH

Faith was sitting in the kitchen sipping a glass of wine. Although she was in recovery she believed it wouldn't do her any harm. She knew that some people believed you had to stay away from all alcohol but she felt like that wasn't her issue and it wasn't a trigger, so if she felt like a glass of wine, she would have it. Of course, she never shared that in the meetings.

Faith was reading the paper when she heard the front door open. *I hope it's not Raheem,* she thought to herself. The past week had been so peaceful. Raheem was away on a business trip and as a result Faith didn't feel on edge, nor did she feel like she was walking on eggshells.

That day she left him in the restaurant, they almost came to blows when he arrived home. What stopped them? She told him she would call the police. Faith recalled the look of disbelief on his face. He packed some clothes and left the house for a couple of days. When he returned they barely said two words to each other. Which was fine with Faith, but now she was ready to talk again.

Raheem's daughter, Sherry, who still had a key, walked into the kitchen. Initially it bothered Faith that Raheem still allowed his kids to have keys to the house. After all, they no longer lived there. But whenever she tried to bring it up, he wasn't trying to hear it.

"This is my house too you know," she told him.

"But they're my kids," he responded.

All that did was piss her the hell off because he acted like he was the one home with them every day cooking, cleaning, bathing and watching after them, when their mother was nowhere to be found.

That was one of the reasons she even agreed to take care of them, because she knew about the whole addiction thing and although she too was an addict, at least she was able to function. Well, at the time that's what she thought.

Yes, there had been times when she neglected the kids in the area of affection, but she made sure they were fed, dressed and clean. After that was taken care of, she'd go up to her room, close the door and do her thing.

Did she feel guilty about it? Sometimes, but she dealt with it the next day by doing something extra special for the kids.

By the time they got to junior high, their mother, Lace, had gotten clean and Raheem let the kids go back and live with her.

Faith didn't have a relationship with the kids' mother. As time had passed, she found herself wanting to call her and ask, why did she and Raheem end their relationship.

After all, they were middle- and high school sweethearts and it usually took a lot for people that had been together since childhood to call it quits.

Faith wondered if it was the drugs or was it infidelity. Maybe that's why he was so good with her in the beginning, supporting her by being there and taking her to NA meetings, maybe it was because he was trying to make up for what he didn't do for Lace.

"Hi," Sherry greeted.

"Hey sweetie." Faith stood up and kissed her on the cheek.

"Where's Dad? I've been calling him and calling him, he hasn't returned any of my phone calls."

"He's away on a business trip."

"You haven't heard from him?"

"No."

"Do you know where he's at?"

"No." There was no sense in lying.

Sherry took a glass out the cabinet. "I'll think I'll join you."

Faith almost told her no she wouldn't, until she remembered that Sherry turned twenty-one two months ago.

As she poured herself a glass of wine, Faith noticed Sherry focusing on her.

"Why are you looking at me like that," Faith asked.

"Because something is up and I'm trying to figure out what it is."

"There's nothing up," Faith denied.

Sherry sat across from Faith. "I'm not a little kid anymore, you can tell me the truth. Are you and Dad finally getting a divorce?"

The word *finally* wasn't lost on Faith. "Finally? Why would you say that?"

"Because I know that you've been unhappy for a long time."

Faith didn't know what to say, should she deny it or should she open up a little? As much as she wanted to open up, Faith knew Sherry was not the one to do it with.

"Plus, you don't hide things very well. It's all over your face."

Faith didn't want to have Sherry concerned about what was going on in their household, she also didn't want to lie. "You shouldn't concern yourself with us, sweetie."

"Why not? It's my dad and you're like my mom. I love you both and I want both of you to be happy and if it takes y'all getting divorced, then maybe that's what you two need to do."

Faith smiled inside because even though what Sherry was saying was out of line, she felt proud of her wisdom.

"I was talking to my mom about it and—"

On that note Faith interrupted Sherry. "You were talking to your mom about me and your father's relationship? I don't like the sound of that."

"Oh, believe me, she doesn't care, she's been over Dad."

"That's not the point," Faith told her. "Me and your father's affairs are just that, ours." Her business was her business to share.

Sherry wasn't getting what Faith was trying to say at all. "Maybe you should call my mother, I know you and her have never really been friends but I think you should be. Y'all remind me so much of one another."

That must be true for your father too. You have no idea how alike we are. Of course Faith didn't speak these words.

"You and Mom really should get to know one another. I don't know why you haven't after all these years."

"I don't know how comfortable I would feel with that."

"Well, you're the one that raised us until my mother got better and she talks about how much she appreciates it all the time."

This was news to Faith, she was pleased to hear it. It made her feel good to know that Lace recognized what she'd done. Raheem damn sure didn't make her feel like he appreciated it.

Sherry stayed for about an hour. As she was walking out the door, she told Faith, "Listen, you and Dad really should consider either getting counseling or getting a divorce. What's the sense of holding onto something that's broken?"

After she left, Faith picked up the phone and dialed Raheem's number. As usual, she had to leave a message. "You really need to call me, I'm still your wife and we need to talk, not yell, not fight, but have a real conversation."

After she hung up the phone, Faith called Susan and asked her if she was going to a meeting.

'Have you forgotten about the get-together Lisa is having?" Susan reminded her.

"Actually, I did."

"Well, that's where I'll be."

"I'll meet you there."

When they hung up the phone, Faith went into the bedroom to change into some jeans, a cute shirt and heels. Faith really didn't feel like a party but she figured what the hell, maybe it would put her in better space. She took a quick shower and got dressed. She didn't bother with makeup, she just put on some lip gloss and brushed some bronzing powder on her cheeks. She looked in the mirror and said, "This is as good as it's going to get tonight."

Faith was on her way out the door when she saw headlights pull up in the driveway. She walked over to the window, looked out and saw Raheem climb out of a limo. *Damn, why does he have to show up just as I'm leaving the house?*

It was hard for Faith to believe that there was time when she would be waiting by the door for him to arrive. There was also a time when he'd bring her home a gift from wherever he'd traveled. That stopped quite some time ago and there was no use reminiscing about what was, when she was trying to get through what is.

Faith left Raheem numerous messages, letting him know that it was time to stop putting off the divorce issue. She hoped that when he finally returned home they would actually have a conversation about it, without becoming emotional.

Faith started pacing the floor, her nerves were on edge. Although she was ready for them to sit down and have a talk, it would to have to wait, she was on her way out the door.

Now that she'd made up her mind to go to Lisa's, she was going. Shit, anything she was invited to from this moment on, she was going to make it a point to go. *There will be no more sitting around feeling sorry for myself, it's time to get out and explore.*

As Raheem walked down the driveway, Faith turned around and headed towards the bathroom. Her heart was racing and she was getting a sick feeling to her stomach. Faith felt like she was having a panic attack. She inhaled and exhaled deeply.

"Faith!"

Faith could hear Raheem yelling for her. She refused to answer him.

"Faith!" he called out again.

He knew she was home because her car was parked in the driveway. He probably saw her shadow through the curtains when she moved away from the window as well.

Damn it, that's why I should have gotten blinds. Faith opened the bathroom door slightly. "I'm in the bathroom," Faith yelled out while trying to get herself together.

How dare he come home yelling my name out like I'm supposed to run and see what he wants. He didn't even bother to return any of the messages I left his ass.

Faith opened the bathroom door and walked out to find him sorting through the mail that was on the coffee table.

He looked up and before he could open his mouth, Faith asked him, "Why didn't you return any of my phone calls?"

Raheem put the mail back on the table. "I was in meetings most of the time."

Faith shook her head in disbelief. "You were in meetings twenty-four hours a day?"

Raheem ignored the question and pulled a small box out of his briefcase.

Faith saw that it was rectangular. Before she could wonder what it was, Raheem was handing it to her.

Faith crossed her arms. "Raheem, what are you doing?"

"I bought you something."

"Why would you do that?"

Still holding the box out, Raheem told her, "It's my way of apologizing."

Faith refused to take the box out of his hand. "Who you need to be apologizing to is your daughter Sherry. You need to tell her why you didn't at least call her back. She came by here upset and worried. She wanted to know if everything was okay between us."

Raheem still held the box out toward Faith, who ignored it. "I needed to think, I needed space, I needed to figure out what to say to you, to make you not leave me."

Faith didn't believe that for one minute. Raheem had the verbal skills that could charm, harm and disarm you. She had fallen for it numerous times and this time she would not.

"You needed time!" Faith heard her voice rising and although she was telling herself, *keep it calm*, she couldn't believe he had the boldness to say he needed time.

"You needed time! Motherfucker, how the hell can you stand there and say that to me?" She was furious.

Raheem finally put the box in his pocket. It was obvious he wasn't getting off that easily.

"You need to watch your mouth," he told her.

To this Faith laughed. "I'm a grown-ass woman; I don't have to watch a damn thing."

Faith had to admit, speaking up and cursing his ass out felt real good. "You've had nothing but time, time to cheat,

time to lie, time to make me feel inadequate, time to—"
Faith couldn't even finish her thought; she was livid.

Raheem picked up his briefcase. His suitcase and garment
bag were still near the front door. "I'm going to take a
shower, when I get out and after you've calmed down, maybe
then we can talk."

"I won't be here when you get out the shower," Faith told
him.

"Where are you going?"

"Out!" She wasn't telling him shit.

"Is that right?" He looked at what she was wearing.

"You're going out in jeans?" Normally, when she was going
"out," as she put it, which she rarely did, her attire was more
upscale.

"Yes, I am." Faith's hands were on her hips.

"Listen, I'm going to take a shower, when you're ready to
talk, you know where I'll be."

"Do I?"

Looking like he'd had enough of the back and forth, he told
her, "I'll be here Faith, for a while. I don't have any business
trips planned. When you're ready to discuss us, I'll be here."

When Faith told him she was going out, Raheem didn't re-
spond the way she wanted him to. She wanted him to be like,
where the hell is out, that's not telling me anything. She wanted
him to be more curious and to feel threatened, instead he
just walked away and left her standing in the middle of the
floor.

A part of Faith wanted to stay and discuss their marriage.
After all, it was the only thing occupying her mind but she
refused to do it on his time, when his schedule allowed.

"I needed time to think about how to make you stay with
me."

139

She couldn't believe he said that to her. What the hell was that about? Why was he fronting, acting like their marriage mattered now?

Faith grabbed her purse from beside the couch and headed out the door. *You know what, I'm going out and hang with the girls. I deserve it, as much as I want to stay here, I'm not. I'll show his ass that I have a life too.*

When Faith arrived at Lisa's house, she noticed the door was wide open. She stood there trying to decide if she should just walk in or ring the doorbell.

She didn't have to make the decision herself, someone was walking by and noticed her standing there looking un-sure. "Come on in."

She did.

"There are people in the kitchen and downstairs."

Faith allowed the sound of conversation to lead her into the kitchen, where a few women were laying out food.

Faith looked down at her hands. Damn, on her way there she was so upset from the confrontation—or should she say argument—with Raheem that she forgot to bring anything.

She was about to turn around and leave when one of the women she recognized from the meeting rooms looked up. "Faith? What's up, girl, didn't you just walk in? Where are you going?"

"Oh, um, I was about to run back out and pick up some-thing to contribute to the party."

"Why would you leave to do that?"

"Because I didn't bring anything and I didn't want to come empty-handed."

"Girl, get your ass in here. It ain't even that serious. Shit, after all you've done for us, you think we're going to be upset that you came empty-handed? We appreciate you, so you get a pass."

Her compliment made Faith feel a little better. "I do what I do from the heart."

"We know you do."

What they were talking about is that Faith often paid for the coffee and refreshments they had at the NA meetings. When there was someone in a dire situation, she would go in her pocket and assist financially. She didn't do it for props or recognition. She did it because she could and she did it because she remembered how when she was emotionally broken down, the women "in the room" helped put her back together.

"Where is everyone else?" Faith asked, she could hear the music playing and loud laughter.

"They're downstairs."

Faith was headed towards the stairs, when she heard Susan's voice. She turned around and saw Susan come in with two bags and her cell phone between her ear and shoulder.

"I'm just getting in the door, I'll call you back." She looked around, spotted Faith and smiled. "Where should I put this?" she asked no one in particular.

"On the table."

"Wherever you find a spot."

Faith walked over to her and took one of the bags. "I'll help you."

"Thanks," Susan said as she released the bag and caught the cell phone before it fell on the floor.

"You see, this is why I need to go ahead and purchase headphones."

After meets, greets and hugs, Susan pulled a couple of bottles of sparkling apple cider, Perrier waters and a fruit salad out of the bags. She and Faith placed everything on the table and in the coolers that were on the floor before going downstairs.

Once they were downstairs, Faith noticed that everything was in full swing. People were playing backgammon, chess and spades. She also noticed a handful of men.

Faith looked at Susan. "I thought this was supposed to be women only."

"I didn't hear that. All Lisa said is she was having a get-together."

Faith frowned; right now she was upset with men and didn't want to exert the extra energy by playing nice.

As they walked across the room, Susan took a good look at Faith. "Are you okay?"

"As well as can be expected, considering me and Raheem got into it before I came here."

"Does it matter that there are men here?"

It really didn't, it's just that Faith thought the women were going to be free to sit around and talk about whatever they wanted to without having to censor their words.

"Nah, you have to excuse me, I'm just tripping, I know I can't take my disgust with Raheem out on all men. I'm just carrying some baggage right now."

"Do you want to talk about it?" Susan asked.

It took everything in Faith's power to keep her mouth shut. She wanted to run down the list of things that weren't right. She wanted to be reassured that leaving Raheem was in her best interest.

"Now's not the time."

Of course, Susan couldn't let it go at that. "What's going on?"

"I don't want to talk about it here."

Susan stopped in the middle of the floor. "Well, we are going to talk before this night is over."

Faith just let it go, because she knew if Susan said they were going to talk, then that's just what was going to happen.

"Come on, let's go mingle." Susan took Faith by the hand

and pulled her towards the hostess. "Lisa, I see you've out-done yourself once again."

Before she knew it, two hours had passed and Faith found herself having a good time. Worn out from her busy day and from mingling, Faith found a seat in the corner near the pool table and sat down.

"Why are you over here by yourself?"

Faith looked up to find one of the most attractive men she'd seen in a long time standing in front of her. "Just minding my business." She didn't mean to be bitchy, it just slipped out.

"My, my, we're in a nasty mood, aren't we?"

Faith apologized. "I'm sorry, I'm just tired and I've had a rough day."

"Why don't you just leave?"

"Because my husband is home and I don't want to be there with him." Those words came out of Faith's mouth before she could stop them.

"So, you're having problems at home?"

Feeling uncomfortable with what she revealed, Faith told him, "Forget I just said that and let me introduce myself. I'm Faith."

The man raised his eyebrow. "Faith, a beautiful name for a beautiful person. I'm Siddiq. I'm Lisa's big brother."

Faith put her hand out for him shake. "Pleased to meet you, Siddiq."

Instead of shaking her hand, he leaned over and kissed it.

How corny, Faith thought, *but how charming.*

"Do you know Lisa from the rooms?" he asked her.

Did Faith want him to know she was an addict? Did it really matter? After all, she probably wasn't going to ever see him again after tonight. "Yes."

Siddiq pulled up a chair and sat in front of Faith. "How long have you been clean?"

"You're asking a personal question for us to just have met."

"Well, I thought we were past small talk, especially since you told me why you don't want to go home," he half-joked.

What could Faith say other than he was right about that. "For a few years."

"Good for you, I've been clean for eight," he revealed.

This revelation made Faith look at him with more intensity. Was this his way of letting her know it would be okay to open up to him? Hopefully, it wasn't just a come-on line.

Faith eyed him up and down.

He took notice. "Make sure you get it all in," he teased.

There was something about him that just pulled her in. You see, this is the shit that used to get her into trouble with men. She'd jump into things and see the possibilities way too fast.

Faith stood up. "I have to go."

Siddiq held onto her arm. "Why? We were just getting to know one another."

"I'm married."

"I know, you already told me."

"Then why would you want to get to know me?" She looked at his hand, which was still on her arm.

"I was just trying to make conversation." He dropped his hand.

"Well . . ." Faith saw Susan coming her way and gave her a "help me" look.

Susan walked over and grabbed Faith by the arm. "Faith, I've been looking all over for you. Come on." Susan pulled Faith along but not before acknowledging Siddiq.

When they were out of Siddiq's earshot, Susan asked, "Was Siddiq bothering you?"

"You know him?"

"Girl, please, anyone that's around Lisa knows her brother, she adores him. She talks about him all the time."

"I see why," Faith said under her breath.

Susan stopped in place and teased, "Oh, do you? What exactly does that mean?"

"Nothing."

"Come on, let's go outside near the pool and talk."

As they walked through the house, Faith snuck glances at original pieces of art, very expensive knickknacks and high-priced technical gadgets throughout. "I didn't know Lisa had money," Faith observed.

"No, her brother does, this is his house."

Faith felt like a fool. "I'm embarrassed."

"Why?"

"I was rude to the host."

Susan waved that comment away. "Don't even worry about that. Let's talk about what's really bothering you. But first let me call Timothy."

When Susan hung up with Timothy she asked Faith, "What's up?"

"I envy what you have."

"What could you possibly envy that I have?"

"A happy marriage."

Now Susan understood why Faith seemed preoccupied. "You've finally decided to admit it, huh?"

Faith frowned. "Admit what?"

"That your marriage is in trouble."

They sat near the pool. "How long have you known?"

"How long have you been coming to the meetings?"

Faith didn't know what to say to that. It's not that she tried to keep the state of her marriage a secret, she just didn't go around advertising that her husband cheated on her every chance he got and that she allowed it because she felt un-

145

worthy. It really wasn't anyone's business. Some things she didn't mind sharing with people but this was one topic she did.

Why? Because she knew people would tell her to leave him and if there was one thing she couldn't stand, that was when she gave advice or told a person something they already knew over and over only for them have it go in one ear and out the other.

This is why when she counseled people, she guided them into seeing the solution. She let them think the next step was their idea. Well, that's what she tried to do.

"Are people talking about it?" If people knew her marriage was failing, surely they were discussing it amongst themselves.

"Now don't you think that the people who come to NA and AA meetings have bigger concerns than you and your marriage? I only recognized it because I'm your friend."

"Well, how come you never asked me anything?"

"I figured you would talk to me about it when you were ready."

Faith appreciated that because now she was ready and she was going to need as much support as possible. "I'm leaving him."

This surprised Susan, because even though she knew things weren't what they should be in Faith's house, she didn't think it was that bad, either. "Have you tried counseling?"

"We're way past that."

"What's going on?"

Faith went on to tell Susan about Raheem's numerous affairs and how she just wasn't willing to take it anymore.

"Why did you stay in the marriage so long anyway?"

"He saved me from myself."

"And you sacrificed your dignity because of that?"

"He took care of me, he was my hero, he helped me get clean and I love him."

Susan leaned over and looked in Faith's eyes.

Faith shifted in her seat. "What? Why are you looking at me like that?"

"You said you love him."

"No, I didn't."

"Yes, Faith, you did."

"Well, I still care for him. I always will but I'm not in love with him anymore."

"Do you think couples stay in love?" Susan asked.

"Yes, I do. Aren't you and Timothy still in love?"

Susan leaned back in her seat. "I don't know. I think what we have is a mature love. Before you make any rash decisions, you really need to ask yourself and be sure that you're not operating off of hurt. Maybe you do still love Raheem. Maybe that's why you've put up with so much and maybe that's why you're so unhappy. If you didn't have any feelings left for him, you wouldn't care what he did. It wouldn't affect you this deeply."

Faith didn't disagree with Susan and she didn't have the energy to go back and forth on it. She knew what she was she going to do and it wasn't open for discussion.

After talking a little while longer, Faith decided it was time for her to leave. She was walking to her car when she heard someone walk up behind her.

"Hey, pretty lady."

Faith turned around. It was Siddiq.

"You're leaving so soon?" he asked.

Faith looked down at her watch and continued walking. "I've already been here a couple of hours."

"You could stay all night if you want to," Siddiq flirted.

Faith could hear the playfulness in his voice. "I apologize for being rude to you earlier."

"Your apology is accepted."

Faith unlocked her car door. She looked at Siddiq, who

looked like he wasn't leaving his spot. "Well, I have to go."
She opened her car door.

"Can I see you again?" Siddiq asked.

Faith sat down, closed the door and rolled down her win-
dow. "I'm married."

Siddiq wasn't fazed. "So you keep saying."

"I don't date," Faith told him.

"I'm not asking you for a date."

Confused, Faith said, "But you just asked me out."

"No, what I asked is if I could see you again. That could
just mean over coffee or a quick lunch. It's your call."

No words came out of Faith's mouth and seeing that she
was stuck verbally, Siddiq pulled out a business card and
handed it to her.

As she took it and read it, Faith asked him, "You carry
business cards in your own house?"

Siddiq laughed and shook his head. "I'm not that much of
a player. I saw you leaving and grabbed one out of the
kitchen drawer."

"Oh." Faith was flattered.

"Don't throw that card away, call me when you're ready. It
doesn't have to be a date. There's nothing wrong with hav-
ing a male friend."

Faith put the card over her visor. "Bye."

"See you later, beautiful."

Faith smiled all the way home.

That night when Faith arrived home, Raheem was in the
living room asleep with his legs up on the table, head thrown
back and a book across his chest. For a brief second Faith
stood there looking at him. She looked at him and remem-
bered the happier moments. Moments when she stopped
getting high for a long period of time and it was like their

relationship was brand new. They were in love and enjoyed being in each other's company. She would come home from work late and he'd be up waiting on her. If he wasn't waiting on her, he'd be asleep on the couch with a book, like he was now.

Faith tried to glance at the title; she had no idea what his interests were now. She tried not to get too close, after all she was still pissed at him and she didn't want to wake him. Faith took her off her heels, so she wouldn't be heard and went straight into the bedroom that used to be theirs but was now hers. She closed the door behind her.

She sat on the bed and asked the Lord to give her strength, the strength to leave Raheem.

"Faith?"

Faith looked at the door and then her clock. It was after midnight. "Yes, Raheem?"

"Can I come in?"

She didn't want to deal with him this late.

"Why?" Faith stood up and moved towards the door.

Faith could hear the exasperation in Raheem's voice. "You know what, never mind, we'll just talk in the morning."

When Faith didn't respond, Raheem told her good night and she heard him walk away.

She placed her forehead on the door and felt her eyes well up. Her marriage was really coming to an end and there wasn't anything that could be done to save it.

Faith went into the bathroom and turned on the light. She stood in front of the mirror and stared at herself. *What's wrong with me? Why does everyone leave me?*

This wasn't a new question she was asking herself, she'd asked it each time a man left her, cheated on her or mistreated her.

It had to be her, maybe there was still something she was

doing or wasn't doing enough of. *Maybe it's time for me to give up this whole relationship idea and realize that I should just be by myself.*

Faith wouldn't have been able to stop the tears from falling if she tried, so she just let them run down her face. Faith shook her head, blew her nose and got undressed. She was too tired to take a shower and decided to take one in the morning. She washed her face, brushed her teeth, pulled a pair of sweats out of her closet and took a T-shirt out of her drawer. She put them on and climbed under the covers. She laid down and stared at the ceiling. She thought about what Susan said: "If you didn't still love him, you wouldn't care as much as you do."

Faith closed her eyes and begged sleep to come. She didn't want to be up all night thinking about her failing marriage, but her mind could not stop racing, snippets of happier days with Raheem kept flashing before her, conversations they had, vacations they'd taken and the few times they did something eventful with his kids.

What happened? When did it go wrong? Perhaps Raheem grew tired of being her caretaker.

She sat up in the bed and sighed. She knew it would take more than lying down for sleep to come, and she was going to go to sleep one way or the other, even if it mean taking a Tylenol PM.

Dear Journal,

I had a good time at Lisa's party tonight, met her brother and I must tell you he was charming. I know, I know, Raheem was charming when we first met too. I also know that I'm still married and really shouldn't be thinking about calling him. But you know what I am. Two wrongs don't make a right, but

maybe the attention Siddiq would like to give me would at least make me feel better.

I'll sleep on it before I make my decision on calling him. Coffee wouldn't hurt, plus maybe he can give me a man's perspective on things.

Is tomorrow going to be the day, Raheem and I actually come to terms about our marriage? Will he finally accept that it's over and we're just wasting each other's time?

Damn, I wish it hadn't turned out this way but I'm done, worn out and beat down. I can't fight for us anymore, I can only fight for me.

Love and Peace, Faith

CHAPTER THIRTEEN

ELSIE

Elsie finally decided to have dinner with Trey after he called her every day for damn near a week and asked her to join him. The day he called the Center and she tried to call him back, he had made other plans just that quick, after that it was just hard to clear her schedule.

She knew he wanted more than "just dinner." She could hear the flirtatious tone of his voice in each conversation. Tonight over dinner, she would definitely have to let him know about her sexual preference.

Prior to Elsie arriving, Trey told the hostess he wanted to be placed by a window with a view. She did him justice by placing them so that they faced the beach. The view was romantic enough for anyone to stand a chance, if they were hoping to get lucky, which Trey was.

Elsie glanced out the window and could see the sun going down, it looked liked it was landing in the ocean. The reds, yellows and orange rays were coming in through the windows, jazz was playing softly in the background and Trey was ready to get his mack on.

Elsie had to laugh to herself because even back in high school she remembered the girls teasing Trey, saying he wanted to be "Dr. Lovesexy." It was so obvious that's who he was trying to be at this moment. It was a shame she was going to have to burst his bubble.

"So you finally decided to stop turning down my dinner invite?"

"I've just been busy." Elsie told him. "I finally got a free evening."

"Well, I'm glad you decided to spend it with me."

Okay, I really need to let him know, I'm not interested in him like that. "Trey—" Elsie began.

He cut her off. "So tell me, what's been going on with you? How have you been? Last I heard, you were Ms. Super-model."

Elsie laughed. "I don't know about all that."

Trey leaned back in his chair and if Elsie wasn't mistaken, he licked his lips LL Cool J–style. "Well, you are a beautiful woman."

"Thank you," Elsie said, blushing.

"Then you became an attorney, opened your own firm and now you have a nonprofit organization. I'm impressed, you've been a busy little bee."

Well, damn if he knew all that, he should know that she only dated women. "How do you know all that?"

"I stay in touch with people."

That still didn't answer Elsie's question. "People like who?"

Trey smirked. "Wouldn't you like to know?" He thought he was being charming.

That was not what Elsie wanted to hear, she couldn't stand when people played games and the "guess who?" game wasn't going to make it with her.

Trey must have saw the frustration on her face because he

apologized. "I'm sorry, I'm just playing with you. I know a lot of attorneys, especially in my line of business and they talk amongst themselves. My attorney here in Jersey mentioned your firm and I recognized the name."

Even that bothered her just a bit, but she decided to just try and let it go, because when you or your business are talked about in the corporate arena, it usually meant you were doing a hell of a job or that you were their competition.

"How'd you go from law to what you're doing now?"

"I wanted to make a career change."

"It's more than a career change, it's a life change."

He was right; that's just what she made, a life change.

"Tell me about you, what have you been up to, why movies?" Elsie wasn't just asking this question to take the focus off of her, she really was curious. When they were in school, Trey was a bookworm, always studying and an honor student. What surprised people is that he also had a little flavor and a way with the girls on top of being smart. She recalled he was voted most likely to succeed. Half the school expected him to become a doctor, lawyer or politician—the last category she would have put him in was entertainment.

"I love movies, on the weekends when I was growing up, that's what I did, spent my days at the movie theater."

"Really?" It was then that Elsie remembered them going to the movies a couple of times and Trey trying to talk her into staying to see two movies. "I don't think I can sit that long," she remembered telling him.

"Yep, I knew back then that I wanted to do something behind the scenes in Hollywood, I just didn't know what. So I studied and got straight *A*'s because I knew if I did that I would be able to get a scholarship to the school of my choice."

Elsie found that fascinating; here he was a teenager, plotting his future.

"So I went as far as law school."

"Law school?"

"Yep, I thought I wanted to be an entertainment lawyer but realized that remembering codes, clauses and laws wasn't holding my interest. So long story short, I moved to California and started working for one of the top agencies and from that experience, not only did I meet people, but I found out about various opportunities and here I sit doing something I love, producing movies."

"Doing something you love," repeated Elsie, "must be the best feeling in the world."

"It is, because even when I'm having a bad day, I'm having a good day."

Elsie wanted to reach that point in her life, when a messed-up, stressed, I-can't-take-it-anymore day, wasn't that bad because in the end, she was accomplishing what she'd set out to accomplish.

"So tell me, what have you been up to, who are you seeing, did you ever get married?"

Finally, the opening Elsie had been waiting on. She decided to hell with it, she wasn't going to beat around the bush. She was going to be up-front and let him know. "Actually, I'm gay."

Trey sat up, as straight as a rod, with the quickness. "Did you just say you're gay?"

"Yes."

"Gay or bisexual?"

Elsie laughed because she knew what he was getting at, if she was bisexual he possibly felt he still stood a chance. "No, honey, I'm just what I said, gay."

"Wow!" Trey sat back in his seat and crossed his arms. "I think I'm in shock, and here I was hoping."

"You were hoping what?" Elsie asked.

"Do I even need to say it?"

Elsie laughed. "I guess not."

Trey couldn't move on. "Were you gay when we were in school?" He had to know.

"I was something, I just didn't know what to call it at the time. I do know there were a couple of classmates I was attracted to."

Trey cut her off. "Like who? Damn, I wish I had known, maybe we could have—"

"Don't even go there," Elsie warned, knowing he was talking about every man's dream.

"I'm playing, but for real, who were you attracted to?"

Elsie shook her head. "Look at you, acting like you're getting a piece of gossip. You are too funny."

"Well?"

"I plead the Fifth."

"Well, have you ever been with a man."

"Why so interested?" Elsie wasn't used to sharing information like that.

"I don't know, I think I'm just in shock because you're so beautiful and you don't look gay." Trey paused. "Then again, with the way things are today, what does gay look like?"

Elsie picked up her up glass and asked, "So does this change your game plan?"

"I hate to say it, but no."

"It should."

"Well, I'm a determined man."

Elsie laughed.

Still curious, Trey wanted to know if Elsie wanted children.

"I do eventually." *Eventually* wasn't a true answer, she wanted children now, today, tomorrow, in nine months if it was possible. "Do you have any children?"

Trey shook his head. "Nah."

"Wow, either you've been very lucky or extremely careful."

"I'd like to think it's the second option. I mean, don't get me wrong, I've come close to it a couple of times but one was a false alarm and the other, well, she made her choice."

"Do you want kids?" Elsie asked.

"Yes, yes I do."

Hmmmm, Elsie thought. *He's smart, ambitious and good-looking. He just might be the one.* That idea was something she was going to have to ponder when she was alone. Would he say yes to fathering a child and not taking part in the kid's life. After all, he was a busy man. In his line of work, he had to travel and be free, not be tied down. Could this be the reason he suddenly appeared in her life? Was this God's way of answering her prayers?

After they ate dinner and made small talk, Elsie could feel herself getting tired and was ready to turn in. She pushed back from the table. "I think this night is just about over, I've had a long day."

Trey, not the least bit offended that she was ending the evening, asked, "Can we get together again, I'd like to stay in touch with you."

Elsie told him, she'd like that too, *especially since he just might be the potential father of her child.*

Trey called the waiter over. "We're ready for the bill."

The waiter nodded and walked away.

Trey stood up and walked around the table. Elsie stood up. Trey gave Elsie a hug. "We'll talk sooner than later."

"Thanks for the dinner, good food and good conversation." Elsie hugged him back. When she turned to walk away she could feel Trey's eyes on her every move.

She knew not to turn around because he might think she was expecting him to look. Elsie couldn't help but be amused, she knew when she told him she was gay that it was going to blow his mind. She also knew that he was hoping for some

interest on her part. Well, now he knew that wasn't going to happen.

Even when she left him, she could see there was still some hope. It was all in the way he touched the arch in her back when he hugged her bye and the way he looked at her with lust even after she revealed to him she was gay.

Elsie wondered if she asked him to father her child, would he be interested in doing so. Maybe she should have hinted around the topic or maybe she should have just been forward and asked: Would you ever consider fathering a child out of wedlock by donating your sperm? If he said yes, she wondered what his expectations would be from her, if anything. Elsie knew she was getting ahead of herself but the excitement of approaching him on this was growing in her heart.

Maybe she needed to run her idea by someone first. She was definitely jumping the gun, this whole have-a-child thing had become her secret and she was ready to share.

Who could she share something like this with? Which one of the women she knew was open-minded and wouldn't judge her decision?

Elsie considered this question her whole ride home and the person she came up with was Crystal. She'd talk to her about it. If she decided to use a sperm donor, she wouldn't want to go through the process alone, she would need support.

When Elsie arrived home she collapsed across her bed and looked at the phone. She'd been thinking about calling Summer for a few days now, but kept putting it off. She didn't want to be rejected. How rejected could she be when the only reason she was calling was to say hello, to catch up and maybe if she agreed to see her, to have lunch.

Elsie glanced at the clock and saw that it going on 11:00 PM. She wondered if it was too late to call Summer's house; if

it was, she'd just deal with it. She needed to hear Summer's voice tonight before she went to bed.

What if she doesn't want to talk to me? What if she hangs up on me? What if, what if, what if? Elsie made the decision to stop what-if-ing and just pick up the phone only to hang it up again.

Dear Journal,

What do you do when you end a relationship for all the wrong reasons? What do you do when you really miss a person and have no idea if they miss you? What do you do when you finally realize you made the biggest mistake of your life by trying to move on when the truth is you haven't moved an inch?

I want to call Summer so bad, I want to hear her voice, I want to feel her touch, I want to taste her again. Even though some time has went by and I've dated other people, she's always been the one. Will she continue to be the one I can't shake loose? Will once I speak to her I realize that I built her up to be more than she is and more than we were? Or will what I thought be real? That our love was one of a kind. There's only one way for me to find out and that is to call her.

It's just that everytime I pick up the phone, I lose my nerve.

Okay, for real, I'm going to call her this week and hope she misses me as much as I miss her.

Your friend, Elsie

CHAPTER FOURTEEN

BELLA

"Good morning." Bella turned over to find Brother James in her bed. He had the nerve to be on his side with one of his hands propped under his chin like he had watched her sleep.

It freaked Bella out because this was not what was supposed to happen and she hoped he knew that it would never happen again.

"I enjoyed you last night," he told her when she looked him in the eyes.

Didn't he realize that last night was a mistake, a huge one? Didn't he know that he was supposed to wake up with regrets, apologizing and trying to get out of there as soon as possible?

Obviously, he didn't, because he was chilling and looking like he wasn't trying to go anywhere.

"James?" How was she going to ask him to leave without being rude? Should she just straight-out tell him they were going to hell and the longer he stayed in her bed, the longer they would burn. Would that do the trick?

"Bella?" James wasn't dense, he could see the unsettled look on Bella's face and knew what she was going to say before she said a word.

"I, um, I think—"

"You think I should leave?"

Bella sat up in the bed, holding the blanket over her body. It wasn't like he hadn't seen it already, the damage was already done, but she still felt it was necessary. "I do." She couldn't bring herself to look at him.

"Why? We're adults, we're free to do whatever we want to, whenever we want to."

"Yeah, but we should also know better. I'm a pastor." She faced him. "I'm your pastor."

"We knew that last night when we climbed in this bed together."

He was right about that.

"I also know that you're a woman with needs, Bella, needs I can satisfy, needs I want to satisfy."

Satisfy them, you did. She turned her back to him and pleaded, "Please James, I just need some time, time to process this, time to process us."

James sat up. "So, are you saying there's a chance for us?"

"I don't know what I'm saying, James, this is all so sudden, too sudden."

Bella knew there wasn't a chance for a *them,* there was no way she could or would see a member of her congregation. It would be too awkward. What was she thinking? That was it, last night she wasn't thinking. She was feeling and reacting and that wasn't a good thing.

James stood up. Bella couldn't stop herself from looking at him. He was naked and her flesh was saying, "reach out, touch him, tell him to get back in this bed," but her mind was telling her, "let him go and not just today but forever."

"I'm going to take a shower and then I'll leave, but know this one thing, Bella: we have to talk about this, it's not something we can run from. We both wanted it."

That I did, she admitted to herself and if she didn't feel guilty right now, she'd want it again and again and again.

James surprised her last night with his body and his love-making skills. Who was she going to tell this to, her journal once again? She needed a confidante and she needed one fast.

An hour later James had left, but before he did, she took the time to make him some breakfast and kept the conversation between them light. At the door, he bent forward to kiss her and she turned her cheek.

He didn't comment on it. He just pulled back and told her, "I'll call you."

The second Bella closed the door, she went into her prayer room and got down on her knees. She didn't know what she wanted to say to God but she knew she had to say something, she knew she needed to ask for his forgiveness, grace and mercy, not only because it was the right thing to do but because it was the only thing she could think of doing. Even though she felt guilty, that guilt wasn't enough to make her not want to do it again.

What happened last night? What led to them making love? Was it something he said? Was it something she said or was it just the devil? *Am I losing my mind?* Bella wondered. *Maybe I need to hand in my pastorial title, maybe it's not in my makeup to be preaching to people, telling them how to live right, when I can't even live right. Perhaps I've finally come to accept that I've bitten off more than I could chew, that I've chosen the wrong profession.*

* * *

The previous evening Brother James had come to her office after the men's committee left. They were meeting at the church to discuss an event for the young men in the community.

Bella was at her desk reading when he poked his head in the office. "Do you have a moment?"

Thinking nothing of it, she told him to come on in. Bella wanted to speak with him anyway because ever since he'd asked her out on a date, she felt a little uncomfortable when he was around. It always seemed like he was watching her out of the corner of his eye.

He stood across from her desk.

"Have a seat," Bella told him.

"I'm not going to stay long, I just wanted to see if you would like to grab something to eat with me. You've been cooped up in your office for most of the day, you must be starving."

She was, but she wasn't going to tell him that. "We need to talk," Bella told him.

"Uh-oh, maybe I do need to take a seat. Whenever a woman says we need to talk, it means, I have some bad news for you. Just put me down easy," Brother James told her.

"Brother James," Bella started. "Any single woman in this church would be more than pleased to be seen with you. Why don't you ask one of them out?"

"Because it's not them that I want, it's you."

He definitely knew the right words to make a women feel good.

Brother James reached across her desk and took her hand. "Come on, since you're turning me down, you might as well let a heartbroken man take you to dinner."

Bella paused and against her better judgment she agreed. "This is not a date," she let him know, "it's only dinner."

Brother James stood at attention with a smile on his face. "Whatever you say."

When they walked outside, Bella said, "How about I meet you where we're going."

"Well, where do you want to go."

"I'm not sure."

"Somewhere close?" Brother James already knew the answer to that one.

When Bella didn't answer, Brother James told her, "Listen, let's take your car to your house, I'll drive us to this restaurant I know about. It doesn't make sense for you to meet me somewhere that's out of the way, since I know you don't want to be seen."

It made sense, so she agreed.

On the way to her house, Bella couldn't help but wonder what she was doing. She tried convincing herself that it was only dinner and dinner never hurt anyone. He knew where she stood and that they could not be anything other than friends. Therefore, dinner was safe.

When she pulled up to her house, she told him she was going to run inside, change clothes and that she would be right out.

"Is it okay if I come in?' Brother James asked. "That way you can take your time changing. You don't have to rush."

Coming from where she came from, which was the streets, Bella couldn't help but wonder if he was trying to set her up. She wanted to think the best of him, so even with that question in mind, she told him he could come in. If she trusted anyone it was God not to put her in a situation she couldn't get out of, if she wanted to get out of it.

This is where Bella knew she went wrong, she knew she should have told him to wait in the car, but sometimes women make decisions they end up regretting, decisions

that they think about days later and wish they could go back and change. The next day, they'd wonder, "Why did I?"

Bella even wondered if on a subconscious level she set herself up. Was she that desperate and lonely? Was she that in need of companionship? If she got honest with herself, she'd have to say she was.

Brother James followed her inside and the smell of baked chicken hit his nose.

He sniffed the air. "It smells like food in here."

"Oh, shoot!" Bella walked into the kitchen and turned off her Crock-Pot. She'd forgotten that earlier that afternoon when she stopped home, she had thrown a small chicken into the Crock-Pot. It was a good thing she had put it on low. She lifted the top and the smell of rosemary, onions, garlic, red potatoes and chicken made her stomach growl.

"I guess you won't be going out to eat with me?"

Bella put the top back on the Crock-Pot and looked at him. "Maybe you can stay here and have dinner with me."

Bella could see the expression of surprise on his face. "Are you sure?"

This was her chance to do the responsible thing, but she ate alone all the time and she really wouldn't mind his company.

"Yes, I'm sure."

"Is this still not a date?" he joked.

"It's still not a date," Bella told him. "Make yourself comfortable in the living room, I'm going to freshen up and then I'll be out to make our plates."

"I'd like to use your restroom," he told her.

"Use the one in the hallway." She pointed in the direction of the bathroom.

"Bella?"

She raised her eyebrow.

"I can call you that outside of church, right?"

"Yes." After all, her entire being was not that of a pastor, she was a person with feelings, emotions and so much more. It was a relief for someone to recognize it.

"I have some champagne in my car."

"What are you doing with champagne in your car?"

"One of my clients brought me a case," Brother James told her. "Would you like for me to bring a bottle in?"

Not really a drinker, Bella could never resist champagne. She always enjoyed the taste of it. "Yes, do that."

Bella went and put on a long linen skirt and a white cotton T-shirt. When she stepped into the kitchen, James commented on how comfortable she looked.

"Thank you," she told him.

Bella made them each a plate and poured both of them a glass of champagne.

"This is nice, thanks for letting me in your presence."

Bella took a sip of her champagne, then another sip, then another. The next thing she knew they had drank two bottles and the conversation between them was flowing.

Bella forgot that she had planned on talking him into dating one of the women from the church and to stop pursuing her. She forgot how good it felt to just be a woman.

When Bella really took the time to think about last night, she couldn't pinpoint when it went from casual to personal, nor when it went from personal to sexual.

Did the champagne have that much of an effect on her? She guessed it did. She did know that she enjoyed his company more than she should have and she did recall telling herself at one point, she should ask him to leave, but she talked herself out of doing that as well.

* * *

When James left that morning, Bella wanted to place the blame on James entirely, he knew her situation, he knew how she felt, he should have respected her boundaries and put an end to the night. She wanted to blame the devil for playing tricks on her and for sneaking up on her.

She also wanted to place the blame on God for her being single and for giving her free choice because the choice she made that night was one of the flesh and not the spirit. Although she wanted to place blame, she knew the only person she could blame was herself.

Bella took the linen off her bed and threw it in the wash. Then she called Crystal. She was going to invite her out to lunch, feel her out a little and see if she was someone she could confide it.

Crystal picked up on the first ring. "Hello."

"Good morning, may I speak to Crystal?" Bella asked. She thought it was Crystal's voice that answered, but one could never be to sure.

"Speaking."

"Hey, it's Bella."

Bella could hear the questions in Crystal's voice. "Bella? Hey, good morning."

Suddenly Bella felt uncomfortable. *How do you ask someone to be your friend?* "I was wondering if you would like to have lunch with me today or tomorrow, whenever you're available."

"I'd like that. Is everything okay?"

"Everything's fine, I just figured . . ."

What was Bella going to say, she just figured what, that they could be friends, that Crystal was someone she thought she could tell her business to? Bella decided to be honest. "Here's why I'm calling: I'm going to keep it on the up-and-up with you. I know you attend my church often. We've

talked on numerous occasions and have seen each other out and about. This may sound real corny, but I need a friend."

Crystal laughed on the other end. "Girl, we all need friends."

"I mean, being a pastor is not as easy as people think, not that anyone thinks it is, but it's hard to have outside friendships because of the pedestal we're on."

Crystal told her she understood. "It's like you're not an everyday person with regular wants, needs, likes and dislikes."

Bella felt so relieved that Crystal got it. "Exactly."

"I'd love to have lunch with you and get to know you on a more personal level."

"So you're saying yes, you'll be my friend," Bella joked as she tried not to sound too eager.

"Yes, I am."

"So when are you available for lunch?" Bella asked.

"How about tomorrow?"

Bella agreed, they set up a time and place, then hung up.

Dear Journal,

What does it feel like to have a friend? Someone you can confide in, someone you can talk to about anything, someone you could share secrets with, laugh with or just plain old connect with.

I wouldn't know because I've never been one to get along with other women, with my past profession and all I was afraid of, afraid that they would turn on me, afraid that they would judge me, afraid that people would discover who I am. Well, now I am ready to take a chance. I've always believed or convinced myself that I didn't get along with women. I'm ready to change that.

I hear that a lot, "I don't get along with women." Is it that women don't get along with one another or that they just

choose not to? Is it jealousy or insecurities? What's the real rea-son? I know it's hard opening up and allowing others into your space, place and thoughts. What things are best left kept to self? Where do you draw the line? How do you know who to trust, how do you know who to let into your life?

I'm going to find these things out. I'm going to make myself available and allow someone in. I just hope God sends me the right person.

Fully Blessed, Bella

CHAPTER FIFTEEN

HARMONY

"You need to tell me something," Shareef asked Harmony. He was livid.

"I don't know what to tell you, he's called collect a couple of times and—"

Shareef looked at her in disbelief. "What do you mean, he's called a couple of times, how come I don't know this?"

Harmony just stood there looking busted. Although to her she really wasn't, because a phone call didn't mean a damn thing, it's not like she was sneaking off and seeing him.

"When is he calling?"

He was calling when Shareef wasn't there but it wasn't planned that way. It just kept happening that way. Shareef started pacing the floor, if Harmony wasn't mistaken, Shareef seemed to be shaking, he was so angry. She looked down at his hands, which were balled up at his sides. "I can't believe you, Harmony, this is something you should have told me. You just don't accept collect calls in my house from another man that's in prison." Shareef was stunned beyond

belief. It just so happened that he had to run back in the house to grab some papers off the counter, when the phone rang.

"Hello?" he answered.

The next thing he knew, there was a recording talking about, "You have a collect call from an inmate." At that point Shareef was holding the phone away from his ear looking at the phone like, *I know this ain't Ny'em calling my motherfucking house.*

He accepted the call and called Harmony into the living room. He didn't tell her who it was, he just passed her the phone.

"Who is it?" she asked as she placed the phone near her ear.

When she heard Ny'em's voice, she tried to appear calm, which was hard to do especially with Shareef standing there in front of her, staring in her mouth.

"Listen, I asked you not to call here." That was a lie, she didn't ask Ny'em not to call but she felt like she had to play if off because Shareef looked like he was ready to go upside someone's head.

"No, no. That's just not going to happen." Ny'em was asking Harmony if he could call later and speak with his son, Shacquille. He asked that same question each time he called the house and the answer was always the same. "Listen, I have to go, bye."

As she placed the phone on the hook, Shareef lost it.

"Why is he calling my house?" Shareef asked again.

"Our house," Harmony said. It was the only thing she could think of to say, because she knew he was right. She was dead wrong for not letting him know about Ny'em's phone calls. "This is our house, we live here together."

Shareef didn't even dignify that with a response, he turned his back to her and took a deep breath, trying to

calm himself down. "You would really betray me like this? Where's your loyalty?" he asked her.

"Betrayed? Loyalty? What are you talking about, Shareef? I think you're overreacting."

Shareef shook his head in amazement. *She really doesn't get it.* He turned back towards Harmony—he was going to make her get it. She really needed to see that her ass was dead wrong.

"Listen, Harmony, you saw the movie *Baby Boy,* right?"

She nodded and wondered where the hell he was going with this.

"Remember in the movie when Snoop started calling old girl from prison?"

Harmony waited for him to get to the point.

"Well, the next thing you know his ass was being paroled to her house. Harmony, you don't know how them jail nig- gas think. When you allow them to call, especially when they know you have a man, they start to think your relationship can't be that serious if you're letting them call you at your man's house. They start to think they still have a chance."

"But he doesn't," Harmony told him. "We both know that shit has been over for years. Me and his relationship was dead before he even got locked up. Any chance he had with me is buried and gone."

"What you say and what he believes could be two different things. Let's turn the table. Would you have a problem with any of my exes calling me on the house phone?"

Harmony rolled her eyes. "What you think?"

"Exactly," Shareef said, knowing he was proving his point.

But Harmony wasn't done with that one. "Ain't no ex- girlfriend of yours got any business calling here anyway, you don't have kids by anyone other than me so there should be nothing to discuss."

"Tell me this then, Harmony, you and Ny'em have been apart for years, he's never even seen his son. So what the hell do you two have to talk about other than the old times, how much he misses you and what he thinks he's going to do for you when he gets out?" Shareef was getting worked up all over again. "I can see that motherfucker now, getting all worked up, masturbating to the sound of your voice and the vision of your body. I don't like that shit and I did not sign onto this relationship to assist your ass in doing a bid with another nigga. I'm not having it. When we met, you said he was out of your life for good and I moved forward with you believing that."

Harmony realized how deeply affected Shareef was about this whole thing, so she told him, "Look honey, I can see how this might seem like I've disrespected you and for that I can't apologize enough."

Shareef wasn't hearing it. "Just think about this while I'm gone today. I've worked too hard to get us to this point in our relationship and I don't want anyone to come between us. I don't want you giving him false hope and have him thinking he has an opportunity to get back into your life. Also ask yourself, how am I supposed to see the difference between a nigger knocked up and a nigger on the streets when you're talking to him behind my back?"

"You have to understand that he's not just any man, Shareef, he's Shacquille's father." The second she said those words Harmony regretted it.

If there was one thing Shareef took seriously, one thing he did not play with, it was the kids, all the kids. She knew he was more of a father to the two that weren't his than their own fathers were.

"You would really stand there and say that to me?" Shareef asked with hurt evident in his eyes.

Harmony reached out and put her hand on Shareef's chest. He pushed it away. "I apologize, Shareef, I didn't mean it the way it sounded."

"You would really stand there and disrespect what I do to my face." Shareef looked distraught and Harmony felt responsible for the expression on his face.

She tried apologizing again. "Shareef, please listen to me." She stepped closer to him, trying to bridge that gap. "I'm so sorry, I know you are all the kid's father."

Shareef wasn't going to make this easy for her. He stepped back. "I'm Shacquille's father, not that man who has been locked up since his birth. I'm the one that's been there for him in his formative years. I'm the one he calls Daddy. I'm the one he runs to when he gets hurt, I'm the one he likes to discuss girls with and you will stand here in my face talking about Ny'em is his father. He hasn't even seen Shacquille."

"You're right, Shareef."

"Don't try to placate me by telling me I'm right." Shareef threw up his hands. "You know what, let me get out of this house before I lose my mind and say or do something I shouldn't."

Harmony didn't want him to leave with all that anger inside. "Wait, let's talk this out."

"I don't feel like talking a damn thing out." Shareef stared at Harmony like she had two heads. "I guess with Ny'em being back in the picture, me adopting Shacquille is out of the question, huh?"

"Why would you even say that?" Harmony asked him. They had discussed Shareef adopting both the boys once they got married. It was what Harmony wanted more than anything in the world.

"Because at this point I don't know what the fuck is going on."

Harmony intended for them to be one big happy family

and her intentions were sincere, it's just that when Ny'em called and told her he was getting out of jail soon and wanted to be a part of his son's life, it threw her off course.

Harmony hadn't heard from him since he'd been locked up on drug possession and that was a couple of days after she found out she was pregnant.

When he called her house the first time, to say she was struck speechless was an understatement. When she asked Ny'em how he got her number, he told her he'd asked Supreme to get it from Lala, a girl she used to hang with. She got it and gave it to Supreme to give to him.

"Well, how did she get my number?" Harmony wanted to know, because she had cut Lala off a long time ago.

"I couldn't tell you."

Well, Harmony wasn't going to just let that pass. The next time she saw Lala she was going to ask her because the bitch knew she was wrong. Everyone knew that Harmony had a new man and a new life now. Lala was one of the hoochies that had tried to step to Shareef when they first got together. It's a good thing she had an honest man. What made it even worst was when Shareef turned her down, Lala tried to tell him lies about her, saying things like she was cheating on him and that she would never be a faithful bitch.

Harmony already beat her ass once. She really hoped she wasn't going to have to do it again, because she was getting too old for this shit.

"Why now, Ny'em? Why the sudden interest in Shacquille so many years later?" Harmony asked him.

"Because I'm a changed man," Ny'em told her.

"You don't have much of a choice but to be a changed man in prison. It's not like you're out in the streets," Harmony told him.

"Listen, I know this is coming as a surprise to you, but if I

had not gotten locked up prior to you having my son, you know I would have been there for you."

Harmony was astounded at this lie. "Do I?"

Harmony's recollection of the day she told him she was pregnant was not one for the books. He wasn't happy about having another child at all. Especially since he had two other children by two different women.

"He's my son, Harmony. He came from my seed."

"Your seed, man, please. Don't give me that shit." Harmony knew she should have just hung up the phone, but she just couldn't bring herself to do it.

"What about your other children, will you be reaching out to them as well?" She needed to know how sincere he was. Were these just words to see if he could get with her when he got out of jail or was he going to make a real effort to be a father?

"I've reached out to their mothers as well and they too have given me a hard time."

Harmony needed to process this whole conversation. "Listen, I have to go, my man will be home from work soon and he and I have to talk about how we want to handle this." Harmony hung up before Ny'em could say a word.

Harmony then went into her bedroom and in the top of the closet pulled out a box that had old pictures in it. She shuffled through them and came upon one of her and Ny'em. Why she was still holding on to them was a question she asked herself, she should have thrown them away a long time ago. She knew if Shareef had pictures of him with any other women, all hell would break loose.

Harmony stared at the picture and recalled the day it was taken. They were at Great Adventure with a group of people and were laughing up a storm. They looked so happy in the picture. It was one of the few genuine moments they shared.

Those moments were distances apart because Ny'em was always hustling and she knew not to stand in the way of a man and his hustle. Plus, the more money he made, the more money she had in her pocket, the more jewelry he brought her and the more shopping she could do. They were hood rich and in those days her priorities were all fucked-up.

Harmony enjoyed being a drug dealer's main girl. She knew there were others but all that mattered at the time was her being the main one and everyone knowing it. She was the one he took around his boys. She was the one the other women were warned not to mess with. She was the one he spent most of his free time with. Eventually that got old. His coming and going when he felt like it got old and his cheating on her got old.

When she realized that she was pregnant, she was preparing herself to break off what they had, but she just couldn't do it just yet. What if this baby changed their relationship for the better? She still couldn't believe she thought their relationship would improve because of a child. That's what his other baby mamas thought, not her, but she was caught in the cycle.

When Harmony told Ny'em she was pregnant, he didn't show any emotion. His main and only concern was, "So what are you going to do about it?"

"What do you mean, what am I going to do about it?" She knew what he was asking but she wanted to be sure she heard him right.

"Are you going to have an abortion? You need money?"

Pissed and hurt, she walked out on him and went to Jewell's house.

The second Jewell opened the door, Harmony started crying. "I'm pregnant."

Jewell shook her head with disappointment. She didn't

want her cousin to be weighed down with a bunch of babies, she already had one by a dirty-ass old man, who Harmony used for money when she was young and dumb.

"By Ny'em?" Jewell asked.

"Yeah, and you know what he had the nerve to tell me to do."

Jewell didn't have to guess. "Have an abortion."

Harmony looked stunned that she knew.

"Don't look at me like I don't have a clue. Ny'em is an ass, I told you that a long time ago, when you first got involved with him. I warned you. You know what you've got to do, right?"

"What?" Harmony asked, like she didn't know the answer.

"Leave his ass," Jewell told her. Jewell didn't like Ny'em at all. She hated the way he mistreated Harmony and she hated the way Harmony allowed it.

Harmony turned to walk out the door.

"Where are you going?" Jewell asked.

"I didn't come here for the I-told-you-so and look-what-you-got-yourself-into talk. I came for support, for a shoulder to cry on."

Jewell pulled Harmony into her arms. "You know what, you're right. I apologize, let's go sit down and talk this through."

Jewell led Harmony to the couch.

"I don't think I can do this by myself, take care of another baby." Harmony didn't want to be like everyone she knew and have baby after baby by someone who could care less.

"Girl, please, do you know how many girls are doing it by themselves? If you decide to have the baby it's going to be a challenge, but I'll be there for you."

Harmony looked in Jewell's eyes. "You're always there for me."

"That's what family is for."

"I am going to think about having an abortion, though."

"Well, whatever you decide to do, I've got your back."

That night when Harmony left Jewell's house, she promised her she was going to think about whether she wanted to have the baby or not.

The next morning when Jewell called her for her decision, Harmony still had not made up her mind.

"Don't wait until it's too late," Jewell warned.

Harmony waited around all day to hear from Ny'em. Day turned into night and one day turned into the next. Harmony didn't think much of it because that was the way he operated, being a hustler and all. But after two days of not hearing from him and with her situation at hand, she called up one of his boys. "Have you heard from Ny'em?"

"Your boy got picked up last night with product."

This is not what Harmony wanted to hear. "What! Please tell me you're lying."

"I wish I could, but I'm not."

Well, come to find out, one of his old runners snitched on him and he ended up having to do some serious time. Harmony in the back of her mind planned on having an abortion but she kept putting it off and time slipped away. Before she knew it, Harmony was four months along in her pregnancy.

"Do you think it's too late to have an abortion?" she asked Jewell, one night when she was visiting.

Jewell wanted to knock her upside the head, but instead she said, "Don't you know that at four months the baby's heart is beating? Girl, that's a life inside you now. If you wanted to have an abortion, you should have done that in month one or two. If you were to do some stupid shit like that now, you'd be committing murder."

179

When Jewell put it that way, Harmony knew she wouldn't be able to go through with an abortion.

So she had the baby and just as she predicted, it was a struggle doing it on her own.

Shareef was still standing in front of Harmony, waiting on an explanation. "Why didn't you tell me he was calling here, why did you keep it from me?"

Harmony told him the truth. "I was afraid to."

"If you were afraid to tell me then you must have known it was wrong."

Harmony walked over to the couch and collapsed on it. She was mentally drained. "Shareef, I don't know what else to say. I can apologize until I'm blue in the face, but that doesn't mean you will accept it. I know I was wrong but you have to understand, I got caught up in the moment. I know that's no excuse but it's the best I could offer."

Shareef didn't even let her finish what she had to say, he was disgusted. "I'm out of here."

Harmony wanted to stop him but with the way the conversation was going and from the look on Shareef's face and the tone of his voice, she figured *what's the point.*

"What time will you be home?" Harmony followed him to the door. She was going to make this up to him some kind of way.

He didn't answer her, he just opened the door, stepped through it and slammed it shut behind him.

Harmony knew she fucked up. She knew she should have told Shareef when Ny'em called the first time. The only person she had to blame for this situation was herself. She should have listened to King when he told her to tell Shareef right away.

* * *

After the first phone call from Ny'em and his request to speak with Shacquille, Harmony should have known that wasn't a topic that was going to be dropped.

"Why now, Ny'em?" she asked him. "Why are you reaching out after all these years?"

"Because my plan was to do this bid by myself," he told her. "I didn't want to involve you or any of my other children's mothers."

That was typical Ny'em style, selfish as always.

"You see," Ny'em continued, "I've been taking these classes and going to group and it's made me see who I really was and I'm a changed man. With me changing, it got me to wondering how my son was doing."

That shit threw Harmony for a loop, she had nine years of anger built up in her. His ass didn't even want her to have Shaquille. She was ready to let him have it.

"You wanted to see how your son was doing? The son you didn't want? The son you told me to abort? The son I had to support by myself." Harmony, who had been standing, had to sit down on that note, because she felt like she was about to pass out from anger. "How dare you! How dare you act like you care. Ny'em, I know you."

She told him of something she suspected all these years. "I know that before you got locked up you hid money somewhere. You were always bragging about it. Did your ass once call me and offer me anything? No! Did you send me a message? No! My life has not been easy. Your son's life has not been easy. Thank God I met Shareef, he's a good man, better than you ever were." Harmony felt like patting herself on the back, that was some shit she'd been holding in for a long time.

"I'm not even going to get upset by that statement," Ny'em told her, "because I know you're trying to hurt me and that's okay."

181

Ny'em's tone was way calmer than Harmony expected it to be.

"I'm a changed man," he continued, "more than you will ever know and I want to make up for that lost time with my son. I want to make up for what I've done to you and what I didn't do for you. If jail taught me anything it taught me how precious life is and I need to make amends to you, Shacquille and my other children."

Ny'em said this with such intensity that Harmony almost gave in, but it was not going to be that easy. During his speech, she had figured out what he was trying to tell her. "Are you telling me you're getting out soon?"

"Yes, I will be getting released soon. I am unsure of the exact date, but I know it's within thirty days."

Shareef is going to have a fit. "Ny'em, you've got children with other women, Shacquille is doing good right now, Shareef is a great father figure and we have a family. Please, consider leaving Shacquille alone and making amends with your other kids. As a matter of fact, I release you from all your fatherly responsibilities and forgive you fully for not being there."

"Listen, Harmony, I am going to see Shacquille, you need to understand that and you also need to understand that I am not the same man, I am going to break the fatherless cycle in my family. I no longer want to do what my father did to me and what his father did to him. I am not abandoning any of my children once I get out. I am adamant on this."

It was then the operator interrupted and told them they had thirty seconds to complete their call.

Harmony had to get the last word in. "Well, Ny'em, I don't feel good about your selfish-ass decision. You should consider Shacquille's mental health and how it might negatively impact him after not hearing a word from you ever." To really dig the fork in deeper because she was pissed off to a new de-

gree, Harmony continued, "I actually told him that you were dead and when I found out you got the kingpin charge and your lawyer said you would never be free again, I believed him."

Ny'em screamed through the phone, "You told him what? Well, you better tell him something because I will see my son."

Harmony slammed down the phone. She knew this shit was going to happen just when she was getting her life in order. *Damn, can it ever be easy?*

It's when he called back the third time, talking that same, I want to see my son shit, that Harmony called Jewell. She needed to talk this out.

The only thing was Jewell wasn't home and King could hear the distraction in her voice.

"What's going on?" he asked her. "Is everything okay?"

Not able to hold it in, Harmony told him, "No, everything is not okay. You know that motherfucker Ny'em's been calling me, telling me he'll be home soon and that he wants to get acquainted with Shacquille."

"You're straight lying."

"I wouldn't lie about this and that's just part of it. I kind of told Shacquille that his father had died."

"Damn, Harmony, why would you tell him that shit?"

"Because I didn't know what else to tell him."

"If I'm not mistaken, didn't Ny'em get the kingpin charge?"

"Exactly, so now I can't help but wonder why his ass is getting out now."

"What does Shareef have to say about all this?"

Harmony didn't answer him.

He repeated himself. "What does Shareef have to say about all this?"

"I haven't told him."

"What! Are you crazy? You know what, never mind, don't even answer that. Let's just put this shit in order. Your first concern should be the impact that Ny'em will have on Shacquille and correcting that lie you told about him being dead. Secondly, you really need to tell Shareef what's going on. Knowing my boy, he's not going to handle it well but it's better to tell him now and deal with the consequences than for him to find out some other way. Also, even though I hate saying this, you need to understand where Ny'em is coming from. When men are locked down they go through changes. They see other dudes corresponding with their families and they think this is what they want and need. I wouldn't put too much stock into anything he's saying while he's locked up. Because when men are in prison time stands still. They create pseudo-realities for themselves to survive, until they get out and reality sets in. Once Ny'em gets out and that nine years of back child support attacks his ass, rent, cable and the rigors of a job—that is, if he can find one and doesn't go back to hustling—the last thing he's going to be thinking about is your son. You and I both know Ny'em has never worked a honest day in his life. Two seconds after he's free he's going to be chasing that money on the block. I say all this to say, you need to tell Shareef and you and him had better come up with a plan."

Damn, if only she had listened.

CHAPTER SIXTEEN

ELSIE

"Come on, girl, one more mile to go."

Elsie looked at Angel and rolled her eyes.

"You can roll your eyes all you want. You're the one who thought of this. You're the one who called me up talking about you want to do a triathlon."

Elsie didn't know what the hell she was thinking when that idea popped in her head. Well, actually she did, she figured if she did something physical, something to challenge her body then maybe, just maybe, she'd be able to get this baby thing off her mind.

Well, it wasn't working.

Earlier that morning, Elsie made an appointment with a doctor she read about that specialized in sperm-donor procedures. She wanted to find out more about the procedure and discuss her options. The appointment was scheduled for later that day so until then she was going to fill the up the hours by working out and handling business for the center.

"Come on, speed it up," Angel demanded. "Mind over physical, mind over the physical."

Elsie stopped in her tracks. "Okay, enough of this shit, let's walk."

Angel laughed. "Tired?

Elsie stopped, bent over and caught her breath. "What do you think?"

"Well, you might as well get it together because you are going to finish this last mile."

Not bothering to respond, Elsie stood up and took off; after all, this is what she paid Angel for, to work her ass out.

Less than ten minutes later they were sitting on a bench, sipping Gatorade. They were deep in a discussion when a woman stopped in front of them. "Elsie?"

Elsie looked up, it was Savannah, the woman from the mall. She was dressed like she'd been working out as well. "So you're a runner?" Savannah asked her.

"It might look that way, but looks are deceiving," Elsie told her. She looked at Angel and said, "Savannah, this is Angel, my trainer, Angel, this is Savannah."

"Nice meeting you," Savannah told Angel.

"Same here." Angel stood up. "Call me when you're ready for your next appointment," she told Elsie.

"I'll do that."

As Angel walked off, Elsie asked Savannah, "Do you have anywhere to be in the next hour or so?"

"No, why?"

"Want to go grab a cup of coffee?"

"Sure, I'd like that."

They were both familiar with the coffee shop that was a few blocks away. They decided to walk.

"So how's your nonprofit going?" Savannah asked.

"Better than I expected."

"That's good to hear. Don't forget I'm available if you need me, I didn't give you my card for nothing."

They entered the coffee shop and stood in line to order.

"So what's your schedule like? When would you be available to come and speak to the girls?"

"My schedule is flexible. I share a practice with three other doctors and we rotate. Just so you know, Tuesdays and Thursdays are my busiest days, so any other day would be your best bet. Just give me some notice and I'll be there."

"Can I help you?" the girl behind the counter asked.

They told her what they wanted and waited off to the side while it was being made.

"How long have you been running? I haven't seen you in the park before today," Savannah asked.

"This is a new thing for me. I've decided to try a triathlon."

"Get out. I do triathlons as well."

Elsie inconspicuously snuck a peek at Savannah's frame and liked what she saw.

"Well, maybe we can train together sometimes."

"I'd like that, because whenever you train with someone it's less of a task, less daunting."

"Your drinks are up," the cashier called out as she placed them on the counter.

Elsie and Savannah paid for their order then looked around to see if there were any open seats. They spotted a table in the corner and headed in that direction.

As they were sitting, Elsie glanced towards the window and noticed a profile that looked like Summer. She shook her head and wondered if it was a figment of her imagination.

It wasn't. Summer walked in holding hands with another female. Elsie couldn't help but stare and Savannah noticed.

"Do you know them?" Savannah asked.

Elsie could feel the green-eyed monster coming on.

Elsie stood up and unable to control herself, told Savannah, "Excuse me, I'll be right back." She started to walk toward Summer and her friend. As she took each step she tried to think of what she was going to say.

Damn, Summer still looks fine. Summer's back was turned, therefore she didn't see Elsie walk up behind her.

"Summer?"

Summer recognized Elsie's voice before she even turned around. "Elsie, how are you?" She reached out to give her a hug.

Elsie hugged her back. She must have done it a little too long because the woman Summer was with had attitude written all over her face.

"How's Winter?" Elsie asked.

"Winter's fine, thanks for asking."

There was an awkward moment when neither of then said a word. "I've been thinking about you a lot, I've been wanting to call you," Elsie told her.

Of course, Summer's friend wasn't going to let that comment go. She put out her hand for Elsie to shake. "Hi, I'm Sunny."

Elsie almost threw up as she thought, *Summer, Winter and Sunny, how cute.*

Realizing how rude she was being, Summer apologized. "I'm sorry, Elsie this is Sunny, Sunny this is Elsie."

From the way Sunny raised her eyebrows, Elsie wondered if Sunny recognized her name. She hoped so because if she did, it meant that Summer still spoke of her and if she talked about her, she thought about her.

"Nice to meet you," Elsie lied.

Sunny didn't bother to fake the funk. "I have to go to the ladies' room, I'll be right back."

The second Sunny was out of earshot, Elsie asked, "Is she your lover?"

Amused, Summer crossed her arms and nodded her head towards Savannah, who was sipping her coffee and patiently watching the interaction. "Is she yours?"

Why Elsie decided to lie was beyond her but she found herself saying, "she's someone I'm seeing."

The next thing she knew, Summer started walking toward the table. "I'd like to meet her."

What was Elsie suppose to do now that she'd stuck her foot in her mouth? *Shit, shit, shit.* When they reached the table, Savannah put down her cup and greeted Summer.

Instead of introducing herself, Summer said to Elsie, "I see you still have good taste, she's a beautiful woman."

Savannah looked at Elsie but didn't say a word.

"I'm Summer."

"Savannah."

Elsie tried to think of a way to get out of the situation before her lie was revealed but no such luck because Sunny walked up and greeted Savannah: "Dr. Matthews, how are you."

As luck would have it, Savannah was Sunny's doctor.

"Isn't this a small-ass world? So you know Elsie's date?" Summer asked.

Sunny was stunned by this news because as far as she knew Savannah was married. She wondered if this was one of those "down low" situations.

Savannah finally caught on and before she could decide what to do or say, the cashier called out to Summer and Sunny.

Elsie watched them walk away. Her gaze was interrupted by Savannah saying, "So, we're lovers, huh?"

Embarrassed, Elsie sat down and placed her head in her hands. "I'm so sorry about that."

"She's your ex?"

"Yeah."

"You still love her?"

Elsie answered honestly, "sometimes."

Savannah touched her hand. "Girl, don't sweat it, but know this. Your ass owes me big-time."

"Just let me know how I can pay up."

Savannah winked and told her, "I'll think of something."

Elsie wondered what was up with the wink, what was behind it. Was she flirting? Fuck it, she decided to find out. "Are you gay?"

Savannah smiled. "I've dipped and dappled a few times."

Elsie looked down at Savannah's hands. She noticed a wedding band. "It looks to me like your married."

Savannah leaned in and said, "and?"

Elsie was not one to play with fire or to have casual affairs with women, but for Savannah, whom she found extremely attractive, she just might consider throwing caution to the wind. She was tired of being an uptight, frustrated, under-sexed lesbian.

It was time to rock the boat.

CHAPTER SEVENTEEN

FAITH

Faith had just finished a session with the girls at the center and she was fumbling with Siddiq's card. Her intentions were to throw the card away but she never did because there was something about him that intrigued her. She was definitely captivated by him.

I can't believe he tried to run that friend line on me. Grown-ass women and men cannot just be friends.

Faith believed that and she also believed that when a man says *let's be friends* that what he meant was he was willing to be a little more patient than the average man.

Maybe, just maybe, Siddiq would prove her wrong. She was willing to give him that chance.

Faith looked at the card and dialed his number.

"Hello? Siddiq Bradley speaking."

Feeling flustered, Faith almost hung up. She felt like a teenager calling a boy she liked for the first time. "Siddiq?"

"Yes?" Of course, he had no idea who he was speaking with.

"This is Faith. I don't know if you remember me, but we met the other night, at your house, your sister's party."

"I don't need to be reminded of who you are. You're my new friend."

Faith laughed. "Oh, is that right?"

"As right as can be."

"So how are you?" Faith asked.

"It's all good. I'm shocked you called me. I didn't think you would, I wrote it off as my loss."

"Oh, so you wrote me off, huh?"

"Well, you were trying to give me the cold shoulder."

He was right and Faith told him so. "I know, it's just that I'm—"

"Married." He paused before asking, "are you reminding me or yourself."

"Both of us," Faith told him.

Siddiq was impressed with her honesty. "So tell me, what kind of things do you like to do with friends?"

"Why? Is there something you would like to do?" Faith relaxed in her chair and propped her feet up on her desk.

"Is that a trick question?" Siddiq did not want to play himself and speculate that she was teasing him.

"No, it's not."

"It depends on the person I've befriended."

Deciding to be adventurous, Faith asked, "Well, what are you doing this evening?"

"Are you asking me out?" Siddiq wanted to know.

"Maybe."

"How about we do something different and spontaneous."

"Like what?"

"Go to Seaside Heights."

"The beach?" Faith asked.

"Yep."

Faith hadn't been to Seaside Heights in a long time, since Raheem's kids moved out. She would take them there to get on rides and to play in the ocean and sand.

"I'd like that," Faith told him.

"How are we going to do this? Are we going to meet some-where and ride together or do you want to meet me there?"

Finding a parking spot in that area was difficult, finding two was going to be even more a challenge, so Faith told him, "Let's ride together, we can meet at one of the rest stops on the Parkway and go from there."

"I'm looking forward to it," he told her.

"Yeah, me too."

Together they picked a time and a spot.

"See you soon," Faith told him.

Later that evening as Faith waited for him to pull up in the rest stop, she questioned her true motives. Was she really just trying to be friends or was she attempting to be more?

She spotted him right away. He told her he would be driving a white Lincoln Navigator. So when she saw one pull up, she climbed out of her car and started walking over to where he was parking.

Before he turned the engine off, she knocked on the driver's window, causing him to jump. She could hear the music play-ing outside the truck and watched as he turned it down.

"Mmm, I see you like your music," she teased.

"That I do," he answered back while taking her in with his eyes. "Get in, beautiful."

Faith walked over to the passenger's side and climbed in. She put on her seat-belt, adjusted her seat and leaned back.

Siddiq watched her every move. "Comfortable, are we?"

"Very."

"All right, here we go."

On the way to Seaside Heights, they talked about every-thing except her marriage and that was fine with Faith.

"Let me ask you something," Faith began. "Do you really think a man and woman can just be friends?"

"Yeah, actually I do."

"What about if they're attracted to one another."

Siddiq looked at her and asked, "Are you asking me that for a reason?"

She was but she wasn't going to tell him that. "Let me ask you something else."

"Go ahead."

"When a man tells a woman I just want to be your friend, is that a slick way of getting the woman to sleep with you?"

"Maybe for some men, but not for me. I don't play games like that. If I'm trying to sleep with a women I come right through the front door, I don't hide my intentions."

"Mmmm." Faith wondered if he wanted to sleep with her.

"Also," he went to say, "right now, I'm practicing celibacy."

Faith leaned towards the door and looked at him with skepticism. "Yeah, right."

"Why you say that?"

"Celibacy? Come on."

"I speak only the truth. I've had enough sex to last me a lifetime. I'm looking for someone to love, honor and cherish. I'm a Harlequin romance novel waiting to happen and if it means getting to know a female outside before knowing her insides, than so be it. Not to mention all the diseases that are spreading. You have to be extra careful with who you deal with."

Faith knew just what he was saying. As much as she thought about it now, she didn't really know how she would be able to handle dating. Maybe that's why some people stayed married when they didn't really want to because it was easier than being on the hunt for a mate.

That night they relived their younger years, got on rides, ate hot dogs, cotton candy and laughed up a storm. They

didn't take their being together too serious. They just decided to take it for what it was, a good-ass time.

As the night came to an end, Faith wondered if he would try and kiss her. If he didn't, she had to admit that she would be disappointed.

They were back at the spot where they met and were still sitting in the truck.

"So, did you have a nice time?" Siddiq asked.

"You have no idea," Faith told him. "I had more fun with you these past couple of hours, than I had in years."

"I did too," he told her.

For a couple of seconds neither of them said a word, that is until Siddiq asked, "Am I going to see you again, or was this just a one time thing?"

Faith had already made up her mind that she would be seeing him again. "Yes, yes, you will."

Siddiq turned in his seat to face her. She turned to face him.

"Are you nervous?" he asked.

"Yes." Faith was honest.

"Why?"

Faith decided to be honest again. "Because I want to kiss my new friend."

Siddiq leaned over so that their faces were almost touching. "Do you think that would be wise?"

Faith brushed her lips against his. "No."

Before either of them could stop themselves, they started kissing.

Faith felt herself get moist within a matter of seconds and pulled away. "I guess being celibate doesn't include kissing."

"No, kissing is not included," Siddiq told her.

"I have to go," Faith said. "I'll call you."

"You do that," Siddiq responded.

Angel M. Hunter

* * *

Siddiq watched her get into her car and pull off. As Faith drove home she thought about Siddiq and how connected she felt to him just from spending those couple of hours together.

She knew he was someone she could fall for, hard and fast. *I'm going to have to be careful with him.*

CHAPTER EIGHTEEN

BELLA

She did it again. After all the praying, after asking for forgiveness and after making deals with the Lord, Bella slept with James again.

What was it about him? Or was it really about him at all, maybe it was about Ramsey and how she felt after she left him at the restaurant last night.

Bella knew she should have went with her gut instinct and told Ramsey no when he asked her to meet with him. Ever since the 1:00 PM appointment they had at the church was cancelled due to an congregational emergency, he'd been calling and calling, begging to see her.

She'd already told him no numerous times, but he was tireless in his efforts. She knew if she kept saying no, he would show up at her church over and over until she said yes. She knew this because he told her he would.

She also knew before going that nothing good would come out of it. What could they possibly talk about? Why did he want to see her so bad? What did he think they were

going to do, relive the past, talk about the old times? She knew that wasn't going to happen, she wouldn't allow it to.

Why go then? Because curiosity got the best of her. She wanted to hear what he had to say, she wanted to hear about what he'd been up to and she had to admit, she was curious about the old neighborhood and what happened after she left.

Bella didn't want to meet him at the church because people showed up unexpectedly and she didn't want to meet him at her house for the obvious reasons.

"Well, where do you want to meet?" he asked while wondering why she was making this so difficult.

"Let's meet at your hotel restaurant."

Bella still didn't know how Ramsey ended up being in the same town as her, she did know he was staying at the Hilton in Eatontown because the few times he called that's what showed up on the caller ID.

Bella must have changed her clothes over five times before she settled on a simple pair of cream linen pants that fit loosely and a cream short-sleeve body suit, with a pair of ankle-strapped heels to match. The look she was going for was casual, not overdone, not churchy and definitely not old. She did want him to notice that she still had "it" and notice he did because when she walked in the restaurant he whistled.

"I'm glad you finally said yes to seeing me."

Standing here in front of him, outside the church environment, she admitted to herself that she was too. "It was obvious you weren't going to stop asking to see me unless I said yes."

Ramsey stood up, walked around to her side of the table and pulled out her chair. She sat down.

Neither of them said a word, they just sat there looking at one another.

Finally Ramsey broke the silence. "Wow, life has really thrown us some curves, hasn't it?"

Afraid to let her guard down, Bella said, "Yes, it has, but God is good, He can do all things."

Ramsey knew she was being cautious and told her, "You don't have to do that, Bella."

"Do what?"

"Be the pastor. You can be yourself. Remember, I knew you when and you knew me when."

"What do you mean 'be the pastor.' That's who I am now."

"Is it?"

Not wanting to be put on blast, Bella stood up. "I'm leaving. I didn't come here to be insulted or questioned about my faith."

Ramsey stood up. "Bella, please sit back down, I didn't mean to offend you or hurt you. All I was trying to say is, you can be yourself, you can let your guard down, I'm not here to talk about what was, I'm not here to do you any harm, I just thought we could get together like old friends."

Bella didn't move nor did she say a word.

"Remember what we used to have, remember how we were with one another."

She did and that was the problem, when she saw him walk into her church, all sort's of emotions ran through her. She used to love this man standing in front of her and she believed he loved her too but their pasts, him being a drug dealer and her a hooker didn't mix.

Bella sat down.

Ramsey sat down too. "So?"

"So?" Bella repeated. "What are you doing here?"

"I sort of do what you do," he told her.

"How is that? Are you a minister?"

Ramsey laughed. "No, but I do help people change their lives."

"Really? How?"

"I've started an organization called Changing Courses and Directions, where I speak to young men and women who are about to be released from prison and back into mainstream society."

"Wow, I'm impressed." Bella was sure he was excellent at what he was doing because even as a drug dealer, he had a way with the kids in the community. If it wasn't for the money that kept him in the game, she used to wonder if he'd be doing something else.

"What ever happened to Rock?"

"What do you think happened?"

"Is he in prison?"

"No, he's dead."

This didn't surprise Bella because killers often get killed. She had to ask, "Did Rock kill Leon?"

"Yeah, he did."

"Why didn't you tell me when I asked you before?"

"Because at the time I wasn't sure, but later he bragged on it."

There was nothing Bella could say other than, "Isn't that something?"

"Yeah, and ultimately that's what got Rock killed, him bragging on his conquests."

"Is that what made you change your life?"

"That and a few other things, but I will say Rock's getting killed made me realize that other than always having dough, he is also what kept me in the game, he was my boy and he saved my life a couple of times." Ramsey reached across the table and lightly caressed Bella's face. "I was feeling you,

Bella, more than I was anyone back then. It's just you know how we both were living."

"Yeah, I know," Bella responded.

"I didn't realize how much I missed you until I saw you standing in that pulpit," Ramsey said.

Bella wanted to jump across the table and tongue him down but she knew she had to control this instinct and from that point on Bella was uncomfortable because sitting across from Ramsey made her realize that the inner struggle she was currently enduring wasn't going anywhere any time soon, no matter how much she prayed. Is that what being a pastor meant, that you have to give up on the possibilities?

On one hand, she was content with the direction her life was going in but on the other hand, she missed the freedom of possibilities. The possibility of a relationship without rules and the possibility of not being held to a higher standard, being able to mess up and it be all right.

When Bella and Ramsey ended their meal, it was obvious they both wanted to take it further but knew it wasn't an option.

They departed with the promise of seeing each other again.

That night when Bella arrived home, there were flowers at her door. *Who could have sent these?* she wondered.

She unlocked her door, put her purse down, bent over, picked up the flowers and pulled the card out of the center of the arrangement. The flowers were from James. She closed the door behind her and read the card. *Here's to our night of passion,* it read.

He can't be doing things like this. Bella knew she was going to have to put an end to any ideas James had about them having a relationship. It wasn't going to happen, especially with Ramsey in town.

She wanted to see him on more than a "let's catch up" level. She came to this conclusion in the middle of their conversation. She liked him and enjoyed his company way back when and she enjoyed his company now.

As Bella headed towards her bedroom, there was a knock on the door.

Who could that be? Bella didn't even bother to ask who it was, she just opened the door. It was James.

"What are you doing here?" Bella asked. His just showing up at her door, uninvited and as though he knew she'd just arrived home, unnerved her.

"I just wanted to make sure you got the flowers."

Bella couldn't believe he was actually standing here in front of her like it was kosher for him to pop up, like he was her man.

"What I'm asking is, what are you doing popping up uninvited?"

"I wanted to check on you. I called the church, I called your home phone and your cell, there was no answer anywhere, I was getting worried."

Bella didn't know what to say. She started wondering if James was crazy. She looked into his eyes and tried to read what was there. Hell, some of her johns back in the day were maniacs and had stalker tendencies. She hoped she would be able to tell if something wasn't right in the head with James.

She determined there wasn't and knowing they needed to have a serious talk, she opened her door wider, moved to the side and told him to "come in."

James followed her into the kitchen. She went to pour herself something to drink and he asked for something as well. She obliged.

"Let's sit down, we need to talk." Bella led him to the table. She put their glasses down and just as she was about to sit, she could hear her cell phone ring.

She had left her purse in the living room with her cell phone in it. "I have to get that, I'll be right back."

The second she was out of the kitchen, James looked around and once he knew she was away from the door, he reached inside his pocket and pulled out a small vial that had clear liquid inside. He poured the liquid into her glass and hurriedly placed the vial in his pocket. He then sat down like he wasn't doing anything and sipped his water.

When Bella returned, she started to drink her water as she said to him, "James, I know you care for me but as I told you before, we can't do this." She went on and tried to let him down easy and to her surprise he accepted everything she said.

Fifteen minutes into the conversation Bella started feeling nauseous. "I don't feel well. I think I need to lie down."

James stood up and took her hand. "I'll help you to your room and see myself out."

The next morning when Bella woke up, she stretched and wondered how long she'd been asleep. Her body felt like she'd been sleeping for two or three days. She felt heavy.

Bella turned over and noticed that the space next to her looked like someone had slept there. She heard a noise coming from the bathroom and became frightened. She jumped out the bed and realized she was stark naked.

God, what have I done?

She grabbed her robe off the side of the bed and ran into the kitchen, where she grabbed a knife. She tiptoed back towards the bedroom. As she was on her way, James startled her by exiting the bedroom. She had the knife in the air.

James threw his arms up. "Whoa, whoa. What are you trying to do, kill me?"

Bella stood there with the knife still in the air. "What are you doing here and why am I naked?"

203

James backed away from Bella. "First, you need to put the knife down and second, you're naked because we made love last night."

Bella lowered her arm. "I don't remember that happening. How come I don't remember?"

"I can't answer that," James told her, "but I can say this, that doesn't make me feel good."

Bella turned around to go into the kitchen with James behind her. She placed the knife on the counter and tried to recall last night's events. "The last thing I remember is me telling you, we couldn't see each other on an intimate level and you understanding and agreeing." Bella knew knew she wasn't going insane.

"I don't recall any such thing, I remember me telling you I love you and your telling me you love me back."

Now Bella knew those words would not have come out of her mouth. There was no way that happened, but how else could her being nude and his being in her house as though he stayed the night make any sense.

"James, I really don't remember that conversation and I think it's best if you leave right now. I have some things I need to sort through."

"What is it you need to sort through? I'm clear on my feelings for you and what you expressed to me last night verbally and physically shows me that you're clear on your feelings as well."

Bella started to become anxious. "James, please just leave."

James stepped towards her and Bella reached for the knife.

James jumped back and told her, "I'm going to leave, but I'll be back."

Bella watched him as he headed towards her bedroom. "Where are you going? I asked you to leave."

"I'm collecting the rest of my things."

"Oh, okay. I'll stay in here until you leave." Bella stayed in the kitchen and didn't leave it until she heard the front door close.

It was then that she broke down.

Dear Journal,

James just left my house talking about I told him I love him. I know there is no way I could have done that.

The last thing I recall was meeting Ramsey for dinner, coming home to find flowers on my porch and James showing up unannounced and uninvited. I poured us something to drink and my phone rang.

Something is not right. What? I'm unsure of. I feel like I'm hungover or was out partying. God, please give me some clarity into what took place last night.

And God, forgive me once again.

Your Humble Servant, Bella

CHAPTER NINETEEN

HARMONY

"You mean to tell me you really got this bitch calling my house?" Harmony was irate. She was ready to fuck something or someone up.

"What bitch, Mommy?" her three year old asked.

"Not now, baby, Mommy and Daddy need to talk."

Shareef knelt down and picked his son up. "We'll talk after I give little man his bath."

With her hands on her hips and fire in her eyes, Harmony told him, "little man can wait." Making her tone a little sweeter, she kissed Shareef Jr. on his cheek. "Ain't that right, baby."

Shareef turned away from her and went towards the bathroom with his son in his arms. Harmony was hot on his heels.

"What do you think you're doing?" he asked her.

"What does it look I'm doing, I'm following you in the bathroom."

Shareef put his son down and told him, "I want you to go to your room. I'll be in there to get you in a minute."

"Okay, Daddy." Little man looked at his mother and frowned.

She caught it and chose not to comment on it, all her children were sensitive and couldn't stand to see Mommy and Daddy argue. Thankfully, the other two children were at a birthday party.

When junior was out of earshot, Shareef grabbed Harmony's arm and pulled her towards the bedroom. "Let's take it in there."

When they stepped inside, Shareef closed the door behind them. He kept his voice low but you could hear the anger in his tone. "You really have some nerves," he told her.

She knew what he was getting at the second he said it, so she let him finish.

"You got another motherfucker calling here collect and you throw it up in my face when Maria calls."

"You're damn right. They are two different things. Ny'em is Shacquille's father and that Puerto Rican bitch is someone who used to work for you that came onto you." Harmony recalled every bit of drama Maria bought into their lives.

Harmony knew something was up with her ass the second they met and what was up is she wanted Harmony's man.

"I don't want her working for you," Harmony told Shareef the first time she laid eyes on Maria.

Of course, being the man that he was and not knowing the ways of a woman on a mission, he asked Harmony what the hell was she talking about. "She's more than qualified. She's has her own bookkeeping business and my concern is not who wants to get with me, it's hiring someone that knows the ins and outs of a financial statement."

"What she would like to know is the ins and outs of your bedroom," Harmony told him.

"You know what, Harmony, I don't even know why we're

arguing about this shit, it is not your decision. King is my partner and he's the one who found her."

"Well, I don't give a fuck who found her ass and I'll tell him just like I'm telling you. I don't want her around."

Harmony and Shareef went back and forth for no reason at all because Maria ended up working elsewhere. Even with this turn of events, Harmony still felt that something was up with her and Shareef.

Now months later for Maria to call the house, just when Harmony and Shareef were going through it behind Ny'em, was a bit suspicious.

"Why the hell is she calling here?"

Shareef was just as in the dark as Harmony. "I have no idea. You're the one that called me on my cell hollering and screaming about the phone call. Why didn't you ask her yourself what she wanted?"

Harmony didn't have an answer. She was too pissed to think straight. Harmony was insecure when it came to Puerto Rican women because back in the day, all Ny'em cheated on her with were Spanish chicks. She recalled him making the comment, that with a Spanish chick you get the best of three worlds: the body of a black woman, the submissiveness of a white women and sex on demand. That shit bothered her to the core and she still held onto it.

Before Harmony could think of an answer the doorbell rang.

Saved by the bell, Shareef thought.

Harmony walked out the bedroom with Shareef behind her. The front door was open and standing behind the screen door was none other than Ny'em.

"Ain't this a bitch," Shareef said, unable to believe what he was seeing.

Harmony was stunned. She was stuck in one spot, mouth open and unable to move or utter a word.

"Let the motherfucker in," Shareef ordered.

Still standing where she was, Harmony asked Ny'em, "What the hell are you doing here? When did you get out?"

Shareef didn't bother to wait for an answer. He was on his way to the door.

Harmony stepped in front of him. "Please, Shareef, let me handle this. I didn't know he was coming here."

They both looked at Ny'em who said, "I didn't come to start trouble, I just came to see my son."

"How the hell do you know where we live?" Shareef asked. He did not feel like talking, he was ready to bust some ass.

From behind Ny'em stepped Lala. "I brought him here."

Harmony looked at Lala, Shareef and Ny'em. She could not believe what was taking place on her doorstep.

"I'm about to beat this bitch's ass." She moved towards the screen door and pulled it open. As as she reached to snatch Lala up, Ny'em grabbed her arm and stepped in the house.

Shareef, seeing Ny'em's hands on his woman, stepped forward to knock Ny'em's ass out and was stopped by the sound of Shareef Jr.'s voice.

"Daddy, I thought you were coming to get me soon."

Everyone turned toward Shareef Jr.

Shareef looked over towards Harmony and told her, "You know what, I'm going let you handle this. You got five minutes and if he's not gone by the time I get back out here, it's on. You started this shit by allowing him to call my house, now you finish it." He then turned towards Ny'em and told him, "Don't fucking put your hands on her again."

Ny'em threw his arms up. "Man, it's not even that serious. I come in peace."

Harmony looked towards Lala with all the hatred she

could muster. "Why would you do this, why would you bring this drama to my doorstep?"

Lala smirked and told Harmony, "Bitch, yo' ass think you're better than us."

Harmony shook her head. "You know what, you are unbelievable. Everything in me is telling me to whip your ass again but I'm not, instead I'm giving you one minute to get the fuck off my doorstep before I change my mind."

"Leap, bitch, leap," Lala told her.

On that note, Ny'em looked at Lala like she'd lost her mind. "I didn't ask you to bring me here for this drama. You need to step before I beat your ass, I'm came here to see my son."

Lala couldn't believe that Ny'em dissed her like that. "You'll really talk to me like that?"

"Step, Lala, step, I'll catch up with you later."

By now Shareef had come from the bedroom. "What the hell are you still doing here?" he asked Ny'em.

Ny'em looked at Shareef and told him, "Yo, I don't mean any disrespect but this has nothing to do with you."

"It has everything to do with me. I've been raising your seed as my son for the past four years, since me and Harmony hooked up. He calls me Daddy, he doesn't even know you exist."

Ny'em looked over at Harmony and asked, "Did I have a child with you or did I have a child with him?"

At this point, Shareef had enough and he moved toward Ny'em. Before he could reach him, Harmony intervened by stepping in front of Ny'em.

Shareef looked at her. "What the fuck are you doing? I'm protecting us."

Harmony placed her hands on his chest, looked into his eyes and pleaded, "Please, Shareef, just let me handle this."

Shareef, not wanting to back down and not wanting

Ny'em to have any reason to step foot back in his house, told them both, "I'll let y'all get this moment to try and figure shit out but just know that I will kill to protect mine."

"I understand that, man," Ny'em responded, "and like I already said, I didn't come her to disrespect you or Harmony. I just came by because I want to talk about seeing my son."

Shareef looked at Harmony. "You need to handle this." He looked at the watch that was on his arm. "You've got ten minutes and then I'll handle it."

Harmony breathed a sigh of relief. She didn't want any bloodshed on her porch.

Dear Journal,

Today there was some serious drama at my house. Ny'em showed up and I almost killed a bitch.

I don't know what I'm going to do about this situation. Jewell said that I should have let Shareef kick Ny'em's ass but Ny'em did help create Shacquille but Shareef is the only father he has ever known.

I feel torn because the right thing to do is not to deny a child his father but Ny'em didn't even want him and it took his going to prison to realize his responsibility.

Should I allow my family to be affected by his revelation, because truth be told, I don't even know how sincere he is.

In need of advice, Harmony

CHAPTER TWENTY

ELSIE

"**I**'m thinking about having a baby," Elsie blurted out as she plopped in the bar seat next to Crystal.

Earlier that day, she called Crystal and told her she wanted to talk to her about something.

"Well, let's go out for drinks," Crystal told her. "We can meet at Stars."

Elsie really didn't feel like going to a bar. Come to think of it, she wondered when did Crystal start hanging out at bars. That's not something she knew Crystal to do. "Why don't I just come to the office?"

"I have appointments all day and I know after I meet with one client in particular a drink will be necessary."

Elsie understood because she'd been there numerous times herself. "All right, what time?"

"I'll call you when I'm with my last client."

The hours passed and just when Elsie thought Crystal had forgotten about her, she phoned. "Let's meet there at nine."

So here they sat with Elsie sharing her news. "You're thinking about what?" Crystal asked.

"Having a baby," Elsie told her.

Crystal waved the bartender over. "I'd like a martini on the rocks." She looked at Elsie. "What are you drinking?"

Elsie told the bartender she'd have the same.

When he walked away Crystal looked at Elsie. "I don't understand, aren't you gay?"

Elsie started laughing. "You think I'm talking about having a baby the old-fashioned way."

"Yeah, what other way would you?" Before Elsie got a chance to reply, Crystal said, "Hold up, are you thinking about adopting?"

"No."

"Then what?"

"I'm thinking about a sperm donor."

"Here are your drinks." The bartender placed their drinks in front of them, while he eyed Elsie.

"Um, thank you," Crystal told him, "we'll let you know when we need you."

He got the message and went to wait on another patron but not before he winked at Elsie.

"Men?" Crystal said. "They are a trip."

Elsie took a sip of her drink. "I wouldn't know."

Together they laughed.

"So you're really thinking about a sperm donor?" Crystal asked.

"Yeah. I'm ready to be a mother."

"But a sperm donor, Elsie, don't you know any decent men out there?"

Elsie immediately thought of Trey. The only thing is, she didn't know how good a man he was. She had not been in touch with him since high school and here they were years

later getting reacquainted. "Not anyone I would want to sleep with."

"I think you really should look into this before you make a decision like that. I don't want you having some madman's baby."

"Girl, me neither."

"You ladies need anything else?" The bartender was back.

Crystal nudged Elsie with her knee, who ignored her.

"No, thank you."

"Whatever you want," he told Elsie, "you just let me know."

When he walked away, Crystal said, "Damn, he's on yours. Girl, that might be your baby daddy."

Elsie was looking over Crystal's shoulder. "Girl, isn't that Lange?"

Crystal almost broke her neck trying to see if it was him. She had not seen him since he left the firm that was in the same building as hers and that was over six months ago.

"Oh girl, yes it is."

They both watched him as he flirted with a very attractive woman.

Crystal could feel herself react in a way she knew she had no business reacting. She was jealous.

Elsie looked at Crystal and noticed that she had not taken her eyes off him or blinked. "Hmmm, you still care for him, don't you?"

Crystal broke her trance, turned around and downed the rest of her drink. "Girl, you know I do. I haven't stopped thinking about him since I chose Roger over him and you see how that turned out."

Crystal thought back to when she started seeing Lange, he was a married man on the brink of divorce. She truly cared for him, she would almost say she loved him. Why didn't she choose him? Because in the back of her mind she couldn't

get the thought out of her head that he would cheat on her just like he cheated on his wife.

"Why is it when women get with a married man, they expect him to be faithful to them?" Crystal wondered out loud.

They finished their drinks and Elsie waved the bartender over. "We'd like two more, please."

"Yours is on the house," he told Elsie.

Elsie didn't want to lead him on, so she leaned over the bar and said in a real low tone, "There's something I need to tell you."

He leaned in closer to her. "What? Your number?"

"No," Elsie hesitated. "I need to tell you I'm gay, that I don't do dick."

He pulled back and looked at her, smiled, leaned back over and said, "I don't mind."

Elsie sat back up. "I do."

Not to be put off, he told her, "You know what, I don't care, you're fine anyway and this drink will be on me." He left to pour their drinks.

Crystal was taking it all in. "Ain't that some shit, here you are, turning brothers down and they're still buying your drinks. You go, girl."

Elsie didn't think it was amusing at all, she knew that most men fantasized about being with two women and maybe her telling the bartender she was gay would make him be that much more aggressive thinking, he could get in where he fit in.

Elsie changed the subject and said, "You think my getting a sperm donor is a bad idea."

"I didn't say that, plus I'm not one to judge anything a person does; shit, I've made enough mistakes in my life."

"You have?" a voice interrupted. "I hope I wasn't one of them."

Crystal didn't have to turn around to know it was Lange, she'd know his voice from across a crowded room. Should she be cool or should she show her true feelings? That was the question.

She didn't have to answer it because the minute Lange said, "I've missed you," she told him, "I've missed you too."

Elsie just shook her head.

Lange noticed. "Why are you shaking your head?"

"Because it's obvious you two should have stayed together."

"Well, she chose another man." Crystal could tell in his tone that Lange was still bothered by that, after all this time.

"Well, they're not together anymore," Elsie revealed.

"Is that right?" Lange asked.

Before Crystal could respond, the woman he was flirting with was standing behind them. "I've been waiting on you to return."

Lange turned to face her. "I ran into someone I know."

The woman looked at Crystal and frowned. "Well, I'm ready for my drink."

Crystal touched Lange's arm. "My number is still the same, call me."

Lange kissed Crystal on the cheek. "I'll do that," and to Elsie he said, "It was nice to see you."

Just to piss his female friend, companion or whatever the hell she was, Elsie replied, "And it's always nice to see you, Lange."

When Lange was gone Elsie mocked Crystal. "My number is still the same."

Crystal smirked and looked Lange's way. "That is one handsome man." As an afterthought she added, "and good in bed too."

Elsie followed her gaze and told her, "Maybe you two can

start over, have a new beginning. You know what they say, if it's meant to be, it will be, if it's not, oh well."

"I don't know about us having a new beginning but it would be nice to see him sometimes."

They continued looking his way and noticed he was whispering in his date's ear. She looked up, noticed them watching and rolled her eyes.

"Want me to put her out for you?" The bartender had watched what transpired.

"Didn't I tell you I was gay?" Elsie smiled so that the bartender would know she wasn't being a bitch.

"You did indeed, but you can't fault a brother for trying."

"No you can't," Elsie agreed.

"Elsie," Crystal interrupted.

"Yes?"

"This must be your night."

"Why do you say that."

"First the bartender is acting like he's all in love with you and then there's this lady, who keeps looking your way."

Elsie turned to look around. "What lady? Where?"

"Look behind you."

Elsie began to turn around but Crystal stopped her. "Wait, wait, at least play the shit off."

"Girl, I'm to old for that." Elsie turned around anyway to see who Crystal was talking about. It was Savannah.

"Oh, you know her?"

"Yeah, she's a friend of mine." Elsie noticed that she was with a man and turned back around.

"Oh, oh, she's on her way over here," Crystal told Elsie.

Elsie turned back around just as Savannah arrived at the bar.

"Elsie? I thought that was you."

Elsie stood up to greet her with a hug. If she wasn't mistaken, Elsie felt Savannah's hands touch her ass.

She stepped back and noticed Savannah was smirking, like she had a secret. "So who's your friend?" Savannah looked at Crystal and raised her eyebrows, "or is she more than a friend?"

Elsie could tell that Savannah may have had one too many drinks.

Crystal answered the question. "No, no, no, I'm just a friend."

Elsie introduced them to one another.

Elsie looked past Savannah and asked her, "Is that your husband?"

"Yes."

"Well, it looks like he's waiting on you."

Savannah looked his way. "Well, he can wait a little longer."

Neither Elsie nor Crystal responded.

"Crystal, would you excuse us for a minute, I'd like Elsie to walk with me to the bathroom."

Elsie couldn't help but wonder why Savannah needed her to tag along but she agreed nonetheless.

"I'll be right back," Elsie informed Crystal.

"I'll be right here, watching the sights."

Elsie got that Crystal was talking about Lange and his date.

When Elsie and Savannah entered the bathroom, Savannah looked in the stalls.

"What are looking in the stalls for?" Elsie wondered if Savannah was past tipsy to drunk.

"I'm seeing if we're alone."

"Why?"

Once Savannah was sure they were alone, she locked the door and stepped closer to Elsie. "Remember at the coffee shop when we pretended I was your girl?"

How could Elsie forget, she'd never been so embarrassed.

"Well, I'd like to collect on my debt."

Elsie was lost. "What debt?"

Savannah moved closer and placed her mouth near Elsie's ear. "Did you like it when I grabbed your ass?"

Elsie stepped back. "Okay, Savannah, I think you may have had too much to drink."

Savannah grabbed Elsie's ass and pulled her so that their bodies touched. "I don't think so."

Elsie had to admit that she was turned on. "What are you doing?"

"Seducing you."

Elsie glanced around the bathroom. "One, I hope you're not doing this just because you're drunk and two, look at where we are."

Savannah knew that Elsie was right about the "where they were part" but she was not right about Savannah wanting her just because she had more liquor in her system than usual.

Savannah placed her lips on Elsie's and moved her hands towards her ass. Elsie was surprised with Savannah's aggressiveness. She knew she should push her away but the shit was turning her on.

Savannah pulled slowly away from the kiss and whispered to Elsie, "Turn around, look in the mirror."

Elsie complied. Once turned, Savannah attacked her neck and ears.

Savannah's hands were everywhere; her nipples, her ass and finally she started to slide her entire hand down the front of Elsie's pants.

Elsie grabbed her hand and for a moment was fearful that

someone would attempt to enter the bathroom, but the warmth of Savannah's hands combined with the kisses on her neck made Elsie allow her to continue.

When Savannah's hands finally reached their goal, Elsie let out a deep gasp, which delighted Savannah as she increased the pressure on Elsie's clitoris.

At this point if someone came into the bathroom, Elsie would not have cared. She started grinding against Savannah's hands, trying to assist in her bringing her to an orgasm. Elsie could not believe they were doing this in the bathroom.

It was when Savannah's heard a low moan and when Elsie arched her back that she knew Elsie was about to come. She took her free hands and squeezed Elsie's nipples through her shirt.

"Fuck! Fuck! Fuck!" Elsie repeated over and over.

Savannah slowly removed her hand from Elsie's pussy and told Elsie to turn back around.

When she did, Savannah slowly sucked her fingers dry.

While Elsie gathered herself together, Savannah winked and walked out of the bathroom.

Elsie was left standing there thinking, *I know she didn't leave me here like this.*

Elsie heard the bathroom door open. She quickly checked herself in the mirror.

It was Crystal with a smirk. "Did you have fun?"

Elsie just laughed and walked out the bathroom.

When she sat back down at the bar, she looked across the room for Savannah and her husband. Neither of them were anywhere to be seen. *Yep, I'll definitely call Savannah tomorrow, after my meeting with Faith.*

CHAPTER TWENTY-ONE

FAITH

"What do you mean, he's in the hospital?" Faith asked, but the person hung up.

Faith pulled the phone away from her ear and looked at it.

"What's going on?" Siddiq asked.

"Someone just called and said Raheem's in the hospital."

"Did they tell you what happened?"

"No, they just said I need to get there as soon as possible, then the line went dead."

Earlier that day Faith and Siddiq literally ran into one another with their shopping carts at the grocery store. Both looked up at the same time.

"Hey beautiful," he greeted.

Faith was pleasantly surprised to see him. "Good morning, how have you been?" Faith asked him as she took in his relaxed look. Siddiq wore a lightweight baby-blue Sean John sweat suit. On someone else, it would have looked just plain wrong but not on him.

"You look smooth," she complimented.

"Thanks." Siddiq pulled his cart next to Faith's and peeked in. All he saw was vegetables and fruit.

"So, healthy eaters are we?"

Faith laughed because if only he knew how addicted she was to junk food.

It just so happened that she recently made the decision to try and go cold turkey and not have anything white, which included flour, sugar and salt. It was making her cranky as hell. "I'm trying," she told him.

"Listen, what are you doing later?" he asked her.

They'd seen each other a few times since the beach outing. Faith had to admit that Siddiq had gotten into her system. She was truly feeling him, so much so it frightened her because she knew she was headed for trouble.

"I'm open, what are you doing later?" Faith replied.

"Let's get together, maybe go to this little theater I heard about in North Jersey."

"Yeah, I'd like that."

They made small talk a little longer and agreed to meet up later.

On the way home, Faith stopped by Susan's to say hello. When Susan asked Faith what she'd been up to, Faith told her, "Well, I've kind of been seeing Siddiq."

"Siddiq? Lisa's brother?"

"The one and only."

"Girl, are you crazy? Why? Why are you doing that? What about Raheem?"

"What about him? I told you how he does me. Shit, this is the first time I've ever stepped out of my marriage."

"Well, two wrongs don't make a right," Susan offered.

"I know, but I'm tired of letting him be the one enjoying

his life doing whatever the hell he wants to do, whenever he wants to do it, with whoever he wants to do it to."

"But still, you need to think about this. You're going from one relationship to another. Actually, you are still married. In the rooms, you've stated that going from relationship to relationship is one of your issues. Why are you doing this to yourself?"

"You're acting like I'm going to marry Siddiq, I'm just having a little fun, enjoying his company, that's all. I've been unhappy and in a half-ass marriage for a long time, Susan. I deserve this."

Susan looked at Faith like she was crazy. "Girl, you don't think it's too late to be talking about you want to have fun?"

Faith didn't think it was too late at all. She'd never casually dated. She's had boyfriend after boyfriend, caretaker after caretaker and her drugs.

When she really gave it some thought she realized that she'd never truly been in a relationship sober, clean or drug-free. She was either under the influence or in transition. This was the first time she'd been confident of her sobriety and wanted to experience life in a new way.

She wanted a relationship where she just didn't go through the motions, where the small habitual things you did together made you a couple, the waking up, getting in each other's way, brushing your teeth and maybe even drinking coffee before running off to work.

Was she fantasizing, was it wishful thinking? Did this kind of relationship even exist in this day and age or was it just what was shown on television, in the movies or read about in books?

"I respect what you're saying, Faith, believe me. I understand how you feel about enjoying life in a new way, but please think about what you're doing. A lot of times, when

couples are going through rough patches in their relationships and they start seeing someone else, it's usually just a Band-Aid that covers a wound."

Faith knew that what she and Siddiq shared was more than that.

Susan went on. "What if you could work on your marriage? What if Raheem was open to counseling? What if it can be turned around?"

It's not that Susan was on Raheem's side. Faith revealed to her his many indiscretions and Susan knew that if Timothy cheated on her with such disregard, she knew beyond a shadow of a doubt that she would not be the type of wife to accept it. As a matter of fact, she'd probably end up in jail for assault or something, assault on Timothy and the female.

Susan shook her head to get out of that whole thought process. There was no need to go there mentally. She and Timothy had overcome much worse, more than the average couple, and that was why she believed Faith should try and make it work. Marriages were worth fighting for and people could overcome anything when they really wanted to.

"Do you not think your marriage is worth saving? Is that why you just want to end it?" Susan asked Faith.

Faith believed that the relationship was done and that's just what she told Susan. "I'm done."

For some reason Susan couldn't seem to let it go. "Faith, you need to give this some more thought. Look at all you put Raheem through. Those nights you disappeared and went missing for days at a time, how you would be clean for a while and he'd think everything was good between y'all, only to one day come home and find that you've had yet another breakdown or relapse. I don't know Raheem that well but what I do know of him, he could have left your ass a long time ago, he could have left you when you needed him the most."

"Well, damn, Susan, how long do I have to repay that debt? Is that the debt that never gets paid up? Is that the debt that will leave me broke emotionally? I cannot live like that, feeling I owe somebody my life, not today and not ever again. Don't get me wrong, I don't want to sound ungrateful because that's the last thing that I am but my mind is made up."

Faith was irritated with Susan because this was not the shit she wanted to hear, she wanted support and encouragement, not to be questioned, doubted and made to see Raheem's point of view. She knew two wrongs didn't make a right but hell, something that feels so right can't be but so wrong.

Her marriage was done. She was going to pack up her shit and move out. The question was when.

Later that day, Faith was looking for something to wear on her date with Siddiq and nothing was suitable. She looked at the clock and noticed she had two hours to get ready.

She decided to run to one of the boutiques in downtown Asbury Park.

Faith walked into Le' Chic, a swanky boutique on Madison Avenue. The store was empty of customers, so she wasn't surprised when the salesgirl rushed over and asked if she needed any help.

Faith glanced around the store and looked at the girl and said, "You're that bored?"

The salesperson laughed and said, "Yes, yes I am."

"Well, I'll let you know if I need you." Faith walked away and started to peruse the store.

About a half an hour later, she was at the cash register pulling out her wallet when the bell chimed, alerting the salesperson that a new customer was entering.

Faith turned around and when she saw who it was she turned back around with the quickness.

"Here you go." She handed the salesgirl her credit card. As Faith tapped her feet she could fell her impatience rise. It seemed like this girl was taking forever to ring up her shit.

The young lady started to put her items in a bag, when the patron who entered called out, "When you're done I'd like some assistance."

"I'll be done shortly," the salesgirl told her as she handed Faith her receipt. "Thanks and have a good day."

Good, Faith thought, she just might get out of the store before Raheem's ex-wife, Lace, recognized her.

She and Lace were casual with one another, had always been, even when Faith was raising her children, but that was it.

Faith turned around with her head down, thinking she could get out unnoticed.

No such luck, right when she got to the door the salesgirl called out, "Ms. Faith?"

Faith turned around but not before she glanced at Lace, who had just recognized her.

"Your credit card." The salesgirl was holding out her card.

"Faith?" Lace was walking towards her.

"How are you?"

Faith took the credit card and told Lace, "Fine and how are you?"

"Doing well."

There was an uncomfortable silence between them that was broken by Faith when she said, "Well, I have to get going, I have an appointment."

Lace moved to the side. "Oh okay, I don't want to hold you up."

As Faith walked toward the door, Lace told her, "Faith, call me sometimes. I'd like to talk to you about something."

Faith paused before replying, "I will." She had no intentions of doing so.

On her drive home Faith wondered what Lace could possibly want to talk to her about. She hoped Sherry hadn't opened her mouth and told her mother about the conversation they had.

Over the phone, Faith and Siddiq agreed to meet for dinner prior to seeing the show. She tried to put what Susan said to her out of her mind.

When she pulled into the parking lot of the restaurant Faith could feel her heart beating.

She turned the car off and looked around to see if she spotted anyone she knew. She always did this; she saw no one. She went inside the restaurant and stood by the entrance looking around.

"Looking for someone special?" Siddiq whispered in her ear. He had snuck up behind her.

Faith jumped and placed her hand on her chest. "You shouldn't sneak up on a girl like that."

Siddiq placed his hand on the small of her back and pushed her through the door with a light touch.

"Mr. Bradley," the hostess greeted. "It's so nice to see you again."

"So you're a regular here?" Faith noted.

"Let me show you to your seat," the hostess said.

If Faith was not mistaken, the hostess was walking extra close to Siddiq. She led them to a table in the corner.

"She likes you," Faith informed him when she walked away.

"You think?" Siddiq asked, amused.

"You know she does."

Siddiq looked in the hostess's direction. "She's like what? Twenty? She's a little girl."

"Well, today's twenty is yesterday's thirty," Faith pointed out.

Siddiq agreed but made it a point to let her know youngsters weren't his style.

"That's good to know."

"What? That I'm not a pervert?"

"Exactly."

Siddiq picked up the menu that lay on the table.

Faith followed suit. "What's good to eat here?" she asked.

"Everything."

"Well, what do you suggest?"

"How about I place your order and surprise you?"

"I'd like that," Faith said.

Siddiq called the waitress over and placed their orders. He ordered the salmon dish.

When she walked away Siddiq leaned back in his seat. "Faith? What are we doing? We can't keep seeing each other like this," Siddiq told her.

"We're having dinner." Faith tried to act like she didn't know what he was talking about.

He knew the game she was playing. "Talk to me, tell me what's really going on in that heart and head of yours. I'm feeling you, girl, and I believe you're feeling me."

He was right, she was feeling him. Siddiq made her laugh, made her feel valued, made her feel appreciated and beautiful. All the things she hadn't felt in a long time.

"I thought we were just supposed to be having dinner."

"We are having dinner, but we need to discuss this 'friendship.' "

"What's there to discuss?"

"I think we're more than friends." He had put her on the spot. "I need to know how you feel about me," he told her. "I think you care more than you're admitting."

He was right but she wasn't ready to tell him that.

"Have you made a decision about your marriage?" he asked.

Faith told him, "I am getting a divorce."

"Well, what does that mean for me, for us?"

"I'm not sure what it means, Siddiq. There's no denying that we both are developing genuine feelings for each other. You've awakened something in me that I thought was dead a long time ago."

"Do you remember when I told you that when I want something I don't go through the back door?" Siddiq asked her.

"Yes."

"Well, I want to make love to you."

"I thought you were celibate."

"I thought so too, but a man can only be around a woman he desires for so long."

"I want to be with you too," Faith told him.

"Stay with me tonight?" Siddiq asked.

Faith didn't respond.

"Well, what do you have to say?" Siddiq asked.

Faith figured *to hell with it.* "Truthfully, Siddiq, we can skip the play."

"Are you saying what I think you're saying?" he asked.

"Yes," Faith told him. "I'm saying let's go back to your place."

Siddiq called the waitress over and told her, "Make our orders to go."

When they arrived at Siddiq's house, they didn't waste any time going into the bedroom. They stood in front of the bed and looked at one another.

"I want to taste you," Siddiq told Faith.

"I want to taste you too," Faith responded.

Siddiq moved closer to her and started to undress her slowly. Faith didn't want him to take his time. She was ready to be naked and made love to. She felt like she'd waited so long for this moment. Her breath was caught in her throat.

She took a step back and said, "I've got this." She started to take her clothes off. The second she was naked, Siddiq stepped towards her and gripped her ass. He pulled her into him.

"Aren't you going to get undressed?" Faith asked.

"After I kiss you everywhere," he told her.

When Siddiq's lips met hers, it sent a shock wave through Faith. She thought she could feel his every breath. He grabbed the back of her head and tilted it. He ran his tongue across her throat.

Faith moaned.

Siddiq let go of her and pushed her back on the bed.

"I've been wanting to do this since I met you."

And before she knew it, his face was between her thighs.

"You smell so good," he told her and he opened her pussy lips and ran his tongue down the center.

Faith lifted her hips up to meet his face. "Don't tease me," she told him. "Give it to me."

Siddiq stuck his tongue as far up in Faith as he could go and started pressing his tongue against her walls.

It was obvious that he enjoyed the taste of her. He went from licking her insides to running his tongue across her clitoris.

All Faith could do was moan over and over. She tried to grip his head but he grabbed her hands and held them on each side of her leg. It was then that he attacked her clitoris, not letting up until he felt her bucking beneath him.

When she finished coming all over his mouth and chin, she told him, "Your turn."

Faith had never begged for any man's dick to go in her mouth, but she wanted to taste Siddiq so bad, she wanted him to fill her mouth up with his thickness, she wanted to swallow everything he had in him.

Siddiq stood up and took his clothes off, before he could

even get his pants down his legs, Faith grabbed hold of his dick and squeezed it. She pulled it and him towards her mouth and covered it with her lips. She tried to take in every inch of him, tried to make him touch her throat.

She started to move her head up and down the length of him. She came all the way up, licking the head and going back down, massaging his balls the whole time.

"I need to lie down," he told her. "I can't take it."

Faith didn't want him to lie down, she didn't want him to be able to take it so she ignored his request and pushed his legs open and started sucking between his balls. One at a time, she played with them inside her mouth and stopped to go back to his dick.

"Oh no you won't," he told her as he pulled her up and placed her on the bed.

Siddiq climbed on top of her and told her, "I'm going up inside you now." There was nothing she could do but wait as he rubbed the head of his dick against her pussy.

"You want me inside you, don't you?" he asked.

What was she suppose to say? No? "Yes, Siddiq, I want you inside me."

Slowly he slid his dick inside her and pushed up as far up as he could go and slowly he slid out. Faith could feel her pussy walls stretching, it had been so long since she'd had this feeling, too long. She closed her eyes and gave herself to him.

He placed his hands under her buttocks and pushed himself deeper and deeper inside her. "Oh girl, you're going to make me explode inside you."

Faith could care less all, she brought her mouth up to his and tongued him down while he erupted inside her.

It was when Faith and Siddiq had just finished making love and and were still basking in the afterglow that she received the phone call that changed everything.

231

Who knew that her day would end up with a potential tragedy. She definitely didn't.

However, the conversation she and Raheem had that morning should have been a sign that it would be an eventful day.

When she woke up that morning she didn't know Raheem was home until she walked into the kitchen and saw him reading the paper and sipping on coffee.

"Good morning," he said as he placed the paper on the table.

"Good morning," Faith replied. Just because she decided to leave him it didn't mean she had to be a bitch. Her best bet would to be to end this marriage in a civilized manner.

"Did you get a good night's rest? I thought I heard you up watching television half the night."

"I was up watching *The Twilight Zone.*"

"Old habits die hard, don't they," Raheem joked.

"Some of them, but not all."

They were talking about two different things; he was talking about when they first met how she was addicted to science fiction shows. She was talking about him and his ways.

Faith went over to the coffeepot and poured herself a cup.

"Would you like me to make you some breakfast?" Raheem asked.

"No, thank you." Faith turned to look at him. She leaned on the counter and frowned. *What is he up to?* she wondered. *Whatever it is, I'm not trying to hear it.*

Faith stood up and walked over to the chair opposite him.

Before she could get a word out, Raheem announced, "I don't want a divorce."

"Huh?" Faith sat down.

"I don't want divorce. I also don't expect us to go on in the matter that we've been going. I'm ready to do whatever it

takes to keep you. If it means counseling, I'll do it. If it means me working from home for a while, I'll do that too."

Faith stood up to leave the kitchen. She couldn't believe that he finally said what she wanted him to say a long time ago.

"Where are you going? You're one that kept saying, let's talk, let's talk, let's talk. Well, I'm ready to do more than talk, I'm ready to change."

Tears formed in Faith's eyes before she had the chance to stop them.

Faith leaned over and kissed Raheem on the lips. "It's too late for all that," she told him and turned to walk away but he grabbed her wrist to stop her.

She looked at him. "Let me go, please just let me go." She meant it in more ways than one. "Please just let me go," she repeated.

He released her arm and told her, "I can't, I didn't realize it until now, but I can't. I've only loved two women in my life, you and Lace."

Faith shook her head, how could he pull this, how could he declare all this love when she no longer felt any? Is this the way it happened? Was God really that spiteful? Did he really play these kinds of tricks on people?

"Answer me this one question, Raheem."

He waited.

"Why all the other women? Why out in the open? Why hurt me that way?"

"Faith, you really need to understand that when I cheated on you in the past it had nothing to do with you. I mean, all that time that you were getting high I looked at it like you were cheating on me or should I say cheating on us. I felt that if I stayed in this relationship with you and never committed an indiscretion I would forever be angry at you.

When I cheated it was like my equalizer, you did us wrong and I made it even. I never met anyone of substance. I never fell in love with anyone else and I wasn't looking to."

Faith let him continue.

"When you would get high, I always thought of the worst-case scenario, like you were in the crackhouse having sex with multiple partners, or having these crazy sex sessions with your dealer. I don't want you to think that I'm trying to make you feel guilty. That's not what I am doing. I am not trying to make you feel guilty about anything in the past. I just want you to understand a little of what my world was like. When we got married and the reverend said for better or worst I took that shit serious, more serious than I did with Lace. So Faith, I'm asking you to please just think about us a little more, think about what we meant to each other and what we can mean to each other again."

Faith couldn't make him any promises and even with the speech he just gave her, she felt like her mind was made up. "I have to go," she told him and went into the bathroom, dropped her robe, took off her panties and bra, turned the shower on as hot as she could stand it and stood under the water, letting it beat against her body. She tried to release all the emotions she carried with her and all the confusion she felt down the drain with the water.

Afterward she got dressed and left the house. That was when she went to the store and ran into Siddiq.

Now here she lay in his bed telling him, "I have to find out what hospital he's in. I have to go."

"I'll help you," Siddiq offered.

Faith looked at him in disbelief, she couldn't believe he was willing to help her locate her husband. "You don't have to do that. I'll call Susan."

"What if I want to?"

"I can't let you." Faith sat up. "I'm going to call Susan,

take a shower and go to her house. Once I know something, I'll call you."

Siddiq told her, "Make sure you do that."

"I will."

On the drive to Susan's house, Faith couldn't even think about what had transpired between her and Siddiq; she was too preoccupied with finding out what happened to Raheem.

Together, Faith, Susan and Crystal—who was visiting Susan—called several hospitals to try and locate Raheem.

"What if it's one of his women, just trying to upset me?" Faith asked Susan.

"What if it's not?" Susan told her. "This is not something you should take a chance with."

They finally tracked Raheem down to a hospital in North Jersey. They wouldn't give Faith any information over the phone, other than, "You need to get here."

Faith hung up the phone in a state of shock. She couldn't even get the words out to Susan and Crystal. Seeing what kind of state she was in they both told her they'd ride with her.

In the car, no one said a word. Susan and Crystal knew that anything they could possibly say simply would not be heard. They knew to wait and see what they were getting themselves into.

"I'm here about Raheem Banks," Faith said when she approached the reception area.

The person behind the counter punched in his name and told her, "He's in ICU."

"We'll wait here for you," Susan told her.

Faith felt like she was in a daze. Could this be for real, was he really in ICU? ICU meant intensive care, which to her

meant death. Was he going to die? What the hell happened? Who was it that called her? How did they even know to call her?

As she asked herself these questions, Faith was being led into ICU.

The nurse stopped in front of a door and told her, "He's in there. Are you ready?"

"Yes," Faith told her.

When they stepped into the room, Raheem was lying in the bed, hooked up to tubes and apparently unconscious. Faith couldn't help but ask, "Is he asleep?"

"No, sweetie, he's unconscious," the nurse told her, already knowing Faith was his wife.

Faith couldn't bring herself to move.

"Go ahead," the nurse nudged her. "Go to your husband, talk to him, and let him know you're here."

Her husband? The man she wanted to divorce the man who said he wanted to try and make their marriage work was unconscious and Faith wasn't sure what she felt or how she felt.

"Get it together," she mumbled under her breath. "Get it together."

Faith thought about a family that came to the hospital she used to work at. She tried recalling their names. Oh yeah, the sister's name was Layla Simone, her brother was in a car accident and was in a coma. Through the power of prayer and faith he came out of it.

What remained to be seen was if Faith had faith. If she didn't, she knew she was going to have to conjure it up some kind of way.

Faith stepped closer to the bed and took Raheem's hand. It was then the tears fell. Just because she wanted a divorce, it didn't mean she wished harm on him. This was the last thing she would have wanted.

Faith looked around for a chair and saw one in the corner. She walked over to it and just happened to glance out the door where she saw Susan and Crystal.

Faith placed the chair next to Raheem's bed and went to let them know what was going on.

They spotted her as she approached them.

"What happened? Is he okay?"

"No, he's not okay," Faith told them. "He's unconscious, he was in an automobile accident."

Neither of them knew what to say.

In order to ease the discomfort, Faith told them they could leave, and that she was going to stay there.

Neither wanted to leave, but Faith insisted. "There's really nothing either of you can do here. Believe me, if I need anything, I'll call you."

Susan took Faith's face in her hands and told her, "If you need me for anything, just call me, I don't care what time it is. You hear me?"

"Loud and clear."

They left her standing in the middle of the hall. When they were no longer in sight, Faith pulled out her cell phone. she dialed a number, it was only right to make this phone call.

When a female's voice answered, Faith said, "Hello? Lace, this is Faith. Are the kids around?"

An hour later, Faith, Lace and Raheem's children were gathered around the bed. They were all holding hands in silent prayer when Faith felt her phone vibrating.

She knew it was probably Siddiq.

"Amen," someone said.

When everyone let go of each other's hand, Faith excused herself. Not wanting to take any chances, she stepped just outside of the hospital doors and called Siddiq up. Prepar-

ing herself to let him know they probably couldn't talk for a few days, if not longer, she was surprised to her his voice mail click on.

"Siddiq, it's Faith, you just called me. I'm here at the hospital. Raheem is in ICU and he uncon—"

Faith stopped in mid-sentence because the other line on her cell phone beeped. She removed it from her ear and saw the name Siddiq.

She couldn't decide if she wanted to discontinue the message or hang up and speak to him. The decision was made for her when Lace came running out the doors.

"Oh, there you are, I've been looking all over for you. Come on."

Hearing the excitement in her voice, Faith rushed inside with her. "What is it? What's wrong?" She feared the worst.

"He's waking up, Faith. He's waking up."

Faith and Lace entered Raheem's room and he was surrounded by doctors. Before Faith could reach his bed, Lace beat her to it.

"Raheem, we're all here, your family is here."

The doctors moved out of the way and started speaking to Lace as though she were the wife. "Mr. Banks is going to—"

Lace directed them towards Faith. "She's his wife."

One of the doctors noticed that the room was full and suggested they go out to the lobby and talk. "Plus, I have some papers that require your signature."

"I'll be right out, just give me a minute."

Faith went over to the bed and couldn't help but notice that Lace sat at the foot of the bed and was caressing Raheem's legs and looking at him with pure love. Faith almost didn't want to interrupt the moment.

"Raheem," Faith said.

He looked up at her.

"I'm glad you're okay."

Lace looked at Faith like, *That's all you're going to say?*

"I have to go speak with the doctors, I'll be right back." She headed out the room but stopped at the door. "You'll be here, right?" she asked Lace.

"I'm not going anywhere," Lace answered.

After she spoke with the doctors and signed the papers, Faith headed back towards the room. She stopped at the door when she noticed the children had left and that Lace was sitting at the top of the bed, holding Raheem's hand. It looked so natural and intimate that Faith decided not to interrupt, especially after Lace bent over and kissed Raheem on the lips.

Faith turned and walked down the hall as she wondered, *Is that how I should be acting? Lace's response is more wifely than mine.* She wondered if anyone else noticed this.

Faith went outside to call Siddiq and once again his answering service came on. "I just called to let you know I'm okay. Call me. I really need to talk to you."

The second she hung up the phone, Lace came up behind her and said, "Nothing like a smoke when in time of despair."

"And this is one of those moments, huh?"

"That it is. That it is."

They leaned back against the wall while Lace smoked her cigarette. She took a drag and asked Faith, "Have I ever thanked you for taking care of my kids?"

"There was no need to, they were with their father."

Lace put her cigarette out and faced Faith. "No, they were with you. I know the type of man Raheem is and was, I also know that work comes before anything and I just wanted to take this moment to let you know that I have the utmost respect for you and I do need to say thank you."

Faith was touched by her words and had been waiting to hear them for a long time. "You're welcome."

They stood next to one another in silence while Lace smoked her cigarette until Faith blurted out, "Do you still love Raheem?"

Caught off guard by her question, Lace asked, "Why do you ask that?"

"I can see it in your face and I also noticed how gentle you were with him in the room."

"Well, he is the father to my three kids and I'll always love him."

"You know that's not what I meant."

Before they could go any further with the discussion, the nurse came out and said, "Ms. Banks, your husband is requesting your presence."

Faith and Lace looked at one another and they both followed the nurse inside.

Dear Journal,

I'm not your superwoman I'm not the kind of girl that you can let down and think that everything's okay.

Why was that song playing when I got in the car? It struck a nerve, because I feel like that's what I'm going to have to be right now.

If I ever needed a hit, it would be today but thank God, I'm not in that space anymore. As a matter of fact, the wine drinking has got to stop as well. As much as I would like to think that I have everything under control, with all that's going on, do I really want to chance it. I think not.

I have that serenity to accept the things I cannot change and the courage to know the difference. This circumstance with Raheem being in the hospital is something I have no control over. All I can do is pray.

I know I should stay by his side through his recovery and I will. After, all, he was there for me during my lowest of lows and I'll be there for him. I'm sure Lace will be there also.

The question is, will Siddiq be there for me?

Forever loyal, Faith

CHAPTER TWENTY-TWO

BELLA

A couple of days later, Bella was at the hospital visiting a member of her congregation when she saw Crystal walk down the hall.

"Crystal!" she called out.

Crystal turned around. "Bella! Hey."

They greeted one another with a hug. Crystal had become Bella's confidante. She was able to tell Crystal things she would normally keep to herself. This was the first time Bella had a real "sister girl" and it took a lot of weight off her shoulders because she wasn't holding so much in her soul now.

"How's Faith's husband doing?" Bella asked.

"Better, he'll be going home any day now."

"Good for him, he's in my prayers, as is she."

They were walking down the corridor heading for the front door when Bella asked Crystal, "Do you have a minute?"

"Of course."

"Let's go sit down, I need to bounce something off you."

They headed toward the sitting area outside the hospital.

Bella had already told Crystal about James and Ramsey, briefly. She didn't know how much she really wanted to reveal, but she did tell Crystal about her and James going out and about Ramsey being an old love from her past.

When they sat down, Crystal asked, "So what's up?"

Not one to beat around the bush or sugarcoat anything, Bella told her, "I slept with James."

This threw Crystal for a minute. She wasn't one to judge and she believed that people are people, even if they are in charge of churches.

"You slept with James?" Crystal repeated. She didn't know what else to say.

"Well, I'm not even sure if I did it knowingly." Bella needed to run that whole incident by someone because something bugged her. She couldn't understand why she didn't remember how they ended up in bed.

Not only that, but the last couple of Sundays, James would show up at church and stare at her through the whole sermon. It was starting to frighten her. He even tried to enter her office when she'd told him not to. Now, he'd taken to calling all her numbers, leaving stalker-like messages.

"What do you mean?"

"Well, one minute I was telling him he should leave and the next day I woke up naked and he's coming out of the bathroom."

Crystal recognized this pattern of events. Some of the young girls whom she'd counseled in the past told her of similar situations, where they had sex and couldn't recall a thing. It turned out they were slipped a mickey. "Did you have anything to eat or drink when you with him?"

Bella closed her eyes and tried to recall the order of events. She opened them. "I remember getting water."

"Did you leave it unattended?"

"You know what? I did. Ramsey called and I excused myself to go speak with him."

Crystal shook her head and told Bella, "I think he put something in your water."

Bella was stunned. "What do you mean, he put something in my water? He wouldn't do something like that."

"Are you sure about that, Bella?"

At this point Bella wasn't sure about anything and she told Crystal this.

"What I would do is tell your boy Ramsey."

"How am I supposed to tell him, I slept with James?"

"He drugged you, Bella, and he needs to be taken care of. You told me yourself that back in the day Ramsey was a thug and the way I see it, you should let him handle it. Some situations you take to Jesus and some situations you take to the streets."

Bella looked at Crystal and asked her, "Where's the Jesus in that?"

Crystal wasn't trying to hear that. "You know what, Bella, you really should let Ramsey handle it and just ask for forgiveness on this one."

When Bella got to her car, she asked the Lord to please forgive her for what she was about to do. She dialed Ramsey's number.

Over the past couple of weeks, Bella and Ramsey spoke a number of times. He'd stopped by the church and she finally allowed him to come visit her home, where she cooked dinner for him. It appeared to Bella that they were rekindling the old flame.

"Hey sweetie," Ramsey said into the phone.

"Hey, Ramsey, can you stop by the church today?"

Ramsey could hear that something was wrong. "What's going on?"

"Nothing, I just need to talk to you about something."

"Are you sure everything is okay?"

"How soon can you get there?"

"Are you there now?" he asked.

"I'll be there shortly."

"Well, I'm on my way."

When Bella pulled into the church parking lot, she looked around. Ramsey wasn't there yet but James's car was. Furious and tired of the whole situation, she made the decision to confront him. The fact that Ramsey was on his way gave her the courage she needed.

She walked into the church and the only people inside were Jasmine, the church secretary and Antonio, the janitor. She didn't see James anywhere. *Where could he be?*

Bella walked toward her office and there he was, sitting by the door.

"What are you doing here?" Bella asked, as she wondered how long before Ramsey showed up.

"You've been avoiding me."

"You've been stalking me."

"You can't stalk someone that you love."

"What!" *Oh yeah, he's lost all his mind.*

"What about our lovemaking?"

Nervous because she didn't want anyone to overhear, Bella unlocked her office door and pulled him inside.

She decided to get gully on him, because this was getting out of hand. "James, you don't love me and I don't love you. What happened between us the first time was a mistake and the second time, it is my belief that you slipped something in my water."

"Woman, please, I didn't do any such thing. You wanted me just as much as I wanted you. You can't stand the fact that you're a freak just like everyone else and now you want to be in denial about what transpired between us."

It was obvious to Bella that James had lost his mind, that he had gone past the point of no return. "James, I think you need to leave and not come back. I really think you need to find another church."

"You're kicking me out of the church?" James started to laugh like that was the funniest shit he'd heard in a long time.

"And if you continue to stalk me," Bella threatened, "you can best believe that I'm going to call the cops."

James got up in her face and in a menacing tone asked her, "and tell them what? That you fucked a member of your congregation? You would really be willing to let that become public knowledge? How do you think your congregation would feel about that?"

All of a sudden Ramsey appeared out of nowhere. He pulled James back by the collar, released him and asked, "Feel about what? What the hell is going on here?"

Bella looked toward her office door, which was still open.

Ramsey walked over to it and shut it, then asked again, "What the hell is going on here?"

Bella rushed over to Ramsey and stood near him. "This is what I had to talk to you about."

James looked at her. "What? You're going to tell him I fucked you?"

Ramsey frowned, anger spread over his face. "What is he talking about? You slept with this nigga?"

It was obvious that everyone had forgotten they were in the house of the Lord. "It's not what you think, he drugged me."

"I drugged you two times? I don't think so," James taunted.

Bella took Ramsey's hand. "Ramsey, I did have a moment of weakness once, but that was before you came back into my life."

James, fearing what was about to happen because of the look on Ramsey's face, moved toward the door but Ramsey stood in front of it.

Bella continued: "That night I met you at the restaurant in your hotel when I arrived home, he was waiting at my door. I let him in to tell him there could be nothing between us. I believe when you called me to make sure I was home and I stepped into the other room, he put something in my water and the next thing I know I woke up naked."

"Don't believe that shit, don't believe that shit," James was repeating over and over.

"Now he's stalking me and threatening to expose what happened."

Ramsey looked into Bella's eyes and knew that she spoke the truth. He turned towards James, who was two seconds from running until he realized there was nowhere to run to. Ramsey grabbed him by his throat, lifted him in the air and said, "You low-life motherfucker." He threw James across the room and before James could get to his feet, Ramsey started to pummel him.

Bella ran over and begged, "Ramsey, stop! Please stop! We're in the church."

Ramsey pulled him up by the neck and told him, "If I ever see you or hear anything about you again, I will personally see to it that your ass no longer exists."

He looked at Bella and told her, "I'll be back." Ramsey grabbed James by the collar. "Open the door," he told Bella. "I have to throw out the trash."

Bella did as he requested.

When she opened the door, Jasmine and Antonio were standing looking like, *what the hell is going on.*

Jasmine looked at Bella, Ramsey and the bloodied James. "Brother James?"

Antonio, who liked Bella and respected her, but knew all along there was something fishy about James, asked Ramsey if he needed any help.

He told him no.

As Ramsey was throwing James out the building, he could hear Antonio say under his breath, "I never liked him anyway."

After Bella assured them that everything was okay, she told them they could both leave for the day. After they were gone, Bella and Ramsey were in her office.

"I don't know how much longer I can do this," Bella said when Ramsey sat next to her.

He had no idea what she was talking about. "Do what?"

"Pastor a church," she told him. "Look at what I've done, I think that I'm making a mockery of the church. I stand in front of people every day professing that I understand their struggles and I don't even understand my own. I feel like such a phony, such a hypocrite."

Ramsey had learned over the years that sometimes a woman wants your opinion and sometimes she just wants you to listen. He knew that this was one of those times that she needed him to listen.

Bella continued to vent. "I teach forgiveness all the time, but more and more it just feels like words without meaning. Some days I wake up and I feel like if someone comes at me with another problem or another issue, I'm going to explode. That's not how a pastor is supposed to think."

After she was quiet for a moment, Ramsey realized it was his turn to speak. "I once thought about becoming a minister."

Bella didn't expect him to say that. "Really?"

"Yep, but it didn't take long for me to realize that I'm bet-

ter one-on-one. I felt that the structure of the church was too restrictive. After speaking with a couple of pastors, I realized that there are other ways to minister and that's how I ended up doing what I'm doing. Maybe that's something you should think about, maybe running a church is too restrictive. Maybe it is time to do something else."

"You might be right," Bella told him.

"Bella, I have a suggestion."

"What is it?"

"How about you take a leave of absence and come travel with me for a while. You can work with the women in the prisons and I'll work with the men."

"Are you serious?" Bella asked him.

"It'll give us an opportunity for us to get to know one another again and to see if what I think we could have is possible."

Bella opened her mouth to say something but Ramsey stopped her and continued. "It'll even give you an opportunity to decide if being a pastor is what you want to continue doing. Bella, I think we would be good together as a couple. I want to be your man."

Bella looked at him. She admitted to herself that she wanted him to be her man, the day he walked in the church the first time.

"I need some time to think about this," she told him.

"You need know I'll be leaving in two weeks," he told her, "and I would like to be able to see you freely without feeling like we're sneaking around."

Bella wanted to see him as well. She was ready to start being true to herself. Yes, she was living her life for God and she would continue to do so but that didn't mean she had to be without companionship. Bella knew what she wanted to do. Why was she putting off her own happiness?

"If I decide to go with you, I couldn't do it right away,

there are things I have to, like, find someone to pastor the church and—"

Ramsey didn't give Bella a chance to finish or talk her way out of the decision he knew she'd made. He stepped forward and kissed her with such a passion that all Bella could do was thank the Lord.

Bella thought about Harmony, the young lady she met at the center and how she already had a family. Yes, she wished she had started one many years ago, but life circumstances didn't permit. Perhaps it wasn't too late.

CHAPTER TWENTY-THREE

HARMONY

Harmony and Shareef were sitting in the living room discussing Ny'em. That day he showed up unannounced had caused a lot of disruption in the household and they had not recovered from it yet.

He had not shown up again but he'd been calling, making threats to take Harmony to court if she didn't allow him to see his son. *His other kids' mothers weren't giving him any problem, so why was she,* he wanted to know.

"Look, Shareef, I already know what Ny'em is not and what he has never been and I already know all that you are. I don't need to be reminded of that. But what you've got to understand is he's threatening to take me to court and I really don't want to put Shacquille through that. So in order to avoid all that, I think we should give him a chance to be a part of Shacquille's world until he messes up again. You know just like I know that he will."

Shareef refused to respond to what he considered nonsense. He seriously doubted that Ny'em would take them to court, especially with what he had just found out.

"I need you to be with me on this," Harmony told him.

When Shareef still didn't respond, Harmony repeated, "I need you to be with me on this."

"Him taking us to court is not going to happen," Shareef told Harmony.

"How do you know that? You can't say that for sure."

"Yes, I can."

"How? What do you know that I don't know?"

"How about the fact that Ny'em is gay," Shareef told her.

Harmony looked at him like he was crazy. "What did you just say?"

"You heard me. I know for a fact that Ny'em is gay."

Harmony just looked at Shareef. She couldn't believe he would make up some shit like that. "I see you're not ready to talk about this, you just want to play games. I know you don't want Ny'em in Shacquille's life, but I really didn't think you would stoop this low."

Shareef started laughing and shook his head. He looked Harmony in the eyes and told her, "My word is my bond, I'm not lying to you. If there is one thing I wouldn't want to be true, this is it, but it is and we have to figure out how we're going to deal with it."

"How do you know this to be true?" Harmony still didn't believe him but was willing to hear him out.

"Do you remember the other night when I told you that I was meeting with some clients regarding our nightclub account?"

"Go on," Harmony told him.

"Well, the account is that gay nightclub on the beach."

Please do not sit here and tell me Ny'em was in there. This was not something Harmony was prepared to hear because if there was ever a true thug, it was Ny'em.

"Well, you know Perry, right?"

"Are you talking about Perry, the gay video store owner?"

"Yeah. Anyway, as I was leaving I saw him and Ny'em pull up."

"At the gay club, you saw Ny'em pull up at the gay club?"

"Will you stop interrupting and let me finish telling you."

"Go ahead."

"I saw Ny'em pull up. At the time I didn't know it was him, until he turned around and greeted Perry. The next thing you know, I saw Perry get into the car and off they go."

"So what? That doesn't mean anything."

"Why are you defending him? You still have feelings for him or something?"

"No, but just because a person gets in a car with someone it doesn't mean they're fucking."

"Well, this does." Shareef waited to make sure he had Harmony's full attention. "I waited until the next day and went by the video store. I asked Perry if that was Ny'em he was with last night. He told me yes. I asked him what was up and you know Perry tells all his business, he told me that Ny'em was his thug lover."

Harmony felt like she was about to cry. This was some bullshit. "You're lying."

"You know I'm not lying. You also know that when a man has been on lockdown for years, there's always a possibility that his ass may get turned out."

Harmony stood up.

"Where are you going?" Shareef asked.

"I'm going to call him."

Before Shareef could say a word there was a knock on the door. "Wait right here. I'm going to answer the door and then we're going to talk about this some more."

When Shareef opened the door, the were two policemen standing there. "Are you Shareef?"

"Yeah?"

"We need to speak with you about an assault that transpired last night."

Shareef had no idea what they were talking about. "An assault?"

By this time Harmony was standing behind him. "What's going on?"

The policemen ignored her and said to Shareef, "Where were you last night?"

"Why?"

"It's been bought to our attention that you threatened Ny'em Howard."

"Man, please, I don't have time for this. Who would have told you some shit like that?"

One of the cops looked at his notes and said, "La—"

The other cop gave him a look that shut him up.

"Lala?" Harmony asked. "Are you saying that bitch set my man up?"

"We're saying no such thing, miss." They looked past Harmony and asked Shareef, "If he wouldn't mind coming down to the precinct to answer some questions."

"Yeah, I would mind."

"If you have nothing to hide, you'll come and understand that we can do this the hard way or the easy way."

Shareef looked at Harmony and noticed that she was looking at him like, *Did you do it?*

"I'll go, because I didn't do a damned thing."

Before he walked out the door, Shareef looked at Harmony and told her to call King.

Harmony watched them walk to the police car and wondered if she should call Elsie too, since she was an ex-attorney and her boss.

CHAPTER TWENTY-FOUR

ELSIE

Elsie had an idea she wasn't sure if she should present to Savannah or not. This was some next-level shit. She knew she was reaching, but all Savannah could say was "no," "hell no," or "hell fucking no."

In order to present this idea to Savannah she knew she was going to have to go out of her way and treat her to something special, have her real relaxed and open to the idea.

"Maybe we'll have a day of beauty together, a spa day." Elsie picked up the phone and cradled it on her shoulder. As she started to dial Savannah's number, she was startled by the buzz of her cell phone. She'd forgotten that she had put it on vibrate. She glanced at the caller ID and saw that it said private.

Elsie couldn't stand when people called and the word *private* showed up. She liked to know who she would be speaking with beforehand. *I'll retrieve the message after I speak with Savannah.*

"Hello? Hello?" Savannah was saying on the other phone.

"Oh, I'm sorry," Elsie said into the phone. "Someone was calling on my cell."

"You want to call me back?" Savannah asked.

"No, we can talk now. How's your day going?"

"Busy as usual, I had a lot of running around to do and my husband needed me to see a client, to stand in for him."

"It must be a challenge having two doctors in the family."

"You don't know the half of it. Sometimes we go days without seeing one another."

Is that why you're seeing me? "Listen," Elsie asked, "are you busy tomorrow?"

"I have a few things I need to do early in the morning, why?"

"I wanted to spend some time together, maybe go to the spa."

"Mmm," Elsie could feel Savannah thinking. "That sounds like a good idea."

"Call me when you know what time you're going to be free so I can set up an appointment."

"I'll call you in the morning if I'm home alone."

This was the exact reason Elsie didn't want to get involved with someone that not only had a man but was married to one. What was she thinking? What did she think would become of this? Why was she wasting her time? That's what she was doing, wasting time, hers and Savannah's.

Or was she? Maybe there's a reason for everything. Maybe her plans for a baby might come through via Savannah. One never knows, one can only hope.

Elsie remembered that someone tried calling on the cell phone. She wondered if they had left a message. She snatched her phone off the nightstand and checked her voice mail.

"You have two new messages," the recording told her

She pressed one to listen to both.

"Hi, Elsie, this is Summer, I was thinking about you. Please give me a call when you get a chance. I'd love to her from you."

Elsie listened to the second message. It was Trey telling her he was back in town and wanted to take her out to dinner. "Don't worry," he said. "I know you're not interested in me, but I enjoyed your company the last time I was here and would love to see you again."

Elsie deleted both messages. She was surprised to hear from Summer, yet pleased. She had finally gotten up the nerve to call her but each time she did, no one answered and she would end up leaving a message.

As for Trey, she'd call him back and accept his dinner invitation. She enjoyed his company the last time they were together also and one never knew what could happen. If Savannah turned her suggestion down, Trey just might be the one to say yes.

Elsie knew she needed to get on with her day. That afternoon she had to attend a fund raiser given by Waves of Courage, another local nonprofit organization. She was slated as one of the speakers. She would be speaking about going back to community and doing your part. She had to pick up Harmony, who was going to introduce the speakers.

A few hours later, when they arrived at the fund raiser, Cora Lee, the Executive Director of Waves of Courage greeted them and thanked them for taking part in the event.

"You're welcome, I'm honored to be here." Elsie glanced around and was surprised to see so many people. "You have a nice turnout."

"I know, I'm so pleased and it helps that Queen Latifah will be making a brief appearance," Cora responded.

"*Brief* being the operative word," Elsie pointed out.

Elsie was the one who set it up, she used one of her old modeling contacts that knew someone that knew someone and that someone made a phone call who made it happen.

"Is there anything I can do for you right now?" Harmony asked Cora.

"Yes there is, when the queen arrives, show her to the office and make sure she's comfortable, that she's not bombarded by fans."

Harmony wanted to hug Elsie for hooking up this opportunity. She also wanted to do something special for Elsie for being there when she and Shareef needed her.

Harmony smiled at them both and said, "You can count on me."

Elsie, knowing Harmony had three kids, told her, "Why don't you walk around, see it there's anything here for your kids?"

The fund raiser was called "Kept Kids." Various stores donated children's clothing, tapes, games and items, that low-income families couldn't normally afford to be given. There would also be a number of speeches and a small concert by a local.

Elsie was proud to be a part of the event.

As she walked around, Elsie spotted Savannah's husband. She made a quick decision to go over and say hello but she stopped in her tracks when she spotted a woman approach him and place her hand intimately on his lower back. The woman leaned over and whispered in his ear.

He laughed, hugged the lady's waist and pulled her into him.

"What the hell?"

"See someone you know?"

Elsie turned around to see Crystal standing behind her. "What's up, girl?" Elsie asked.

Crystal followed Elsie's gaze. "Isn't that your friend's husband?"

"It sure is."

"Well, he sure looks mighty friendly with Ms. Thang."

Elsie agreed, before she could say anything more, she heard her name being called over the intercom.

"Go motivate the people," Crystal joked.

"I sure will."

Later that night, Savannah and Elsie sat up in the bed together. They had just finished watching a movie. Savannah had surprised Elsie by coming to her house.

"I thought we weren't supposed to see one another until tomorrow," Elsie said.

"Well, I was able to get away tonight."

"Where's your husband?" Elsie asked.

"He got called in."

Elsie thought to herself, *I bet he did.*

"So what do you want to do?" Savannah asked her.

"You tell me," Elsie said.

Savannah rolled over and pushed Elsie back on the bed. She unbuttoned the shirt Elsie wore, pushed the bra up and ran her tongue between Elsie's breasts.

Savannah then stuck her thighs between Elsie's and starting grinding her knee into Elsie's pussy.

"Why are you playing with me?" Elsie asked.

"I'm not playing," Savannah told her.

Elsie pushed Savannah over and laid on top of her. "Let me please you."

Before Savannah could respond, Elsie pushed up Savannah's skirt and pushed her panties to the side. She placed her fingers on her pussy and was surprised to find it was already moist. She then dove two fingers inside her, causing Savannah to shiver and wail out loud.

This only made Elsie place two more fingers inside her and pump her faster. "This is what you did to me in the bathroom," Elsie told her. "I'm returning the favor."

Savannah couldn't say a word, all she could do was rear back against Elsie's hand. "Harder," she told her, "harder."

The next thing you know, Savannah was screaming out loud and holding onto Elsie's hand while it was still inside her.

"I shouldn't be here," Savannah said.

"You can leave anytime you want to," Elsie told her, knowing she wouldn't.

Caressing Savannah's face, Elsie said to her, "I'm thinking about having a baby."

"What?"

Elsie, unable to hold in what she wanted to ask Savannah, said, "How would you feel about asking your husband to donate his sperm to me?"

Savannah removed Elsie's hand and sat up. "Are you crazy? There's no way I could ask him something like that. You're joking, right."

Elsie could feel her throat tightening. This was some serious shit to her, it wasn't a joke and Savannah was treating it as such. Elsie felt her body tremble and not from pleasure. "You think this shit funny? You think this a joke?"

Startled by Elsie's response, Savannah leaned forward and told her, "I apologize if I was out of line. Please forgive me." She waited on Elsie's response, when she didn't receive any, she went on. "I know this is important to you, but look at what you're asking me to do, ask *my* husband to father *your* child when we don't even have any of our own."

Elsie realized that maybe she wanted this so much that she was blinded by her need and was not being realistic.

"I need to be alone," Elsie told Savannah. "I really need to be alone." She didn't wait on Savannah's response, she got out of the bed and walked into her bathroom, and slammed the door behind her.

Once she heard Savannah leave, Elsie came out the bath-

room and sat on the edge of her bed. She knew she had no reason to be mad at Savannah. Shit, if the roles were reversed, she would have thought that Savannah was crazy to make such a request.

Maybe having a baby right now or even doing the artificial insemination wasn't a good idea. It was driving her crazy. Elsie decided to put that whole idea to the side for now.

Elsie looked at the phone. She really needed someone to help her sort through this madness. She picked it up and dialed a number.

"Hello?" the voice on the other line said.

"Summer?"

"Elsie?"

"Summer, I need a friend."

"I'm on my way."

CHAPTER TWENTY-FIVE

FAITH

Faith had finally been able to bring Raheem home from the hospital. Considering the circumstances, he appeared to be fairly upbeat and somehow different, but almost losing your life can do that to you.

Faith was in the bathroom, looking at her cell phone. She wanted to see Siddiq in the worst way. She'd rarely been able to speak with him and when she was able to, the calls were extremely short. Assisting Raheem through his rehabilitation was taking up more time than she thought it would.

She could tell in Siddiq's voice that he was starting to pull away and lose hope.

Something's got to give.

"Faith! Faith! Can you come here for a minute?"

Faith could hear Raheem calling her from the other room. She wanted to ignore him but knew that would be just plain old evil.

Shit, I forgot it's his bathroom time. Faith went into Raheem's room and to her surprise he was standing on his own.

"What? How? Are you?" Faith didn't know what to ask first.

Raheem was grinning from ear to ear as he told her, "I made it to and from the bathroom on my own. I figured I'd give you a break from wiping my ass."

Faith laughed. "I'm so proud of you."

"Can you help me get back in the bed? That walk kind of exhausted me."

"Of course."

As Raheem got comfortable on the bed, he patted the spot next to him.

Faith sat down. "You need anything else?"

"No, but there is something I'd like to know."

"What is it?"

"I'd like to know what's going on with you."

"Why do you think something is going on?"

"Because you seem preoccupied," he told her.

Faith was surprised that he could still read her so well. "I don't know what you're talking about." She averted her eyes from his gaze.

Raheem took her hand. "Faith, look at me."

She ignored his request.

"Look at me. There's something I need to tell you."

Slowly she looked up and waited to hear what he had to say.

"That day of my accident I left the house angry at you, upset that you wanted to end our marriage. My normal mode of operation whenever I was mad at you was to go seek out the comforts of another woman. It didn't matter what woman because anyone would do. This day was different."

Faith wondered if she needed to brace herself for what he was about to tell her. "What are you trying to tell me, Raheem?"

"It's time to free you."

"Free me? What do you mean, free me?"

"Please, just listen, don't interrupt."

Faith waited patiently.

"I needed something different that day. I needed to talk with someone that knows me as well as I know myself. I called Lace."

"Lace?" He had her undivided attention.

"Lace and I ended up having a heart-to-heart. I believe that I got distracted when Lace told me that she had never stop loving me."

Faith thought to herself, *Well, hell, I knew that.*

Raheem went on. "She also told me how sorry she was for all that she had put me and the kids through. She expressed that she wished I would have stood by her like I stood by you as you went through your changes."

Surprised, Faith asked, "She knows about me?"

"She goes to the meetings also and although what's said in the room is supposed to stay in the room, you know people talk."

"So how did you feel with her telling you this?"

"I believe I should have supported her like I did you."

"No, what I'm asking you is how do you feel about her telling you, she still loves you?"

"I'm not sure how I feel."

Faith was not shocked. She knew that Lace still had feelings for Raheem. What she didn't know was that they were on the phone prior to the accident. This explained Lace's behavior at the hospital and why she'd been calling and calling, asking if Faith needed her to come by and do anything.

Faith thoughts were interrupted by Raheem. "Are you angry? Are you upset? Anything?"

"No, I'm not sure sure what I feel."

"Faith, sometimes when you don't realize it I catch you daydreaming. Since I've been home, I've seen you on several occasions in the backyard on the phone talking to someone.

I may be many things, but a fool is not one of them. The behaviors that you are exhibiting, I know them only too well. Faith, you are me and I am you. I know that you are in love with someone."

Faith opened her mouth to say something.

Raheem put up his hand. "Please don't deny it. Who is he?"

"Does it matter?" Faith asked him, not having the energy to even play it off.

"You know what? It doesn't. What matters is you've been here for me, even after all I put you through. I thank you for staying with me throughout this ordeal. However, I need somebody to be here that wants to be here, not someone that feels obligated."

"So what are you saying?" Faith wanted to know.

"What I am saying is that if you want the divorce, I will not contest it. We both deserve to be happy."

Faith was dumbfounded.

"I mean it, Faith, I'm willing to let you go but I hope we can be friends."

Faith, unable to believe the words that came out of his mouth, leaned foward and kissed Raheem gently on the lips. "Thank you."

"No," Raheem told her. "Thank you."

Faith stood up.

"Don't you have a phone call you need to make?" Raheem asked her.

"As a matter of fact, I do." She picked up the phone next to the bed and dialed a number.

Raheem looked at her like she was crazy. "I'm not talking about in front of me."

Faith ignored him. "Lace?" she said into the phone. "Raheem needs you."

Faith looked over at Raheem and was thankful. Thankful for a chance to start over and thankful for the new friendship she and Raheem were going to develop.

When Faith hung up the phone, Raheem reached for her hand. "Faith?"

"Yes?"

"I apologize for everything I've put you through."

She could tell from his sincere tone that he meant it.

"I apologize for what I've put you through as well."

CHAPTER TWENTY-SIX

HARMONY

It seemed like apologies were in order all around.

Shareef, King and Harmony were approaching the hospital room where Ny'em was recovering from stab wounds.

Shareef looked at King. "I can't believe you talked me into this shit."

"Just be cool, man, you need to hear him out."

As they got closer to the room, they noticed Perry walking out. He was with another man who was obviously gay and angry.

"How you gonna come and see that motherfucker?" the man asked Perry.

"He's my friend and he needs support right now."

Harmony overheard the statement and wondered, *what the hell is he talking about?*

Before they stepped inside, Harmony told Shareef, "You must stay calm. Maybe then Ny'em will see our side of things. We'll talk about the fact that he has two other kids that he can focus on."

Shareef agreed to the plan. "We just need some sort of resolution today."

Harmony stuck her head into Ny'em's room. "Is this a bad time?" she asked.

Ny'em shook his head no and they entered.

Ny'em acknowledged Shareef with a head nod and told King, "Thank you for getting them here."

Harmony walked toward the bed, but Shareef stayed in the back, but not so far back that he couldn't hear what was being said.

"How are you feeling?" Harmony asked.

"I've been better. But I didn't have King bring you guys here to make small talk." Ny'em looked at Shareef and told him, "First of all, Shareef, I want to apologize for the police harassing you. Lala knew it wasn't you who stabbed me." He then looked at Harmony. "You really need to watch your back because for some reason Lala has it in for you."

"I ain't worried about that bitch. I'd just like to know why you asked us here."

"I'd like to see Shacquille," he told them.

Shareef took a step forward, but King pulled him back by his shirt but not before he told Ny'em, "That shit ain't gonna happen."

"Let me finish," Ny'em said. "I'd like to see my son, but he doesn't have to know I'm his father."

"You're not," Shareef told him.

King nudged Shareef. "Yo, Sha', you really need to shut the fuck up and listen to this man. He's trying to tell you something but your ass keeps interrupting. The man has already said that Shacquille doesn't have to know he's his father, let's see what else he has to say."

Harmony knew something was up, she could feel it in her gut.

268

Ny'em turned to Harmony. "Harmony, out of all my baby mamas, you're the best one, hands down. I know that you would do anything to protect what's yours and now I see that you have a man that would be willing to do the same thing." He looked over at Shareef and told him, "I ain't mad at you, dog."

Ny'em sat up further in the bed and asked Harmony to pull up a chair.

At this point Harmony had started to feel uneasy. She looked back at Shareef, who was hanging on to Ny'em's every word. "What's going on?" she asked as she sat down.

Ny'em pulled an envelope from under his pillow and handed it to her.

She looked over at Shareef, who nodded his head. She took the envelope out of Ny'em's hand and asked, "What's this?"

"I know that you believe that I'm a deadbeat dad and you might be right, but back then with the lifestyle I was living, the dollar came first. I was too busy making that money and dodging death to be concerned about another life. What you're holding in your hand is an envelope full of money. The money you knew I had stashed somewhere. I want you to split it evenly between all three of my kids."

"Why me?" Harmony wanted to know.

"Because I know I can trust you."

"Okay, Ny'em, you're scaring me. You need to tell me what's going on."

"You know I got stabbed, right?"

"Yes."

"Well, the wound caused an infection."

"Of course the wound caused an infection."

Ny'em reworded what he was trying to say. "What I'm try-ing to saying is I can't fight off the infection the wound caused because I'm already ill."

Confused, Harmony asked, "What are you telling me? Just spit it out, please."

"I'm telling you," Ny'em said as he looked at everyone in the room, "that I'm HIV positive and I have been for quite some time."

Harmony couldn't believe what she heard. There was no way this could be true. "Are you sure?

"I've never been surer."

Harmony didn't know what to do other than look over at Shareef, who was standing with his mouth open.

"Close your mouth, son," King told him.

Harmony couldn't stop her tears from falling and Shareef stepped forward to comfort her.

He looked over at Ny'em and said, "I'm sorry, man, I'm truly sorry. I don't wish ill will on anyone."

From across the room, King cleared his throat. "Um, Shareef, Harmony, don't be angry with me but I knew what this gathering was going to be about and I made a decision."

"What are you talking about?" Shareef asked.

King didn't respond, he stepped out of the room.

"Where is he going?" Harmony asked Shareef.

"The hell if I know."

They watched the door and a few seconds later, King returned with Shacquille and Jewell behind him.

Shareef didn't say a word, when Harmony stepped up and grabbed Shacquille's hand and said to him, "I want you to meet a good friend of Mommy's and Daddy's."

THE END

FOR NOW

Stay tuned for *Turned Out 2* and *Sister Girls 3*.